FREEDOM IN THE MOUNTAIN WIND

CALL OF THE ROCKIES ~ BOOK 1

MISTY M. BELLER

Misty M. Beller

BOOKS

ISBN-13 Trade Paperback: 978-0-9997012-4-9

ISBN-13 Large Print Paperback: 978-1-954810-06-8

ISBN-13 Casebound Hardback: 978-1-942265-40-5

To Robin Patchen,
The best friend and editor any writer could want.

Your friendship, tough love, and never-ending support have been some
of the greatest blessings of my writing journey.
I'm so thankful God brought us together.

And not only that, but we also glory in tribulations, knowing that tribulation produces perseverance; and perseverance, character; and character, hope.

Romans 5:3-4 (NKJV)

CHAPTER 1

They'd made it.

Susanna Wilkins stared across the rolling hills, her gaze seeking snow-capped peaks rising in the distance. But the Rocky Mountains couldn't be seen from this point.

As much as this felt like the end of the journey—the final destination—she and her father had barely finished the beginning. The first part of this trip was nothing compared to the long journey ahead. As long as she could convince her father to keep going.

She turned back to the river as she dug her paddle into the water again, sweeping the liquid behind their dingy. The thick scattering of rock around them meant they must be nearing the first of the Great Falls.

Captains Lewis and Clark had written of this stretch of the Missouri. Had been overjoyed when they reached it, especially when Captain Lewis trekked on ahead of the party and laid eyes on the massive waterfall she and her father would surely find a little farther upriver.

Yet for those explorers who'd come almost three decades before, the effort of having to carry their boats and supplies around each of the falls had nearly brought death to the soldiers. Big, strapping men had been laid low by the work ahead.

What in heaven's name made her think she and Pa could manage the same? Yet she had to, or else Pa would insist they turn around and journey back to civilization. Give up the dream he'd craved as long as she could remember.

She couldn't let him do that. Not when this was his last chance.

A thick, wheezing cough sounded beside her, forcing her thoughts into aching clarity. Her father's illness wasn't healing as she'd hoped it would in this new climate and higher altitude.

But this journey was the one thing he'd wanted to accomplish before his final days. She prayed they had time aplenty. Either way, she'd agreed to follow in the tracks of Lewis and Clark's Corp of Discovery—or rather, follow in the paddle strokes.

If only they hadn't lost their guide. The last in a string of guides, actually. The man they'd left Illinois with—Mason—had disappeared in the second week. He'd bedded down beside the coals of their campfire like usual, but in the morning, there was nary a trace of him. Not a trace of the roasted venison she'd packed away either.

After that, she and Pa paddled for two days up the Missouri on their own, then found a new escort in the next village they passed. That man lasted twice as long as Mason before disappearing too—this time after breaking his fast with them one morning. He'd said he was walking upriver to see what the water looked like around the bend, but he never came back. She should have known by the nervous way he kept adjusting his grip on his rifle. After they searched for him awhile, she discovered he'd taken a day's worth of food from their stores, too. Must have tucked the supplies in his trousers or his possibles bag.

This last guide had led them almost to the Marias River, then disappeared a few hours after they passed another boat going downriver—back to civilization. He'd watched the craft float by them with a yearning in his eyes. When the man said he was going to investigate a crop of rocks, then didn't return, she didn't have to search long to realize where he'd gone. She and Pa were alone once again.

That was two days ago, and in this barren wilderness, they'd be hard-pressed to find another man to accompany them. Maybe they didn't need anyone. The men they'd traveled with were almost more trouble than help—especially this last one. He'd helped paddle some as they made their way upriver, but couldn't be counted on for any assistance otherwise. They were better off on their own.

Now she just had to convince Pa they could keep going with just the two of them. Deep down, she knew the real reason he wanted another man along with them. If the worst happened and he wasn't able to see her back to Illinois, he wanted someone to take her safely to his cousin in Boston.

A place she had no desire to go. The worst simply *couldn't* happen.

The bottom of their dingy struck another boulder with a hard jolt, gripping the front end of the boat fast while the flowing water wiggled the rear.

"This might be as far as we can go with these rocks." Pa's voice rasped from the bout of coughing he'd just ceased. "You reckon it's time to stop and hike to the falls?" He'd promised they would at least see the Falls of the Missouri before turning back.

Now it was her job to convince him that they could keep

going past this point. Her father's dying wish was to see the rugged mountain country Lewis and Clark's expedition had traveled through. She *would* get him there if it took all she had.

She pulled the paddle into the boat and rested it on her lap, eyeing the water flowing around the boulders ahead of them. A bend in the river concealed what lay ahead. She needed to know exactly where they were in relation to the map Pa kept tucked inside his shirt front. His replica of Lewis and Clark's sketch had been hard to come by, but it had proved remarkably accurate thus far on their journey up the Missouri from Illinois.

She swiped at a wad of mosquitos hovering around her face. "How about we make land, then hike up to the first of the Great Falls." And she could see what the terrain was like. Maybe they should leave the boat behind altogether instead of trying to carry it the eighteen miles around all five waterfalls. If she could talk Pa into it, would they be able to make the journey on land the rest of the way? Did he have the strength to hike day after day? If only they had horses to take them on from here.

In truth, she'd rather have had horses for the entire trip. Paddling and poling up the river was just about the hardest work she could have imagined. Why men ever thought a water route was easier than land was beyond her ability to fathom. Maybe if she'd been floating down a smooth river, not paddling upstream as they had these last four months.

As she stepped from the boat into the icy water, a movement at the edge of her vision snagged her focus. She held the craft and spun to scan the land. The hill to their right was topped by a rocky crag that blocked the view beyond it. But something about the form made her study the top.

There. It looked like a shadow among the stone, but the longer she stared, the more the spot looked like dark hair framing the top of a face.

"Is that an Indian?" Pa spoke the question at the exact

moment the words planted in her own mind. He'd climbed from the boat and now stood beside her, staring at the same spot that had drawn her attention.

She squinted, but the figure didn't move again. "I think it's a person, but I'm not certain. And I can't tell if he's Indian or white."

Pa's vision was so finely honed after years as a gunsmith, he could usually make out details better than she could. He raised a palm for her to stay put as he stepped forward.

After half a dozen strides, he halted, then lifted a hand to wave. "Halloo. We come in peace."

Some of the Indians they'd met on the journey could speak broken English, but certainly not all. Would this stranger understand? Maybe he was part of the Shoshone tribe, and she and Pa could barter for horses just like Lewis and Clark had. But trade with this man would only be possible if they could converse with him.

The thought made her want to step forward and take over communications from her father, just to make sure they didn't lose the man. She had to let Pa manage everything he could, though, what with his illness taking away so many of his abilities. A man had to be allowed some pride, and this was something he could do. Besides, the Indian would probably respond more quickly to a man than a woman.

"Friendly white man." Pa pointed to his chest and raised his other hand high in greeting. "We would like to talk."

The shadow on the ridge shifted, then eased up to reveal the face of a man. Definitely Indian, if the black of his hair could be believed. The midday sun glimmered on his tawny face, one more sign of his race. Although after only a few months in these rays, she and Pa could pass for Indian as well. Except for the lighter brown of their hair, of course.

As the man straightened to full standing, the wide set of his shoulders revealed powerful muscles under his buckskin tunic. It was possible he was a French trapper or other mountain man, but something about him exuded a majestic strength. Like that of a well-bred stallion, handled just enough to keep him from being completely wild.

Pa stepped forward again, narrowing the thirty strides or so between them. "Do you speak English?"

The stranger was silent for a moment, and disappointment slipped through Susanna. She hadn't really expected an Indian this far west to know the white man's language, had she?

"I do." His deep voice drifted across the distance, not tugged away by the breeze whipping up. Yet it took a moment for the import of his words to settle in her mind.

He could understand them. And talk back.

"Good." Pa's smile sounded loud and clear in his voice as he took a few more steps forward. "That's real fine."

"You travel with others?" The man's voice held only a hint of an accent. Where had he learned the language?

"It's just the two of us, my daughter and me. We're traveling upriver to see the falls, then beyond. We lost our guide a few days ago, and we're lookin' for someone new to take us forward. I reckon' you know quite a bit about this area."

She wanted to step forward and grab her father's arm. Did he really think to ask this man to travel with them?

The man glanced toward the river. "You will carry your craft around the falls?"

Pa followed the man's gaze. "That's what we're plannin'. If we can find a guide to help us."

This was her chance. Before she could stop herself, Susanna stepped forward. "Or, if you know of any horses for trade, we'd consider leaving the boat." And good riddance.

The man studied her, and even over the long space separating them, she had to fight to keep from shifting under his scrutiny. She raised her chin and met his look.

A moment later, he stepped over the crest of the ridge, then strode down the hill with the sure footing of a goat.

He marched straight toward them, and as he neared, Pa extended a hand to shake. "Glad to know ya. I'm Thad Wilkins, and this is my daughter, Susanna."

The stranger nodded a greeting even as he ignored the outstretched hand and stepped around them. "I am called Beaver Tail." He headed toward the river.

Was he going on his way without even a farewell? But he was aimed toward their dingy.

When he reached the boat, which Pa'd had built especially shallow to manage the sandbar-fraught Missouri, Beaver Tail paused and studied the contents.

What was he doing? Susanna charged toward him. They had few enough supplies. The last thing they needed was to be robbed by this impertinent Indian.

He leaned forward and grabbed two of the packs tucked in oilskins—one that contained their food supplies, and the other their ammunition and tools.

"Don't touch those." She grabbed his arm to stop him, but the rod of iron muscle under her grip wouldn't be swayed by a little thing like her. She reached for the pack in his hand, but he turned and dropped both on the ground.

"Help me empty." He grunted the words as he reached for another satchel, this one containing their extra clothing.

"You can't have this." She snatched up the food case with her left hand, but the pack was so heavy she had to use both arms to drag it away. If she only had the chance to get one satchel from him, she probably should have reached for the one containing ammunition.

He dropped the pack of clothing where he'd placed the others, then with a wide sweep of his arm, he scooped up the canteens and loose items she'd not yet organized into satchels.

"Is there something you need there, son?" Pa had joined

them at the river's edge, but instead of snatching their supplies from this thief, he only watched the man drop his load on the ground at Pa's feet.

The Indian—Beaver Tail—didn't respond, just turned back to the dingy and gripped both sides with his massive hands. Bear Paws would have been a better name for him. He hoisted the craft over his head. The mighty growl that slipped through his tight jaw would have made a lesser woman swoon. Any rabbits and birds in the area had surely fled at the ferocity of the sound. Yet the fact that he could actually hoist the boat and carry it atop his head was hard to fathom.

Maybe he really was a bear, one of the famed grizzlies they had yet to see.

The man splashed through the edge of the water, then marched forward on dry land along the side of the river. He'd left all their supplies, and he seemed to be following a trail worn into the ground.

A portage trail?

She glanced at Pa to see what he thought of the situation. Her father raised his brows, his thoughts clearly taking the same track hers had. Then a corner of his mouth tipped up. "I think he's helping."

Maybe he planned to take the job as their guide. At least that way, she'd not have to argue with Pa about whether they would keep going beyond the falls. Either way, the man was already disappearing over the rolling hill ahead. She looped the canteen straps around her neck, then loaded the other miscellaneous items in the food pack and snatched it up. "Can you bring the clothing?" That satchel should be the lightest, but she'd still have to keep an eye on Pa. His stamina was less than half what it had been only a year ago.

She scanned the ground once more. She'd have to come back for the ammunition and tools. Maybe make two trips because that pack was so heavy. Not something she'd relish since the portage route was said to be eighteen hard miles around the five falls, but she'd manage. There was no other choice.

Over the next quarter hour, she was torn between trying to keep Beaver Tail in sight as he marched onward with their boat balanced atop his head and staying near Pa in case he needed her.

His breathing was coming rougher with each step, and when a coughing fit overtook him, she had to let the Indian go altogether. Her father was more important than that blasted boat anyway.

"Here, Pa." She set her oilskins down and held out the bottle of tonic Dr. Williams had sent. Their supply was dwindling, but when these bouts overtook him, he had to have something to ease the pain carved across his face as he clutched his chest.

With a final cough, Pa straightened and turned to take the container. A trickle of blood seeped from one side of his mouth, tightening a raw ache in her own chest. She reached forward and wiped the crimson with her thumb.

The action left a light smear on his leathery skin, and he raised a sleeve to clean the spot as his eyes met hers. His watery blue gaze—rimmed in red from all the coughing—communicated so much, just as it always had.

His apology that shone there was unnecessary, but the love glistening in his eyes made her want to step into his arms just like she had so many times as a girl. Pa's hugs always made her feel so fully loved, everything else in her upside-down world would surely be righted simply because of his affection.

He took a swig of the medicine, then replaced the cork and tucked the bottle back in the pack. "Let's keep moving. There's a whole lot of country left to see."

She gave herself one last moment to savor his tender smile. If only his love could right the world they'd been forced to face these last few months.

~

*B*eaver Tail forced air in and out of his chest as every one of his muscles strained under the weight of the boat. This was no simple dugout canoe, and he wasn't altogether sure he could manage the burden the entire distance around the falls. At least not in the remaining hours of this day.

But the last thing he wanted to do was make camp with these two strangers. They must be a few lodge poles short of a tipi to come into this land with only the two of them. A sick old man and a young woman? He didn't know the terrain they'd traveled through to reach this place, but he'd sure seen the country ahead of them. They wouldn't last a week where they were headed.

He couldn't be the guide they wanted, but he could at least carry the boat around the waterfalls. From there, they could follow the river's winding path easily enough.

For today, he'd carry the boat as far as he could manage, then he may as well return to his own camp for the night so he wasn't bedding down beside these strangers. Maybe one or two of the other men would come back with him the next day to finish the work. All three would want to come if he told them there was a woman in the party. Especially one as fair of face as Susanna.

His weary body almost smiled at the thought of the reactions they'd have when they saw her. Beaver Tail had never seen a white woman wear men's leggings and tunic, and her clothes certainly didn't hide the soft curves of her lean form. She'd have three marriage proposals the moment the others laid eyes on her.

But Beaver Tail wouldn't be offering one of his own. Women had only caused trouble for him in the past, a trouble he spread to everyone around him. He'd come on this journey to escape that particular type of problem. No reason to invite disaster on himself again.

CHAPTER 2

"This is where you will camp tonight." Beaver Tail fought to keep from panting as he leaned against the side of the boat to catch his breath. In truth, he wasn't sure his legs would hold him on their own, but he couldn't let these two strangers see his weakness.

Although, if a man had to show weakness, surely it would be allowed after hauling this oversized canoe for more than half the sun's journey across the sky this day.

Susanna trudged toward him and dropped both of her satchels on the ground with a grunt. The older man—had he said his name was Wilkins?—trailed her, looking even wearier than his daughter. Although the possessions he carried were considerably lighter than her load had been.

The fellow didn't look well. Maybe because of the bags under his eyes and the way his shirt hung on his gaunt frame. Both of those could be explained by reasons other than illness, but there was something else about him. A pallor to his skin? Despite the fact he was browned from long days in the sun.

"How much farther to the last falls?" Susanna still struggled to catch her breath.

Beaver Tail straightened. "We're a little over half the distance. I'll return when the sun rises to finish the portage."

"Do you live around here?" She wiped her brow with the loose fabric of her shirt sleeve.

"Our camp isn't far."

"Our? Which tribe are you from?"

"Blackfoot." She'd misunderstood his meaning, but he let the misconception stand. Better she think an entire band of Blackfoot camped nearby and stay on her guard.

Something passed through the woman's eyes, then disappeared as her jaw tightened and she nodded. "Thank you for your help today. We would have struggled much more than you did to move the dinghy."

The passage would have been nigh impossible for them, but he wouldn't correct that untruth either. Let her keep her dignity. She seemed to be a scrappy creature, like one of the runt dogs in his mother's camp that fought for the larger bone against animals twice its size.

He turned to the man. "You have food enough for the evening meal?" They'd only brought two packs, which meant the heavier one remained below the rapids. Hopefully it didn't contain anything they'd need this night.

Maybe one of his companions would hike down and carry that satchel tomorrow morning while the rest of them took the boat and these packs. Neither Wilkins nor Susanna looked like they would last another day as difficult as this one.

And no matter how badly he wanted to put distance between himself and any female, he'd never been a man to stand by when someone needed help. He was pretty sure the others would feel the same.

"We have plenty." Even with the weariness thickening his tone, Wilkins's voice held a gentleness that made him wholly likeable. "Can you stay and take a meal with us? It's the least we can offer for all your hard work."

Beaver Tail shook his head. "I need to go." The night would be a short one as it was.

"Maybe in the morning then." Wilkins stepped forward and extended his hand. Before Beaver Tail could react, the older man clapped him on the arm. "God be with you on the trail. Come tomorrow mornin', we'll share a cup of coffee."

The touch was foreign. So unexpected. There wasn't a bit of malice in it, just pure friendliness.

Yet Beaver Tail couldn't remember ever being handled so. Jabbed with an elbow, sure. Pushed in the chest with a hard palm or fist, certainly. But nothing so kind as this man's gesture.

An inkling of memory slipped through his awareness. Just enough to tickle his longing. Someone else had rested a hand on his upper arm. A big hand, massive enough to be a bear paw. Yet the touch made him feel loved. Appreciated.

A sensation he hadn't felt in more years than he could count.

Beaver Tail turned away. He had no time for thoughts like these. Reaching for a new burst of energy, he stepped toward the trail leading upriver. As soon as a hill hid him from sight, he pushed into a run.

≈

Susanna stepped into the darkness to attend to personal matters before returning to her blankets. Some animal sound had awakened her, and she may as well take care of this before she went back to sleep. The night couldn't really be called dark, for an almost-full moon lit the sky, along with more stars than there must be droplets of water in the Missouri River.

Box elders lined the little creek near their camp, and she tucked herself behind one for privacy. A sting pricked her neck, and she swatted hard at the spot. These horrid mosquitos even attacked in the dead of night. Lewis and Clark had written the honest truth when they recorded in their journals that the mosquitos in this area were immensely numerous and troublesome.

A grunt nearby snagged her attention. The underbrush shook, not ten strides away. She gripped the tree beside her. Some creature was out there, big and clumsy. Why hadn't she brought her rifle?

She could only hope it was a beaver or badger, but images of the awful grizzlies Lewis and Clark had written of loomed in her mind. She struggled to see what lurked in the bushes. All she made out was the leaves shaking.

But she couldn't take a chance. Pushing off from the tree, she sprinted back toward camp. She'd barely run two strides before a mighty roar sounded from behind. Hadn't she read that grizzlies could run faster than men? Maybe this was only a harmless black bear. *Lord, let it be.*

The ground seemed to shake beneath her as a thudding noise chased close on her heels. She screamed, but she didn't dare slow down to shout any louder. A glance from the corner of her vision showed a creature so light brown its fur shone almost dirty white in the moonlight. She plowed forward as the fierce grunts closed in on her. Thick prairie grass and prickly pear slowed her as if she slogged through snow.

At this rate, she would never outrun the animal, and aiming straight toward camp had left her out in the open. Veering left toward the creek and its sheltering brush, she jumped a cluster of prickly pear. Her foot landed on a spike, but with the fear coursing through her, she ignored the pain.

If she could just make it to one of the trees ahead… Could bears climb trees? She couldn't remember for sure, but that might be her only chance of escape.

A blow struck her side, knocking her off balance. She screamed, but the sound was swallowed by a roar loud enough to shake her teeth. Her racing heart climbed into her throat as she stumbled forward, doing her best to keep from going down. Should she turn and fight the beast?

There was no way she'd win a battle against the strength she'd felt in that blow. She had to get to the trees.

Just as she regained her momentum, the animal slammed into her back, knocking her forward with a force that tore through her. Her head banged against the ground even as sharp claws flipped her over.

Pain roared through her like liquid fire. Searing her side, twisting her neck as another blow jerked her back the other direction.

This would be the end of her. Would Pa survive in this wilderness alone?

Another hit, this one to her leg, skidded her across the ground.

A rifle shot ripped through the air. The bear roared, the sound fiercer than any of the others.

She wanted to curl into a ball, to hide away from the creature, but every part of her pulsed with a pain more ferocious than she'd ever imagined.

Something hard and sharp clamped down on her leg. Another gun blast.

She couldn't breathe, couldn't think with the agony now honed in on her right thigh.

Then the pressure released.

The rifle sounded again, yet this time it seemed farther away. Through a distant haze.

She tried to fight it, but the haze closed in around her, blacker than the night.

*B*eaver Tail lay on his fur pallet, every part of his body tense. Three shots, so distant they could be from Wilkins's camp. Had danger found the man and his daughter? Or maybe the bullets were only meant to bring down game. Perhaps an elk had wandered near and they'd needed to replenish their meat supply. But in the middle of the night?

And three shots?

Something was wrong, he could feel it deep inside. Yet what could he do? He was two hours' run away from them. He'd have to wait and see how they fared in the morning's light.

Yet no matter how many times he reassured himself, his sleep came in restless fragments. Two hours before the sun would rise, he nudged French awake with his moccasined foot. The man mumbled something, probably in his native language, but his slurred words were hard to decipher.

"If you still want to help the woman and her father, we leave now." Beaver Tail moved on to Caleb's side. "Wake up."

The man groaned when Beaver Tail gave him the same nudge on his beefy shoulder. Caleb Jackson was a massive man, tall and broad enough to make most people quake in their buckskins. But his heart was just as oversized as the rest of him.

"We have visitors to help." That reminder should jar him out of his slumber.

"Why can't we help them in the daylight?" French peered at him with only one open eye.

As he'd suspected, Caleb hoisted himself to sit upright, his short-cut hair poking in all directions. He scrubbed a paw over his face, then blinked in the darkness.

Time to move on to the last man. He turned to Joel and eyed his face. Sleep hadn't softened his intense features much. His mouth formed a thin line, and his brow wrinkled. Maybe it would be simpler to leave him behind. But that would be the easy way out.

Beaver Tail gave him the same toe nudge he'd given the others. Joel—always in perfect control of himself—raised one eyelid. "I'm coming." His voice didn't even sound sleepy. Probably he'd awakened when Beaver Tail first rose and had been feigning sleep. That would be like the man.

Beaver turned away and reached for a piece of roasted meat. Then he grabbed three more for the trail. "French, you go to the bottom of the rapids and get whatever packs they left there. You two, I'm leaving now and I'll be running. If you want a part in this, get moving."

That was all the nursemaiding he planned to do. The rest, they could decide for themselves. It'd be nice to have help hauling that boat and the rest of their things, but he'd do the work himself if he had to.

It wouldn't be the first time in his life he'd had to bear the hard labor alone.

∽

"Those two on the outside look to be the worst."

Susanna forced her eyes open and watched as Pa peered at the tooth marks in her leg. He poured cool creek water over them.

The liquid burned like fire singing her skin, and she had to clamp tight around the stick in her hands to keep from screaming. Crimson-colored water streamed down her leg, reminding her too much of the blood that often leaked down Pa's chin after a coughing fit.

"We need to drain the blood from the bear carcass before it cools." She bit the words through clenched teeth. None of her bones were broken, so she could tend her own wounds. Her clothing would need stitched up too. But that could wait until daylight.

Not too much later than sunrise, though. How early would

Beaver Tail come? A wide swath of fabric hung from her trousers where the bear had clamped on her right thigh. As strong as the creature's jaws had been, it was a wonder his teeth hadn't crushed her bone. Maybe Pa's first bullet had weakened the animal.

Pa raised his focus to her face and eyed her for a long minute. She worked for a reassuring smile. Or at least a look that didn't show the depth of her pain.

She must have accomplished it, because he pushed to his feet. "I guess we'd better not let all that meat go to waste. Maybe our new Indian friend can use some of it too."

Good idea. She'd rather not have to haul around the meat from a full bear carcass, especially while she nursed these wounds. And especially as much food as this massive beast would provide. When Pa had stretched the body out, the creature looked to be taller than she was. From what they'd heard, game should be plentiful as they finished traveling up the Missouri and across the plains. They wouldn't want for food for a while. The mountain country was where hunting would become harder.

While Pa prepared the bear carcass, she struggled to her feet and limped back toward camp. Her head throbbed with every step, making the world around her spin. When she pressed her hand against her forehead, the pain eased a little, but each step took concentration to keep from falling. She had to shake free of the haze that still trapped her mind.

She applied the salve they used for wounds—something they'd had to dip into on this journey more often than she liked —then forced herself to trudge back out to where Pa worked over the bear.

She'd made it across half the distance when he saw her coming. He sat back on his heels, raising a hand to point at her. "You go right back to camp and lie down. I'm sure you have more than a few scrapes and tooth marks than those I've seen. Rest your head and let yourself recover. At least for tonight."

Normally, she'd ignore the warning. Skinning a full grizzly was too much work for him in his current condition, but she wasn't sure how much strength she had left in her.

He must have seen her indecision. "I'm only going to bleed it tonight. In the morning we'll finish the job."

She eased out a breath. He could handle that much. She started to nod, but the knife of agony that shot up her neck stilled the action. "All right."

Clamping her jaw to keep the pain inside, she turned and eased back toward their camp. Her bed pallet had never sounded so good.

CHAPTER 3

*V*oices drew Susanna from the fog of sleep, but it took several seconds before she could place any of the resonant tones.

Pa and…the Indian who'd carried their boat? She forced her grainy eyelids open but had to blink against the bright daylight. The aches in her leg and side gradually worked into her awareness, joining the steady throbbing in her head.

The voices had stopped, and she struggled to make her eyes and her mind focus. The figures finally shifted from blurry into a clearer picture.

A couple strides away, the Indian was crouched, watching her. His black hair was tied back in a leather strip at his nape but looked like it probably reached just below his shoulders. His dark eyes studied her with an unnerving intensity, as though he could see anything she tried to hide.

"Your head aches much?"

She would have thought the rumble of his deep voice would make the pain in her skull worse, but instead it soothed. Her pain must be showing on her face for him to know that much.

She started to nod but caught herself, unwilling to endure the extra throbbing.

Instead, she managed a wry smile. "You've been rolled by a bear before too?"

One corner of his mouth twitched. "Not by a bear, but rolling from a horse brings pain enough."

His gaze scanned the length of her. Not indecently but rather looking for injuries. Her hand closed over the edge of the blanket. Good thing she'd laid the wool covering over her to protect her skin from attacking mosquitoes. It now also concealed her leg from indecent exposure at the rip in her trousers.

Beaver Tail seemed to sense her unease, for he stood and turned to her father. It was then she saw the other man beside Pa. No, two men.

She pulled the blanket farther up her chest, although she still wore the linen tunic that was the only shirt she'd brought on the journey. Pa had protested when she'd donned the men's tunic and trousers, but if she was going to work like a man—rowing the dinghy upriver, hunting, and anything else Pa couldn't manage these days—she might as well have the freedom of men's clothing. She had brought one skirt but hadn't donned it in well over a month. Especially since there was no one in this wilderness who would understand the rules she was breaking, the rules of polite society.

Except maybe the two men standing beside her father would know. White men. Who'd surely come from the States.

"Susanna, this is Caleb Jackson and Joel Vargas. They've come with Beaver Tail to help carry our things the rest of the way around the falls." Pa motioned first to the giant of a man whose shock of auburn hair looked like it might shine copper in the sunlight, then to the smaller stranger, whose dark features fit tightly in his olive-colored face. Spanish maybe?

She mustered as much of a smile as she could in response to

their nods, then forced herself to lower the blanket as far as her waist. Why did even that act make her feel exposed? She'd need to find a way to get the men out of camp long enough for her to stitch up the gaping hole in her trousers.

"These fellas offered to help skin that she-bear before we head up the river. That's where we'll be if you need anything." Pa gave her a smile that held just enough twinkle to show he understood her dilemma.

A surge of love flowed through her. Such a wonderful father he was. What would she ever do without him? But before that thought could summon the burn of tears, she locked her jaw and nodded. "I'll cook some of the meat for us to eat today." Most of their fresh food was gone, so this would be a welcome relief from the heavily salted and preserved fare they'd resorted to the day before.

Pa led the men out of camp, each of them falling into step behind the other as they took the now well-worn path toward the bear. Beaver Tail was the last to go, and he paused long enough to turn a final probing stare on her. What did the man hope to see? Was he simply curious about a white woman? Maybe he'd never seen one before yesterday. Yet his gaze didn't seem to hold any curiosity. More like…taking her measure.

Well, he'd find her more than a match for any man in this territory. If not in physical strength, at least in tenacity.

~

*A*fter they'd skinned the bear, Beaver Tail left Caleb and Joel to ready the meat while he and Wilkins worked on the hide. Cleaning hides was usually women's work among his people, but Susanna didn't look to be in any condition to handle the task. Besides, living on his own meant every role fell to him. There was no such thing as women's work anymore. Just his own responsibilities.

And that was the way he wanted it. He didn't fit among all the women in his family, so it was best he be out on his own.

Caleb, Joel, and French were good companions, each of them handling their own tasks, yet sticking close enough to share safety and food. Clan-members where it mattered, yet not stepping all over his toes. And he could count on them in a pinch.

Or when he stumbled across a sick white man and his daughter who needed an oversize canoe carried around five waterfalls.

Once they had the pair and all their possessions moved to the top of the falls, what did Wilkins plan to do? What was his purpose for coming into the Great Plains, as the whites called this rolling land?

He slid a glance to the man. Wilkins worked with a steady focus, cutting the flesh from the hide. He didn't seem to know much about skinning, but once Beaver Tail had showed him what to do, Wilkins worked at it with an attention to detail many people didn't worry over.

"You've come to the plains to hunt?" He kept his voice as casual as he could. Some people didn't like to be questioned.

Wilkins looked up with an easy smile before turning back to his work. "Came here to see what there was to see. Always wanted to trace the Missouri to its headwaters, especially after I read Patrick Gass's book about his journey with Captains Lewis and Clark. Susanna and I figured now was as good a time as any." He turned his head away as a hacking cough punctuated the words, the sound shaking deep in his chest.

It took a long moment for the coughing to dwindle away, and Beaver Tail gave the man the dignity of not staring at him while he worked to regain control. Should he ask about the sickness? That was probably too personal a question, so he chose a different one. "I've not heard of this Patrick Gass or Lewis and Clark."

Wilkins wiped his sleeve across his mouth, and Beaver Tail

caught a flash of crimson. "Lewis and Clark led a group of men, Mr. Gass among them, by boat up the Missouri, then across the Rocky Mountains and all the way to the great ocean that lies to the west."

Beaver Tail played the words through his mind. With an Englishman for a father, he'd spoken both the English and Blackfoot tongues from his earliest days. He'd picked up a good bit of French from the trappers who passed through their camp. Yet he'd not heard the word *ocean*. He knew better than to show ignorance, though.

Even without knowing what that final part meant, the other words raised caution inside him. "You will go through the mountains?" That land was hard and relentless, not for the likes of a woman and a sick man, even if they traded for horses and packed enough food to see them through. The snows would be starting within the passing of another moon, and he'd seen the icy powder mount up higher than the tallest person. Higher even than Caleb, giant that he was.

"If we make it that far. I also want to see some of those geysers they wrote about where the water shoots straight up in the air. I'd like to meet some of the tribes in these parts. Maybe find out where the best place to winter is."

He could feel the weight of the man's glance.

"I suppose I should ask you, since you're from these parts."

Wilkins went back to his work, and silence fell between them. He was waiting for Beaver Tail to respond.

Would it hurt him so much to tell of his people? Especially when Wilkins seemed a genuinely good sort. "I've only traveled twice through this land and farther south. My people are the Blackfoot in the mountains to the north. I don't know of the geysers, but I do know the mountains you call Rocky are hard when the snows come. Beautiful yes, but the food moves to warmer lands and the winters are such that you could lose a hand or foot in only a few minutes if not prepared."

The lines in the older man's brow deepened. "I'd hoped to at least reach the mountains before winter. I don't know how long we'll be able to stay come spring."

Something about his tone—the sadness maybe—made Beaver Tail wonder why he didn't think they'd stay long. Did the man expect his illness to worsen? What of his daughter if the worst happened? But that was probably a worthless line of thought, for surely the man wasn't at death's door. Everyone obtained a cough at some time or another. This ailment would pass. Surely.

"There's one other thing." Wilkins's voice pulled Beaver's focus back up. The older man had stopped working and now pinned him with a solid gaze. "If something happens to me, I need someone to see Susanna back east. To my cousin in Boston. Her safety is more important to me than almost anything else. This will be hard on her, but I know she'll lean on God to see her through. I just need to make sure she'll be in a safe place where she can start fresh."

Beaver swallowed, his breath clearing from his chest. Take responsibility for another woman? Dealing with females was his greatest weakness. And this one probably wouldn't want the arrangement her father was requesting.

He forced himself to breathe and cleared his face of expression that might give away his thoughts. "I'm not sure I can do that."

The words were pure truth, but for some reason, they didn't make him feel any better.

Wilkins's gaze softened, not the reaction Beaver Tail expected from him. "I understand. If you change your mind, the offer still stands."

~

*S*usanna swatted a cloud of mosquitoes away from her face as she shifted the coffee closer to the fire's flame. Not even the smoke drove these awful creatures away. She'd be lucky if the coffee wasn't littered with the varmints by the time it finished brewing.

She couldn't quite stop the groan when she pushed to her feet, then fought a limp as she strode through the trees to the open area where the men worked. Beaver Tail's two friends were slicing the meat into smaller strips, so she moved toward them. "The fire's hot enough to start roasting." She smacked at a new sting on her hand.

The big man—her pounding head couldn't remember either of their names—held up several pieces of raw meat with a grin that tipped his mouth a little more on one side than the other. "This is ready to cook." He nodded toward her father and Beaver Tail, who were working on the hide. "See if BT has an extra sweetgrass pouch to keep the insects away."

The Indian raised his head at the apparent nickname. He wiped a hand in the grass, then reached under the tunic at his neck and pulled out a leather strap with a fabric pouch hanging from the end. After raising the string over his head, he held it out to her.

Would that little sack really keep the mosquitoes away? The thought was too appealing to turn down. But this one looked like the only leather necklace he wore. She hated to take his insect protection when he needed it as much as she. Yet he was offering…

She stepped forward and took the string before she could talk herself out of it. "Thank you." If it helped even a little, she owed this man more than a cup of coffee, no matter how precious the drink was, with their supply dwindling so rapidly.

He nodded and turned back to the bear pelt. Such a quiet man, this Indian. Was it part of his nature, or because he didn't know many English words? He spoke with such a slight accent, the latter didn't seem to be the case. Maybe all Indians were as quiet as he.

She turned back to the others. Understanding the mind of this stranger was the least of her worries this day. "I'm brewing coffee. By the time you finish cutting the meat, I should have enough of it cooked for our morning meal." Cleaning a hide that large would take longer, but surely all of them would need a break by then. Pa would, certainly.

When she had the food ready and the steaming brew had turned richly aromatic, she called the men. They filed into camp on the footpath, Mr. Jackson leading the way with an eager grin on his broad face. He had just a hint of overgrown boy to his features, which made it easy to like him. Mr. Vargas followed— now that coffee filled her senses, she could remember their names—and Pa settled a grateful smile on her as he entered the camp.

Beaver Tail wasn't among them. As she scooped out cups of coffee, she sent a glance toward the meadow where the men had worked but couldn't see through the trees. Maybe he'd gone to wash in the creek. Of course, the others had done that too and now stood in the camp. Perhaps he'd stayed behind to wash their equipment also.

By the time the other three had seated themselves with freshly roasted bear meat and tin cups of coffee, Beaver Tail still hadn't come. She glanced once more toward the meadow, but no Indian brave emerged through the foliage.

"He's still out there working. Said he ate his fill before he left our camp this morning." Mr. Jackson shrugged. "He's a funny sort, BT is, but a good man. Quiet, hard-working." He grimaced. "Not much for fun, but the kind of fellow you can't help but like anyway." Those final words were delivered with a cheeky grin.

"You're traveling together?" They seemed unusual, this band of three. All a similar age, at least somewhere in their twenties by her guess. As far as she could tell, that and the ability to speak English was the only thing they shared in common. Each of them seemed so different, in looks and personality—and even nationality.

Mr. Jackson took another swig of coffee, then released an appreciative breath. "That's good coffee, ma'am. Haven't had the real stuff in a month of Wednesdays. This tastes better than I remember."

She couldn't help but smile at his pleasure. "I brew it with licorice root to deepen the favor." And to help with Pa's cough, but that part she didn't need to share.

After another gulp, he seemed to remember her question. "Yep, we're on our way southwest to meet up with Joel's brother. We last heard he was travelin' with a Shoshone band down there, lookin' for horses we heard about from the Hidatsa."

So there would be a fourth in their group? Why had these men joined together in the venture? She phrased the question as innocently as she could. "Have you known each other long?"

He shot a sideways grin at Mr. Vargas, who'd been watching them as he sipped his coffee. With those dark eyes shifting from one person to the next as each spoke, he seemed to be almost brooding.

Mr. Jackson answered. "I met up with Joel an' Adam—he's the brother we're lookin' for—back in St. Louis. We all wanted to go west, so we joined up with a group of Frenchmen in a pirogue and almost worked our skinny legs off haulin' and pushin' that boat upriver." He scrunched his nose with the words, making him look even more like an overgrown boy. "We learned an awful lot on that trip, but the best part was that we met French along the way."

One side of his mouth tipped up. "Some days he makes me change that opinion, but he's mostly a good chap."

"French?" Surely there wasn't another in their group. A fifth?

Mr. Jackson nodded toward the north, where they'd left the last satchel of supplies downriver from the falls. "He's gone to get the rest of your things. Should be along any time now—if he's not takin' a nap." He winked at her. "BT woke us in the middle of the night to come help you folks." Then he raised his mug as if in salute. "Glad he did, though. This coffee's worth every minute of runnin' in the dark."

Beaver Tail had woken them in the middle of the night and made them run here? Her gaze wandered toward where he still worked in the heat and mosquitoes. Would he like coffee and just didn't want to stop for it? Surely he needed food for sustenance after exerting himself so much that morning.

She poured coffee into a bowl, since the other men were using their only cups, then gathered some meat and attempted to stand. Fire seared her leg as she used the muscles, and the pain nearly sent her down to her knees. She clamped her jaw against a cry, then set down the food and drink before she spilled them.

"Here, ma'am. Let us help you up." Mr. Jackson's words broke through her tension, but the hands that appeared at her side belonged to the quiet Mr. Vargas. He gripped her arm in a hold surprisingly gentle.

She shook her head. "I can do it." She was no fainting flower, and a leg wound that hadn't even broken a bone wouldn't send her running to a man for help.

"Are you certain?" Vargas had a slight accent that made each word short and a little choppy, yet his tone seemed kind.

"I am." She put more certainty into her voice when she could finally breathe through the pain in her leg.

His hand pulled away, leaving her on her hands and knees. Gritting her teeth, she ignored the burning from all three of her wounds and raised up on her good leg, using the injured one for balance.

Once she'd managed to stand, she eased her weight onto

both legs, but only enough to test the faulty limb. It held, although the muscles trembled.

Mr. Jackson lifted the bowl and plate of meat. "I'd be happy to take these out to BT, if that's where you were goin' with them."

She shook her head. She'd accomplish this short walk even if the effort killed her. Beaver Tail deserved her thanks for working so hard to help them. The least she could do was tell him face to face.

CHAPTER 4

*D*oing her best to disguise her limp, Susanna made her way through the trees and out into the open area. Their Indian guest bent over the dark mat of animal skin, the linen of his tunic turning translucent as the sun shone through, outlining his lean torso. Her mouth went dry at the sight. All that male strength honed on each stroke of his knife blade scraping the hide.

She had to force her feet to move forward, and not because of the pain in her leg. She wasn't one to ogle a man, but she could appreciate the beauty of God's handiwork as well as any other woman. She wouldn't let it affect her actions though.

Raising her chin, she limped onward with as much indifference as she could muster. He didn't look at her as she approached, just kept his focus on each swipe of metal against flesh and hide.

She did the same. Or at least, she tried to.

After stopping in front of the bear, she waited for him to finish and look up. Her gaze caught on the creature's massive paws, the pads large enough to send her flying, and the claws sharp enough to dig through her flesh in a single swipe. She could well remember both sensations, and the memories made her head swim.

She closed her eyes to still the spinning, but that only made things worse. She forced the lids open again. She would conquer her body if it was the last thing she did.

While she'd been taming her wayward reactions, Beaver Tail had risen and now stood in front of her. Watching her struggles with eyes so dark they were almost black. She hadn't even heard him move, although now that she thought about it, the sound of his blade scraping had ceased.

She held out the dishes, hopefully to distract him from her embarrassing display. "I brought you coffee and food." The words tumbled out of her mouth, probably only making things worse. Could he hear her mortification?

He took the offering with a nod, then raised the bowl to his mouth as he dropped his gaze.

"I'm sorry we don't have any more cups. Since it's just Pa and me, we only brought two of everything." Now she was rambling.

He nodded again, but this time his gaze bounced off her face. Those eyes, so dark and piercing. Had she realized how intense they were when she'd met him yesterday? Now she couldn't remember. Couldn't recall much of anything with his presence looming larger than life before her.

She needed to escape back to camp, but there was one more thing that had to be said. His attention shifted away from her as he bit off a chunk of meat, giving her courage to speak. "I wanted to thank you for your help. For carrying the boat. Bringing your friends. All of this." She motioned toward the bear hide. "Things would have been much harder without you." Those last words didn't burn as much to speak as she'd expected.

She hadn't quite said, *We couldn't have done it without you*. She would have found a way. Somehow. Maybe left the boat behind and moved forward on foot until they could procure horses.

That wouldn't have been so bad. On her, anyway. And they would have moved as slowly as they needed to for Pa.

But now they wouldn't have to. They would accomplish in two days what had taken Lewis and Clark's expedition a month to complete—portaging around the five falls. Hopefully when they had everything moved to the upper portage camp, she'd be able to hike down and actually see one of the falls.

Treacherous cliffs and other landscape around the massive waterfalls required this portage trail to veer away from the river and onto smoother land, not allowing any view of the water in most sections. It would be a shame to come this close without seeing any of those natural wonders, though.

Pa would want to see them too. After all, wasn't that why they'd come these hundreds of miles up the Missouri? So Pa could experience this wild country as he'd always dreamed?

"I am happy to help." The quiet depth of Beaver Tail's voice pulled her from her wandering thoughts. He pierced her with those eyes again. Seeing through to her inner depths. Did he see how much she needed him? How relieved she was not to bear the brunt of the labor to move their supplies upriver? Especially with her body still so traitorous after last night's battle with the grizzly.

She couldn't let him see these things. She shouldn't even be thinking them. The first step in maintaining her defenses required her to conquer her thoughts.

Stiffening her spine, she nodded. Now that she had that out of the way, it was time she set to work.

A quick scan of the area showed that Mr. Jackson and Mr. Vargas had finished cutting the edible parts from the carcass. The only thing left was to dispose of the remnants far enough away from camp that they wouldn't draw predators.

The last thing she needed was a wildcat lurking in the trees, its appetite only whetted from the innards of the bear.

She should handle moving the leftovers while the men

rested. After all, they'd done the hard work. But even as she moved toward the bloody spot, her stomach revolted. She hated this part.

In fact, that was one of the good things about always being on the move as they'd traveled upriver—she never had to clean the kill site after hunting. Just cut out the meat, fur, and anything else they needed, then paddle away. They usually set up camp early on such days so she and Pa would have time to clean the hide and cook the meat.

But now, there was no way to get out of the nasty job without shirking her part of the work. And that, she wouldn't do.

She stopped in front of the mess, inhaled a deep breath and held it, then bent to scoop up a wad of intestines.

"Wait." Beaver Tail's voice cut through the air, pausing her reach partway down.

She turned to raise her brows at him.

He motioned toward the organs and bones. "There is much we can use. And the best parts for eating are still there."

Her stomach convulsed at the word *eating*, and she had to take in a few calculated breaths to still the roiling. What kind of savage was he that he thought intestines and the other nasty organs were the best parts for eating? Maybe he'd learned uses for some of these aside from food, but she'd just as soon do without whatever supplies or trinkets he planned to make. The sooner she had this bear far away from her, the better.

Straightening, she pretended to study the contents strewn before her. "I don't think we have time to do anything more with this. I'll just get it away from camp so the smell doesn't draw any more animals. In fact, since we're heading on in the next few hours, maybe we could leave this mess here." That would give them incentive to load up and hit the trail earlier.

He shook his head. "We'll stay here tonight, then finish the portage at first light." He took a bite of the meat she'd brought him.

She stiffened. "Why would we do that? We need to keep moving." What if something happened to send Beaver Tail and his friends away before they finished carrying everything? She wouldn't be able to rest easy until Pa and the supplies were safely ensconced above the falls.

This time, only a single shake of his head. As though the matter was settled. "There is much to do here. Better to do the work well then leave this camp with the rising sun."

The tightness in her chest made her injuries ache worse. If only she could give vent to the frustration building inside her. Yet how could she dispute the need to do this unsavory job correctly? Tell him she'd rather settle for half-right so they could run far away from here? At least he sounded like he planned to stay and finish moving everything.

And since using the bear's insides seemed to be so important to him, he could handle the task. She reached for his knife. "I'll finish scraping the hide. Do what you want with this." She waved toward the mass on the ground, careful not to actually look at the stuff. If he tried to feed her from that pile of innards, she'd bring out her own blade. Or maybe her rifle.

He extended his knife to her, but when she closed her hand over the hilt, he didn't release the tool. That forced her to raise her gaze to his face. To see the tugging at the corners of his mouth and the sparkle in his dark eyes. He thought this situation was funny. Was maybe even laughing at her. And of course, that made the blood surge through her veins, raising her ire all the more.

But she forced herself to relax, to take deep, even breaths. She wouldn't fly into a fit of emotion like a silly woman. She could be every bit as controlled as this Indian, with all his quiet stoicism.

He must have noticed the change in her, for the humor fled

from his expression, replaced by a quiet regard. Then he released the knife into her hand.

Yet he didn't move, which required her to turn away first. She dropped to her knees beside the bear hide, ignoring the pain in her thigh.

After scraping several long strokes over a section, she shifted to check his position from the corner of her eye. Finally, he'd moved to the pile of organs and bones, so quietly she'd not heard even the rustle of his clothing.

She forced herself to ease out a breath, pushing the tension from her shoulders with the spent air.

To be so quiet, this man churned her emotions like no one she'd ever known. And that made him even more dangerous than she'd first feared.

~

*W*hat was he doing with this woman? Playing games and drawing out her ire would only get him in trouble. Hadn't he learned his lesson already?

More than once actually, but that last time had scalded him and his family so badly he could still feel the flames. Hopefully the damage for his mother and sisters was lessening now that his presence no longer tainted the entire family.

He liked to understand the things around him—could study an object until he comprehended the inner workings and knew almost precisely what would come next. But women were the one creature he'd never understood.

As he gathered up the bones that would produce the best soup stock, the sounds of steady scraping drifted from behind him. He'd intended today's delay to give her a chance to heal, but one glance at her resolute expression as she reached for his knife had told him he'd be wasting his breath to send her back to camp. His mother was like that. Never one to back down from a challenge.

Susanna didn't seem all that complicated so far. In fact, her determination and strength were impressive. But underneath it all, he could sense her fear. Was her father's illness the source of her worry? Her anxiety didn't appear to come from the wildness of this land. At least, this country didn't seem to be the root of her fear. She looked to have a healthy respect for this untamed wilderness—she'd be foolish not to—but the distress she tried so hard to hide must be rooted deeper inside her.

He'd seen the panic in her eyes.

But who was he to believe he knew the inner workings of a female? In the past, when he'd been arrogant enough to think it, then that female would reverse direction so fast he never saw the change coming. And he was left staggering in the aftermath.

Never again.

He'd see Susanna and her father to the top of the falls, then he and the others would be on their way. These newcomers had made it this far. They could finish their journey on their own.

There was no way he'd allow himself to be burned and left to bear the consequences again.

A rousing laugh drifted from the direction of the camp. French must be back, charming everyone he met, as usual. Maybe his presence would spur the others back to work, for there was certainly a great deal to do here.

And Susanna needed to rest. She seemed to be trying to cover it, but her limp was easy to detect, as was the squint of pain that bespoke a head still throbbing.

Surely her father would send her to bed when he saw her condition. If he didn't, Beaver would suggest it.

But it turned out he didn't have to. When Wilkins stepped from the trees beside Joel, French trailing behind, his gaze honed in on his daughter. He reclaimed his place scraping fur across from where Susanna worked, and French also joined them, taking up a position at the bear's massive hind paws.

Beaver kept an eye on them as he worked alongside Joel to sort the useful organs and bones, then take them to the creek for cleansing. He couldn't hear anything said by those working the bear hide, but only a few minutes passed before Susanna rose and wiped her brow with a sleeve.

She walked toward Beaver Tail and held out his knife, hilt first. He nodded toward the ground beside him, as his hands were currently covered in bear fat. She laid the blade where he motioned. "This is a fine piece of craftsmanship. Did you make it?"

He sent a glance to the tool, with its elk antler handle. He'd carved a beaver at the base of the hilt and worked the grip so it molded to his hand perfectly. This wasn't the first knife he'd fashioned, but this one had turned out well. He nodded acknowledgement of her words, and that seemed to be enough for her, because she turned and limped back toward camp.

And no matter how hard he tried, he couldn't keep his gaze from trailing her.

CHAPTER 5

*S*usanna blinked against the bright daylight. How late had she slept?

She pushed her blanket off and had to bite back a moan as every part of her body protested the movement.

A motion by the campfire grabbed her attention. Pa, scooping a cup full of liquid from the pot. Coffee, she could only hope. She needed something strong to face the pain rumbling through her.

At least her head didn't throb as much this morning. A reprieve she was grateful for, because the rest of her felt like she'd been dragged behind a running horse for a mile or two.

"This should help what ails you." Pa shuffled toward her, the tin cup cradled in both hands.

His eyes crinkled into the usual deep grooves at the edges, his gaze gentle as it soaked over her like a warm blanket on a cool night. He didn't speak as he lowered himself to sit on a log beside her. He groaned a bit with the effort, which turned into a cough. That awful hacking cough that took over his entire body, jarring him like a massive hand thumping his back.

She pushed up to sit and grabbed for the cup before all the

precious coffee sloshed out. If only she could help him instead of simply saving the drink. But she knew from far too much experience that there was nothing she could do except be there, hoping her presence comforted even a small bit.

God, help him. Take this awful condition away from him. So many times she'd prayed this. If only God would act. She knew everyone had to die at some point, but not yet. Not like this. *Lord, please.*

They'd already tried everything else, including the expensive medicine the doctor in St. Louis had suggested. Even the moist caves and the sulfur springs hadn't brought relief, despite the fact they were touted to have saved the lives of others who'd been near death's door from consumption.

Pa's hacking finally slowed, and he released a last hoarse bark before wiping his mouth with the handkerchief he always kept near. He balled the cotton square quickly, but the flash of blood leapt out at her. Next time, she should turn away sooner.

He cleared his throat, then nodded toward the coffee she still clutched in both hands. "Drink up. The boys have already headed upriver. I told 'em we'd be along later this morning."

The boys. Reality flashed like a slap to her face, bringing with it vivid memories from the day before. The men had lingered around their camp, working the bear hide and sundries, gathering firewood, doing any other chores they could find, and swapping stories with Pa. She hadn't seen her father enjoy himself so much in months.

Mr. Jackson and French were the most outgoing by far, the latter regaling them with tales of his various trapping journeys with the North West Fur Company. It was a wonder how much he'd done being so young, but he said he'd joined on his first expedition at the age of fourteen. The deep weather-worn lines across his brow and under his eyes made it hard to calculate his exact age, but his grin made him look no more than five-and-twenty at most.

Beaver Tail hadn't spent much time lingering in camp. The man worked like a demon drove him, using almost every last scrap of the bear's insides, just as he'd said. Then he'd covered the bloody remains with dirt.

After that, she'd barely been able to get him to stay long enough to eat the stew she'd had simmering all afternoon. When he left, he took his friends with him.

Now, the men must have come and gone, by the look of the empty camp. Only her bedding and the small pot she used to brew coffee or tea remained. And Pa's favorite hunting rifle, leaning against a tree. This was the second one he'd made after perfecting his rifled bore, and it held a special place in his heart. Leaving behind his other guns had been one of the hardest parts of departing from their home. That and all the memories there. But they had each other, and they were making new memories in this beautiful country.

She downed the last gulp of coffee, then pushed to her feet. She couldn't hold back her groan this time. The effort was just too much. And Pa seemed to see her pain no matter how hard she tried to hide it anyway.

Setting the cup aside, she rolled up her bedding, tucking the blanket inside the thick fur she used as a bottom pad. The underside of the hide served to keep her bedroll almost water-proof, a fact she was more than thankful for when water sloshed into the boat during thick rapids.

Within a few minutes, she'd finished her morning ministrations, and they set out on the path. The track along the portage trail was more worn than she'd expected it to be, whether from deer or human feet it was hard to tell. But the half dozen deer, two elk, and plethora of squirrels and other small animals they saw certainly proved this section was heavily traveled.

The longer the morning progressed, the hotter the sun beat down and the more mosquitos they had to swat. The sweetgrass pouch seemed to keep many of them at bay, but the multitude of pests would be a challenge for even the best repellant. At times, the insects swarmed in a tight cloud around them, as thick as gnats around a fresh cow pile.

"Did the men say how far to the upper portage camp?" If she hadn't slept so late, she could have asked them herself. Yet as much as her body ached now, how much worse would she have felt without the extra rest?

"They didn't tell me exactly, but Beaver Tail said he'd go and come back for us. I told him not to worry 'bout that. We'd be along shortly. But that makes me think the hike would be three or four hours."

Three or four hours running or walking? From the stories she'd heard the day before, the men were accustomed to covering the land in a jog when they weren't riding horses.

"You're more than halfway there."

The strange voice sent her heart into her throat, and she fought down a scream as a figure stepped from the trees to their right.

Beaver Tail. She forced herself to breathe normally so her pulse would slow.

He fell into step beside her as though he had no awareness of the shock his sudden presence had given her. Maybe his friends were accustomed to sudden appearances. Or maybe they'd learned to hear him coming. She would do well to pay better attention to her surroundings.

Beaver Tail reached to unburden her father, taking the rifle and a small bag slung over his shoulder. It was surprising Pa allowed the help. He must be struggling more than he let on.

"You youngsters must have been moving at quite a lick to cover all this ground so early." Pa's breathing seemed to be coming heavier than usual.

She forced herself to slow, and Beaver Tail matched her pace, although it must have felt like a crawl to his long-legged stride.

"I was hopin' we'd get to see one of the falls before we move on. Will we pass close to one by chance?" Her father's breath caught on a wheeze, and she slowed even more. Maybe they should stop for another rest.

"There's a trail to one I've heard called Upper Falls. I can take you there."

Something inside her stirred with the possibility. They'd heard the thundering of falls several times, yet ravines, cliffs, or trees always rose up to block their view. What would it be like to stand at the edge of such a vast wall of water? To feel the spray and be deafened by the sound of so much power?

"That'd be nice." Pa's breath hitched. "Real nice." He stopped and pressed a hand to his chest as his shoulders rose and fell with each labored breath.

Fear churned in her own chest as she dropped her bedroll and the small pot she carried and stepped close to him. She laid a hand on his arm but didn't dare apply pressure that would force his body to work any harder than it already had to. "Let's sit and rest a while." She glanced around, but there were no longer trees around, leaving only the gentle slope of the plains. No fallen trunks or rocks to offer a seat.

"Here." Beaver Tail picked up the bedroll she'd been carrying and placed it behind her father. "Sit."

She helped Pa ease down, and he sat with hands on his knees, breath coming in wheezing gasps.

God, help him. Let him breathe.

She glanced over at Beaver Tail, whose brow furrowed as he studied her father. He raised his gaze to meet hers, and for once she could read a little of his expression. Questions churned in his eyes.

How much should she tell him? Pa tried so hard to keep his troubles private. He hated the way some people coddled him once they knew of his illness. Others treated him like a leper, as though his condition could spread through only a glance, even though every doctor who'd examined her father assured them the disease wasn't contagious. A type of cancer in his lungs, they'd said.

Beaver Tail clearly saw her father wasn't well. Maybe if she said something general, it would assuage his curiosity and still allow Pa to keep some dignity.

"He has trouble breathing sometimes. Nothing that's catching, just a pain in his lungs." She pressed a hand to her chest, watching Beaver Tail to make sure he understood. It was still hard to believe an Indian could have such a complete understanding of English like he appeared to possess. Had he been raised among whites?

He nodded, then returned his focus to her father. Pa's breathing had quieted a little now, and the knot in her chest eased.

Beaver Tail picked up the pot she'd dropped. "I'll get water to drink." Then he turned and jogged away, his long legs covering two or three times the distance with each stride that most men could have managed.

$\approx$

The sight of so much water spilling over the edge of the rock, thundering in relentless waves, should have captured Beaver Tail's attention completely. It always had in the past.

But with Susanna standing just ahead of him, her side profile strong against the magnificent backdrop of the falls, he couldn't pull his attention away from her. Those sculpted cheekbones tapered to a pointed chin so delicate, he would hardly have believed it belonged to this strong woman.

Her father stood beside her, his outline stooped with shoulders sagging, making him look even older than he did when seen from the front. A sharp contrast to the strong lines of his daughter's profile.

But Beaver Tail would do best not to dwell on the sight before him. Lingering around this woman would only cause him trouble.

He turned away, staring upriver to where his traps were set. He'd not checked them in two days, which meant whatever he'd caught had likely already become a meal for another creature by now. Maybe he could check a few close snares while this pair lingered at the falls.

Stepping forward, he motioned for their attention. "Stay here. I'll return soon."

Hopefully they wouldn't leave before he returned to help them. While he was around, there was no need for the pair to carry their burdens. Also, they'd want him to show the quickest way to the place where Caleb and the others waited with their boat and supplies.

He'd made it partway to the first trap—an underwater pole device he'd crafted near a large beaver dam—when the rustle of leaves alerted him to the person following. The footsteps came whisper-light, which meant it must be Susanna, and she was probably trying to conceal her presence.

Did she follow him merely out of curiosity? He'd not read anything threatening in her manner so far, yet he'd also not expected her to leave her father alone. She must have a good reason for shadowing him now.

He didn't mind showing her his traps. Especially if it would set her fears of him at ease. So he kept on his route, veering closer to the river in the one place where the cliffs lowered enough to allow him access to the water.

She approached nearer behind him, probably feeling comfortable because of the tree cover around them. He waited until she stopped, then turned to face the tree she'd ducked behind. She did a remarkable job of hiding behind the slender cottonwood. At first glance, he wouldn't have known she was there.

But she had to be. Now he could hear her breathing. And a grumpy squirrel nattered at her from the tree's branches, clearly upset she'd disturbed his work.

Beaver fought to keep from smiling—at both the squirrel and the woman. "Would you like to see what's in the trap?" He looked straight at the tree, but it was three long breaths before she stepped from behind the trunk.

She had her chin raised, her eyes flashing. No sheepishness at being caught, only the spark of irritation. "What are you doing?"

He had to fight harder not to smile. Being riled like this made her even more fetching than before. "I'm checking my traps, the three around here anyway." He nodded toward the river. "Would you like to see if we caught a beaver?"

Her gaze shifted to the water, then back to him. She wanted to see—the desire was written all over her.

So he turned and eased down to the river's bank. She would follow, if he'd read her correctly.

But then, he'd been completely wrong before, and it had been the end to the life he'd been destined for. The end of the life his family deserved.

CHAPTER 6

*B*eaver Tail strode upriver a short distance to the snare he'd set near a small beaver dam. Many people didn't trap in the summer, since these furs would be lesser quality than those he took in the winter. But they needed the meat, and he might as well catch something that could serve as both food and trade goods.

He waded into the water, doing his best not to flinch at the cold. The pole marking his trap was only a few strides in, and he pulled up the cord to see what he'd caught.

The beady eyes of a river otter stared up at him. Not a beaver, but still good for eating. He cut the carcass free, then turned to drag it back to the narrow edge of bank.

Susanna stood there watching him, her gaze a little wide. "Is that an otter? We've seen a few on our journey, but I wasn't certain if it was an otter or another creature."

He nodded as he hoisted the animal out of the water. He should reset the trap before readying the animal for transport.

He waded in again. Maybe he should invite Susanna closer to see how he reset the trap. But she was peering at the otter, so he let her be.

As hot as it was on the plains, this nook stayed cool under the shrubbery that lined the bank and cliffs—and made the perfect breeding ground for mosquitoes. He swatted at several that pierced the skin of his arm. He'd already made a new pouch of sweetgrass to ward them away since he gave his other to Susanna, but the new plant didn't seem to be working as well. In fact, he wore two satchels, since he'd made one for her father too but hadn't give it to the man yet.

A splash by his leg grabbed his attention just as a sharp poke jabbed his skin under the water. He kicked out, and his foot struck a body. Definitely larger than a fish.

Another stab of pain pierced his other leg, this time more like an arrow driving through his leathers, penetrating skin and shooting deep into his flesh. He doubled over, kicking hard to shake away the creature embedded in his leg.

The animal shoved against his other leg, knocking him off balance. Beaver Tail struggled to stay upright, but the animal bit again, driving its fangs lower, just above his ankle. He toppled backward into the water, the icy cold reaching up to envelop his body.

Even while the creature still clenched its teeth around his leg, another set of fangs dug deep into his upper arm. Beaver Tail thrashed to free himself from both attackers.

Two of them.

He had to get back to shore. His hand struck one of the animals again, making contact with thick, course hair. Beaver maybe? Perhaps the creatures whose home he'd set his trap beside. Or maybe another otter. They usually traveled in small groups.

Both animals released him as he struggled to crawl back to the bank. But his effort seemed to anger them, for they struck again with fury. Biting farther up his leg, his side, his hand. They seemed to be everywhere at once. Maybe more than two.

He couldn't keep track, but he finally dragged himself from

the water. One of the animals had a hold on the back of his leg, following him onto the shore.

Only then did his mind register the screaming. Susanna beat at the animal, shrieking like an enraged turkey as she struck the creature over and over with a stick.

Beaver rolled over to pull himself from the grasp of those fangs, catching sight of the long, furry body of a river otter.

The animal finally released him and slipped back into the river. Susanna's screaming ceased, and quiet sank over the area while he struggled to catch his breath.

"Are you hurt?" She dropped to her knees beside him as he sat propped up by his hands, his legs extended.

Blood soaked through his buckskin leggings in several places. The leather was torn in even more spots, and he felt like he'd been mauled by a wildcat. Or maybe caught in a hive of bees, stung all over.

She reached for his arm, pulling back a flap of torn, bloody fabric to reveal crimson trickling from several gashes. "These need to be cleaned, and I bet you'll need stitches."

He raised his focus from his arm to her face, and she met his gaze.

"I have what I need in our supplies you've taken upriver. Can you make it that far?" Concern laced her eyes, a look that bolstered his strength.

"I'm fine." The warmth of her hand on his arm made the pain fade almost completely in that area. As much as he'd like to have this woman tend his wounds, perhaps letting her touch him wasn't a good idea. Not unless he could detach himself from the pleasure of having her so near.

He forced his battered body to stand, and she rose too, stepping back to give him space. He sent a glare toward the river where his trap still stood—half of it anyway.

"Was that another otter that attacked you?"

"More than one." He turned from the water and reached

down to snag the dead animal he'd retrieved from the trap. "I've never seen them attack like that. Maybe they were protecting a den." He started down the trail back to her father. It looked like he wouldn't be resetting the snare. Not much could induce him to walk back into that water. Susanna came up beside him, and he matched his pace to hers.

In the murky river water, he'd not even seen the animals before they struck. What if Susanna had been with him in the water? The thought sharpened the pain of every bite mark, many feeling like they'd pierced all the way to his bones.

Even though Susanna had been spared the attack this time, she and her father were traveling on the river. They could easily be assaulted by otters any time they stepped into the water to board the boat. But otters weren't the only danger, as her run-in with the bear well proved. How could the two of them alone protect themselves?

Yet he couldn't worry about that. He'd see that they and their possessions made it to the camp above the falls, then he and the other men would mount their horses and ride away.

Joel was already pushing to leave out tomorrow morning. Although they'd all agreed to make a relaxed trip to find the Shoshone band Adam was living with, Joel never seemed to understand the meaning of *relaxed*. He fidgeted like a horse with the bit in its teeth every time they stopped for a day or two. Beaver wouldn't be able to talk the man into staying at their current camp for another day.

When he and the others rode out tomorrow morning, Susanna and her father would be on their own.

~

"*I* say we invite them along with us. They're going the same direction we are. They could ride a couple of the pack horses, and we won't be put out in the least."

Beaver Tail stood a little back from his friends, watching the exchange between them. Even though French spoke the words with his usual relaxed manner, the fact that he was standing up to the others showed just how strongly he felt about this decision.

"They'll slow us down." Joel kept his voice low, but it held the usual intensity he'd mastered these days. "They came up the Missouri on their own, they must want to stay alone. They could have tagged along with a boat of Frenchies if they'd wanted help—just like we did."

Caleb shrugged. "We could at least ask 'em. If they say no, we'll ride out this morning like we planned."

"And if they say yes, it'll be a half day at least before we can dig deep enough to cache their boat and any supplies we can't carry." Joel turned his glare on Beaver. "We don't have enough room on the pack horses for two people without leaving some of your furs behind. Shall we bury them in the cache too?"

They all knew the wet earth would damage the hides unless he took the time to protect them, which Joel would do his best to disallow. The man's suggestion was merely his attempt to strike at a soft spot. To gain an ally.

But Beaver Tail would rather stay neutral in this battle. Especially since his desires already warred inside him over the decision. He hadn't told the others that Wilkins had asked him to be their guide through the rest of their journey. French or Caleb would probably jump at the chance to travel with the pretty Susanna. Or maybe he was underestimating them and their loyalty to Joel. He knew what it was like for others to think the worst of him, and he wouldn't do the same to these men who'd proven to be friends.

But in truth, why wouldn't he want one of these men to accompany Wilkins and Susanna? Caleb or French could protect them, and would likely be happy to see Susanna back down the river to the land of the white people if needed.

A pinch nipped at his chest. Did Wilkins really expect to die?

The mountain country wasn't where he needed to be then, especially as winter would be on them within another moon or two. Could Beaver in good conscience leave a sick man and a young woman to face the fierce season in that unrelenting land on their own?

Maybe a warning would suffice. But giving an honest caution would require recommending that they hike back around the portage trail and paddle downriver as fast as they could. Back to the land they knew, a home where they would be safe. And he'd almost rather take French's side and argue to bring the pair along with them than tell Joel they'd need another day or two to carry the boat and supplies back where they'd started.

"What do you think, BT? You've been awful quiet." Caleb must be tired of playing the peacemaker.

Beaver scanned the three faces, much easier to see now that the sun had fully risen. French looked expectant, as though there was only one possible answer that made sense. Joel's scowl said he might be close to heading out on his own, something that didn't sit well in Beaver's gut. The man had saved his life twice now, and they'd all three sworn to help him find his missing brother. Although Joel snarled like an angry dog most days, he really was a good man. The kind Beaver would be thankful to have with him through any trial. Besides, if Beaver'd had a brother, especially one who was possibly lost or held against his will, he'd fight against even an hour's delay in reaching him.

He folded his arms across his chest. Maybe they could still help Wilkins and Susanna without inviting them to travel along. "I'll give them my pack horse. Even with only the one mount, their journey will be easier than paddling through all the rapids that lie ahead. I can move some of my furs to Joel's pack mare." He sent his friend a sideways look. "And the rest will fit on my own mount. This way we can bid farewell to them both without a guilty conscience." At least, not as much guilt.

Caleb tipped his head, as though considering the idea, then nodded.

French shook his head and threw his hands down. "I don't believe you all." Then he turned and marched back to where the animals stood tied, ready to load up and ride out. Was French angry enough to leave their group in order to help these two pilgrims?

For a moment, Beaver stood with Caleb and Joel, watching their friend. Usually not much riled the man. But maybe he was right in this case. Maybe giving Wilkins a horse and sending them on their journey was the coward's way out. Was Beaver letting his longing to distance himself from any sign of a female influence this decision? As much as that really was his desire, he wouldn't put his own selfish whims ahead of another's life.

"Best get packing." Joel's growl jerked them all from their thoughts as the man turned toward camp.

Beaver Tail strode toward the horses to ready the spotted gelding he'd leave with Wilkins.

French was grumbling something under his breath, in his native language of course. Probably nothing Beaver Tail wanted to understand. Before Beaver had his pack animal readied, the wiry Frenchman had loaded his bay pack mare with half her normal cargo and was stomping toward the camp, dragging the animal behind him. The poor horse had to trot to keep up.

Did he plan to start the quarrel up again? He wouldn't bring his animal just for an argument though. Maybe he planned to donate the horse for Wilkins and his daughter to ride. That was the more likely possibility, although it would be a sacrifice for their party to lose two animals. Still, they'd have four horses left to ride and two for packing supplies.

Wilkins and Susanna would be much better off with two horses than in their oversized canoe. They'd have to leave the boat behind, and Joel surely wouldn't allow time for Beaver to stay and bury the craft so they could retrieve it later. Unless he chose to stay on his own, then catch up with the men later. That could be a possibility.

With a sigh, Beaver Tail ducked under the tie rope for the horses and followed his friend back to camp. Nothing was ever easy when a female was involved. True, it didn't seem like Susanna was trying to cause problems in this situation. But her mere presence had created the first argument the four of them had experienced in the weeks they'd been traveling together.

He should have turned and run the moment he'd first seen Susanna Wilkins.

CHAPTER 7

*S*he should be grateful for the horses. And she was. Really.

But as she watched the four men ride away, a weight pressed hard on her chest, smothering. Making her struggle for breath the way Pa did after his coughing fits. For the first time in this journey, the sheer magnitude of what lay before them rose up like a wall reaching to the heavens, impossible to scale. This land was so vast, with so many ferocious animals that could attack from nowhere. Weather that could turn from searing heat one moment to hailstones large enough to bruise the next. And the men had spoken of a winter ahead that could obliterate an entire tribe of people if they weren't prepared.

Were she and Pa prepared? Not for what French and the others had described.

Maybe Pa was right and they *should* turn back. Getting the boat back around the falls would be a trick, but now that they had these horses, they could ride back down the Missouri. Back to civilization and some semblance of safety. Pa's condition would still be just as bleak. But at least it was a danger she knew and could prepare for.

Hopelessness rose up in her chest to strangle her. These thoughts were pure selfishness. Pa had longed for this expedition for years. Not just a chance to discover new country, but also to find peace for him in the majesty of this land. The least she could do was see him through it.

Turning to him, she summoned a smile. "Looks like it's just us again." They'd been here before. Would he insist they turn back now or could she talk him into riding on a little farther?

His gaze cloaked her with warmth, and he settled a hand on her shoulder. "My girl."

That look, that touch, the love in his words—they made every unknown trial worth the struggle.

Pa squeezed her shoulder, then turned toward the horses. "Looks like—" His breath caught on a wheeze, which melded into a cough, and the wracking hacks took over his body, bending him over as he struggled to control them.

"Pa." Desperation rose inside her as she stepped nearer, her hand hovering above his back. If only her touch could bring relief, but the weight of her hand would only make his struggle harder. *Everything* made his struggle harder.

So she turned to their food pack and extracted the pouches containing ground licorice root and garlic. A tea would help more than anything else she could do.

Pa's coughing fit finally faded to a few lingering wheezes, and like a glutton for punishment, she turned to him in time to see him wipe the blood dribbling down his chin. Her gut clenched at the sight, then she forced her gaze back to the pot simmering among the coals.

She worked for a casual tone in her voice. "We can stay in this camp today and repack our supplies for the horses." That would give Pa some time to rest.

She would be everlastingly thankful for the horses instead of the boat. Even though she'd probably need to walk so her horse could carry their supplies, she'd rather hike for months than have to row that dinghy upriver, especially through all the rapids that were supposed to lay ahead.

A shrill whinny sounded from the paint gelding Beaver Tail had left for them. The bay mare beside it raised her own call as both animals stared off into the distance.

Susanna sat back on her heels and studied the horizon where the horses were looking. The same direction the men had ridden only a short while before. She raised a hand to shield her eyes from the morning sun, and she could just see a figure bobbing in the place where earth met sky.

More than one figure.

Her heart picked up speed as she made out four separate shapes, with the outline of one bearing a striking resemblance to Beaver Tail's broad shoulders and regal bearing atop his horse.

Why were they coming back? Had they forgotten something? Decided to take the two horses after all? Surely all four of them wouldn't need to return for a simple errand like that. They must know she and Pa would give the animals back if asked.

It was too much to hope they might be returning to invite her and Pa to travel with them. Did she even want that? She'd appreciated the men's help more than she should've allowed herself over these last two days. Especially carrying the boat and supplies, but also with the bear. She'd allowed herself to relish the assistance more than was good for her.

Now she was letting herself hope for something that would never happen. And even if it did, riding with these men may not be a good plan for them anyway. Pa would need extra time to rest, maybe even more so when they switched to horseback instead of the boat.

She rose and faced the approaching riders. "What do you suppose they want?"

Pa stood beside her, his hand also raised to shield the glare of the morning sun. "I guess we'll see." Something in his voice made her glance over at him. A secret smile turned up the corners of his mouth. He didn't look at her, just kept staring out at the men until they reined in before her and Pa.

Beaver Tail was in the lead and met her father's gaze. "We would like you to come with us. The winter will arrive soon, and there is strength and protection in numbers. We can help each other."

Her stomach did a nervous flip even as her pulse quickened. They were asking. She glanced sideways at Pa. Would he speak to her before making a decision? He knew she would support whichever choice he made. This journey was his dream, after all. She'd only come along to help him see it through.

And because she couldn't imagine life without her father nearby. Since Mama's passing, he'd become her world. Even when they sold their little farm and packed for this journey, the loss of her childhood home had been manageable because she still had her father, and all the memories they'd made through the years.

She forced the thoughts away. Forced herself to focus on the conversation around her.

"Please, *Monsieur* Wilkins." French leaned forward, earnestness emanating from every word. "We cannot let you go on your own, especially since we're all going the same direction. The dangers of this country are too great."

For a long moment, Pa was silent. Then he nodded—a single, deliberate bob of his head. "We'd be glad to join up with you. We'll do our best to be useful partners."

His gaze slid sideways to her, and the corner of his mouth tipped up. "Susanna's a sight more useful than I am, but we'll both help."

Beaver Tail dismounted and strode toward them. "You could be ready to leave today?" His gaze slid from Pa to her, as though he knew she would be the one doing most of the packing. Pa needed to save his strength for the journey.

She nodded and set to work. As she sorted the food and wrapped it into bundles, the other three men dismounted from their horses and began readying the two animals they'd given her and Pa. Beaver Tail moved to her blankets and started rolling, and Pa did the same with his own bedding.

Within minutes, the camp had been cleared, and all eight horses stood waiting patiently, fully loaded with all except their riders.

Joel swung up on his mount. "Let's get moving."

After she made sure Pa was settled on the bay, she climbed aboard the paint gelding. The animal felt strange beneath her after so many months without riding.

"Good boy." She patted his neck as he shifted underneath her. Then she looked up at Beaver Tail. He was watching her, and she met his gaze. "What's his name?"

He raised his brows. "Horse?" He said the word like a question, although she was pretty sure he'd meant it as a statement.

This man needed to lighten his intensity a little. She raised her own brows. "His name is Horse?"

One side of his mouth tipped, and he nodded.

She turned her attention back to the gelding and gave his neck another pat. "A pleasure to meet you, Horse. I think we'll get along famously."

❧

*T*oday just might have been the longest day of his life. At least, the longest day in his recent memory. And that was why he found himself now hiding out with the horses under the pretense of checking on them as darkness settled over the land.

Somehow Beaver Tail had ended up bringing up the rear most of the day, making sure no one lagged behind. Which put him staring at Susanna's willowy figure. He suspected she rode behind her father on purpose, to be there for anything he might need.

But that left Beaver studying the confident line of her shoulders, the way her long braid swished with each step the horse took. He'd do best to keep his mind from lingering on that image now that he was finally on his own for the night.

Horse. He stroked the gelding's black neck, running his hand down the splash of white over the animal's shoulder. He'd never thought to name his horses, but apparently this one had now been christened.

"Food's hot." Caleb's call drifted through the night air from the direction of the campfire, rising above the chirp of crickets and the distant hoot of an owl.

With a woman in camp, surely they weren't going to have to suffer Caleb's cooking any longer. The man tolerated the work better than the rest of them, so they'd all agreed to endure his fare, not that Beaver could cook much better.

But both the coffee and cornbread Susanna had made in their portage camps had been much better than anything he'd eaten in more than one moon. Even her roasted meat seemed to have more flavor and tenderness than what he was accustomed to. That must be his imagination though, or simply his growling belly.

Beaver Tail gave the horse a final pat, then headed toward the campfire and the figures that milled around it. The night had cooled, and a brisk wind whipped his hair. He'd pulled it loose from the leather binding, giving himself that one bit of freedom.

He raised his face to the breeze, letting the air wipe away the frustrations from the day. Out here in the dark, he could be free of the control others expected from him. Released from all restrictions.

As he stepped into the ring of firelight, his gaze found Susanna, who was kneeling beside the fire. She had several small cakes sizzling in a pan. At first glance, they looked like pemmican, but that wasn't a likely food for a white woman to be cooking.

"Sit yourself, BT. Mr. Wilkins was just tellin' us about their trip up the river." Caleb perched on a log, his elbows resting on his long legs and one of Susanna's cakes in his hand. They almost never used plates unless they had to—less to wash that way.

The man motioned toward another log that had been gathered for firewood, and Susanna turned with a plate of steaming food for him. She raised her eyes to meet his as he took the offering. Something in her gaze snagged his and held it. A kindness. An earnestness that drew him.

But he forced himself to turn away. Susanna and her father traveled with them for their safety. But if he wasn't careful, it'd be his own protection he'd need to worry about.

CHAPTER 8

Beaver Tail sat on the log Caleb had offered and tuned an ear to the conversation. But he was careful to keep part of his mind focused on the night sounds around them. Only a foolish man ignored his surroundings, especially when camping on these plains.

"So you see, that first time God sent us through at just the right time to miss those sand bars," Wilkins said. "But when we came through the second time, the river had completely moved, shifting over so the trees that had been on the bank were now an island out there in the middle. We could see the rocks stickin' up on the sandbars high enough to pierce the boat if we'd struck one. Especially movin' as fast as we were."

"We saw the river move many times." French gave a knowing nod. The man's words weren't surprising for how many times he'd sailed up and down that water. "It's a wonder how the Missouri comes alive like a giant sea creature, winding and slithering wherever it has a mind to go."

"Ain't that the honest truth." Caleb piped up. "Lost my best gun when a squall set loose on that sea creature. The waves were tossin' just like we were on a high sea. Knocked me sideways an' I had to grab on with both hands to keep from goin' over the side. Couldn't save my Kentucky though."

He could just picture this giant man gripping a post on the boat, rain and wind lashing all around him. Why anyone chose river travel instead of on a sturdy horse, Beaver Tail would never understand.

"Never have found a rifle I like as good as that one, 'specially not this thing." Caleb nodded toward the rifle perched against the log where he sat. His mouth drooped in a pitiful expression, like a dog with its tail dragging.

"Who made the gun you carry now?" Wilkins' gaze sharpened.

"A Frenchman probably." Caleb cut a sideways grin at French.

The man raised his half-eaten corn cake and chuckled around his mouthful of food. French was always good for a joke, even if he or his countrymen were the source of the humor.

"It's a rifle, I assume? Kentucky model? With a 36- or 42-inch barrel?" Wilkins seemed to scoot to the edge of his seat.

Caleb nodded. "Forty-two. It's a decent gun, just tends to shoot low. I suppose I should tinker with it and see if I can straighten the barrel out."

"I could take a look." Wilkins' eagerness was hard to miss.

"My father is a gunsmith." Susanna spoke up from her place by the fire.

"*Was* a gunsmith." Wilkins sank back on his seat. "Back in Illinois. But I brought a few tools with me. I'd be glad to see what I can do."

Beaver Tail leaned forward before he realized what he was doing. "You built guns too? Or did repairs only?" He'd always been fascinated with the weapons. And they were so hard to come by in this land. If he could learn the skills, he could make guns for his people. Or at least he could learn to repair the parts that always seemed to break.

Wilkins tipped his head as he studied Beaver. "I made a few from scratch, but that's a long, tedious business. Repairs kept me busy enough most days." He raised his brows. "You have somethin' in mind you want made?"

He worked to school his expression. "I would simply like to learn the craft. Perhaps I can watch any repairs you make." Every bit he could learn would be helpful. He'd studied his own rifle at great length but hadn't disassembled it to learn more. He couldn't risk damaging any parts. The gun was too important for both hunting and safety.

Wilkins coughed—a deep, thick sound. Then he wiped his mouth and looked to Caleb. "Where's your rifle, son? Let's take a look."

Caleb reached beside him, then scooted over to crouch beside the older man. "I don't know if the problem's in the barrel or down in the pan. I've tried adding extra powder, but that only makes it kick harder."

The old man turned his head and coughed again, then reached for the rifle and scooted so the firelight shone on the metal of the gun. Susanna appeared at his side and handed him a leather kit. With the gun resting on Wilkins's legs, he loosed the strings of the case and unrolled the leather with steady movements. The pouch contained several pockets, and metal tools poked out from most of them.

With the instruments handy, he turned his attention to the gun, opening the cock and the frizzen, peering inside from all angles. "First off, it needs a good cleaning." He glanced up at Caleb with fatherly admonition in his gaze. "This is a delicate tool. It'll take care of you far better if you take care of it."

The big man ducked his chin with a sheepish grin. "Yessir." Good thing Wilkins was looking at Caleb's rifle first. Beaver wasn't sure his own gun was much cleaner. He did wipe it down after every few uses but probably wasn't as thorough as he should be.

After doing a quick clean, Wilkins used several of the tiny tools from his kit, making little adjustments to the metal of the gun. The first few tweaks, he explained what he was doing, but as his attention delved deeper into the dark cavity of the rifle, his words became rare.

There was no need for them though. Beaver had moved close, squatting beside the man as he bent low to allow the fire's light to shine into the gun. Each of the adjustments he made were logical, but the man's insight into how each angle affected the rifle's abilities could only come from years of experience.

At last, Wilkins straightened, lifting his head from the gun and shifting his shoulders, easing out the kinks from such focused effort. "Alrighty. I think—" A cough broke through his words, but this time it turned into hacking that doubled him over.

Susanna stepped between Beaver and her father, taking the tiny blade from her pa's hand and the leather pouch from his lap. "I think that's all for tonight."

The man was still bent over, coughing up his insides with deep, wracking convulsions that made Beaver's own chest ache. He took the rifle from Wilkins' lap and handed it to Caleb. Finally, the coughs subsided to a raspy wheezing as the man struggled to draw breath. This had to be more than a summer cold.

Wilkins wiped at his mouth as he straightened, and Beaver caught a flash of blood before the man curled his hand to hide the evidence. His face had paled, and his hands trembled, even as he offered a shaky grin.

Beaver hadn't moved from his position in front of the man, squatting on his haunches so he had to look up into Wilkins' face. He tried to return the kindness in the man's eyes, but the worry that had begun to churn in his thoughts made it hard to focus. Something was very wrong with him. An illness greatly advanced, if he was coughing up blood.

Beaver had only seen two others afflicted with such—both old men whose bodies had wasted away within only a few moons of the blood coming with their coughs.

Wilkins clamped his hands on his knees. "Well, I reckon I'd best turn in so I'll be fresh when we start off come mornin'. Been a long while since I spent all day in the saddle like today."

After rising, Beaver Tail almost reached out to offer the man help up. But he caught himself just in time. Wilkins probably didn't want to feel weak and dependent, and as he pushed to his feet, he seemed to manage it decently. Only a low grunt leaked out.

Susanna had quietly spread her father's blankets out behind his log seat, and now she stepped back to the side. As the older man shuffled toward his bed, Beaver did a quick check on his surroundings. Caleb was showing his rifle off to French and Joel. The latter raised his gaze to meet Beaver's, but Beaver Tail shifted his focus to the darkness around them. He and Joel were the protectors in the group. Caleb and French were simply too easy-going to be always on their guard.

Just now, the darkness around their camp echoed with normal night sounds. In the distance, a coyote howled, and some of its companions joined in. Too far away for concern. And coyotes weren't much to worry about anyway, except as nuisances when they broke into foodstores.

He turned back to Joel and gave a slight nod. All seemed well.

"I'm going to the river for water." Susanna's words pulled his focus to her. She held the pan she'd used for cooking, filled with their plates and a spoon.

He shook his head. "French will wash those." Even with a calm night, any number of dangers could attack her. He turned to the dark-haired man.

French was already on his feet. "*Oui, mademoiselle.* I will gladly do that for you."

She hugged the pan to herself. "Actually, I'd like to stretch my legs some. I'm not accustomed to riding all day either." She gave French such a sweet smile, Beaver almost wanted to step in front of the man to absorb that look for himself. He'd been the one to suggest the help, after all.

"If that is your pleasure." French's face took on a silly grin as he nodded, then took his seat again. Clearly, her smile wasn't lost on the Frenchman. Beaver would have to make sure he didn't show such a reaction if he was ever the recipient of that same look.

He turned back to her, shifting his mind back to important matters. Susanna still wasn't safe venturing out of the firelight on her own, especially through the cottonwoods that lined the river. "I'll go with you. Just in case you meet any more bears." He did well to keep his face stoic as he spoke the words, especially when a pink flush swept across her cheeks and ears.

She turned away. "If you wish."

Interesting that she hadn't argued the point. Not surprising really. Anyone who'd tangled with a grizzly and survived would have a healthy desire to avoid the animal in the future. She likely still felt the ache throughout her body, not just in the open wounds.

His gaze slid over her without permission from his mind. By the time he re-captured his focus and reined it over to the fire, the damage had been done. Her lithe body was emblazoned in his thoughts, the image of the graceful sway of her curves as she stepped toward the river. Toward the darkness.

He inhaled a deep breath, then followed her.

~

*S*usanna dipped the pot into the quick-flowing water of the Missouri, letting the chill cool her body from the heat of the cook fire she'd been working over. This was the second night now that Beaver Tail had accompanied her out to wash the dishes from the evening meal.

He didn't speak, not the night before or so far this night, just stood sentry a few strides behind her. Back in Illinois, she would have objected to such overbearing treatment, but in this wilderness…anything could happen. With him guarding her back, she didn't worry about another bear or anything else surprising her.

Perhaps she should worry about the man himself—he was an Indian and a stranger after all. But there was something about his solid presence, his intense watchfulness to his surroundings, which made her feel safe. Besides, if he'd wanted to scalp or assault her, he'd have done it long before now.

Since he didn't speak, she could close her eyes and relish the quiet of the night river noises. She hadn't realized how much she enjoyed the rushing sound of the water as she drifted off to sleep each night.

Too soon, she had all the dishes washed and gathered again in the pot. She stood and turned to Beaver Tail. He reached for the load, and she allowed him to take it. "Thank you." Maybe she should insist on being treated as an equal, but her body still ached from the bear attack, and the weight of the iron pot burned through her shoulders and arms.

He nodded his response—a man of few words, this one. But his silence wasn't awkward. Simply…peaceful.

Before turning back toward the camp, she took one last look around the river. "This is a pretty spot, especially with the moonlight shining on the water."

"We will stay here tomorrow, as well."

She turned to him. "We're not riding on?" Were they resting

a day for her father's sake? He'd had another coughing fit tonight, this one worse than any others. It had left him with barely enough strength to hobble to his bed. Maybe exhaustion from long days in the saddle was weakening his body. Or maybe talking with the men each evening was irritating his throat or lungs.

Either way, part of her sagged with relief at the chance for him to recover. But would these men be angry for the delay? If she and Pa couldn't keep up, maybe they'd be left behind. That thought shouldn't strike such fear in her chest.

As she studied Beaver Tail's face, the moonlight filtered over his features, the sharp cheekbones, strong jaw. The only part she couldn't see were his eyes. And without them, she had no hope of deciphering the feeling behind his words.

He shook his head. "Every few days, we let the horses rest. I set traps and work the hides from the last time we stopped." His tone sounded matter-of-fact, as though everything he said was simple truth.

But she needed to know for sure what these men were thinking. Had to be prepared if she and Pa would be on their own again. "You're not stopping because of us are you? Pa and me?" She hated to single out her father. Besides, maybe they thought a woman too weak to travel day after day on horseback. The thought made her stand straighter, pushing the exhaustion away.

"The break benefits all."

Although she still couldn't see his eyes for the shadows, his voice held no sign of frustration or condescension. He hadn't exactly answered her question, but she'd best not push him further.

She'd simply have to wait and watch. For if there were any sign that these men would change their minds about her and Pa riding with them, she'd need to be ready for it.

CHAPTER 9

*J*ust a few more chores to finish and she could steal a few minutes of freedom.

Susanna straightened her father's blankets the next morning as she strained to hear the men talking. Joel and French were by the tie line, preparing to move the horses to graze for the day. She couldn't hear what they were saying, and that was probably best. She would wear her nerves down if she worried any longer about whether she and Pa were delaying the men. She'd just have to face whatever challenge came their way, even if that challenge included being left to maneuver this wilderness alone again.

For now, the day looked to be clear and sunny, fully of promise. Caleb had offered to bring fresh sweetgrass to ward away these horrid mosquitoes, so that nuisance would soon be lessened. Pa was resting by the river, perhaps the best possible place for him.

Beaver Tail had disappeared early that morning. She'd seen him slip from camp before the sun pinkened the eastern sky but had assumed he'd return within a few minutes. When she had

71

corn gruel heated over the fire Joel had rekindled, Beaver Tail still hadn't returned.

She asked after him, but Caleb had only shrugged. "He goes out early to set traps. Might not be back 'til midday. You never know with him." Then he'd sent her a wink. "Likes his freedom, that one."

She was beginning to see that.

And she could understand it too. Pa had always craved freedom. Wasn't that the real reason why they'd set out on this expedition? If she were truthful, she loved the sense of freedom, too. Of course, a moderate taste of the untamed dangers in this land could be more than enough. Especially when it came to the grizzly species.

Beaver Tail was different though. There was something feral about him, yet the wildness didn't frighten her. Maybe it was even part of what made him seem strong and safe. As if he could conquer anything that threatened them.

But none of that was the reason she'd been rushing to finish her chores around the camp. She simply wanted to see Beaver Tail's process to set up his traps. After glimpsing the results of his snare the other day, she couldn't help wondering at how he selected locations and his process for building the traps.

Maybe he wouldn't want her tagging along, asking questions. But at least she could watch from a distance. If she could find the man.

Once the camp was set to rights and the fire banked, she brushed the dirt from her hands and scanned the land around them. The voices of Joel and French no longer drifted in the distance, which meant they were probably off on another chore. Now she couldn't ask them where Beaver Tail might be, but he was likely near the water.

She started toward the river, swiping at mosquitos as she made her way through the tall grass, then among the scrubby trees. The flowing water called to her as she neared it, and when the bank came into view, her gaze landed on a figure lying on his side.

Pa. For a single moment, her heart froze in her chest. Had he succumbed to his illness? Then her mind caught up to reason, and her pulse began to thump again. He was merely resting in the shade, listening to the sweet murmur of the river.

But still, her feet flew to his side. "Pa?"

He shifted, turning to look up at her with one eye. She must have interrupted a nap. The corner of his mouth curved up, the smile lines grooving his cheeks. "This feels almost as good as heaven will, I think."

Heaven. Not for many years if she had any say so in the matter. She tried to summon a feisty quip along those lines, but the burn stinging her eyes seemed to slow her thoughts.

She blinked the tears away and swallowed the lump in her throat. "I'm going to walk along the river bank for a while. Would you like to come?" Resting here would be better for him, but offering seemed right anyway. If he felt up to a stroll, she'd treasure his company.

His eyes gentled. "I think this is where I should stay for now." His voice had that tender rasp that was his special tone for her. He patted the ground in front of him. "When you're finished, come back and sit with me if you've a mind."

Her own mouth found an answering smile. "I will."

Then she turned her focus to the river, looking first one direction, then the other. Which way would Beaver Tail go? Rocky banks lined the water everywhere she looked, but a few openings allowed access.

"I saw our friend Beaver working upriver a bit. Might be interesting to see how he sets his traps."

Pa had read her mind once again. Maybe she shouldn't be surprised that he knew her so well. Ever since Mama had passed ten years before, they'd spent a great deal of time in each other's company.

For some reason, though, part of her didn't want him to read her mind about Beaver Tail. Maybe because she wasn't sure exactly what she thought of him. Yet none of that mattered right now. She merely wanted to learn more about trapping.

So she nodded and set off upstream.

After walking for at least a quarter hour, she'd shifted away from the water's edge to take shade in what trees grew along the bank. She should probably turn around now, as Beaver Tail had likely left the river to set snares in other areas. The man could be anywhere in this vast country, and with the rolling hills, she'd never spot him.

But then the flash of a figure snagged her attention—down the embankment at the water's edge. She stilled.

Only the top part of his head was visible—his strong, tawny features and raven hair. She crept forward so she could see what he was doing. But she didn't want to startle him. And maybe she'd see more of his work if he didn't know she was watching.

He knelt at the river's edge, studying something in the water. A little splash sounded, then a tiny head rose up from the surface about two arm lengths away from Beaver Tail. The animal didn't move, just sat there with its furry brown cap barely above the water. Another river otter?

Susanna didn't dare draw a full breath, didn't dare move in case she missed something important. This time, she might actually be able to help Beaver Tail if he was attacked again.

But as the creature raised its snout above the water, the features looked suspiciously like that of a beaver. She couldn't help but smile at the endearing little face.

Beaver Tail didn't move as he stared at the creature whose name he'd been given. Neither moved, in fact, as though locked in a stand-off.

Then, slowly, Beaver Tail eased his hand away from his body. He reached to the side, but she couldn't see what he was doing.

Surely he wasn't reaching for a knife or other weapon. This

moment of connection between man and animal seemed too special to destroy for the simple taking of fur and meat.

When he drew his hand back, ever so slowly, he held a leafy branch, about the length of his arm. He extended the foliage out over the water, then lowered it gently to the surface in front of the beaver. Was he luring the animal to a trap he'd set? Water flowed around the leaves, but the branch must have snagged on something under the surface, for it didn't float.

With a slow shifting, he eased backward until he reached the steeper part of the bank and the animal trail that wound up to the grass above. He stayed low as he climbed up the path. At the top of the bank, he paused to look at the beaver again.

The animal still hadn't moved, just sat there with its head barely above the water's surface. She had to look closer to make sure it really was a live beaver. But then she saw the cock of its head. Would it take the bait Beaver Tail had offered? Part of her wanted to yell for it to flee. If there was a trap there, this brave animal should be given the chance to live another day.

Beaver Tail turned from the creature and strode toward the trees. Toward her.

She fought the urge to shuffle backwards, deeper into the shadows. Maybe hide behind a trunk so she wasn't caught watching. Except he'd caught her once before when she'd tried to hide from him.

So she forced herself to stay put and meet his gaze when it finally landed on her. No surprise registered on his face. Of course not. He'd probably known she was there even before she'd spotted him. Ever watchful, this man.

A hint of amusement touched his eyes as he stilled in front of her. He didn't speak, and the silence seemed to draw words from her.

"I wanted to see how you set your traps. For the animals, I mean." Of course he would know that was what she meant. Unless he thought she considered him a savage looking to trap young women. But why would he think that? Why would *she* think that? *Should* she think it? Now she was simply confusing herself.

One corner of his mouth tugged in a hint of a smile, and his eyes danced. As though he could read her thoughts. If her face wasn't already red from the heat, it must be blazing now.

She yanked her gaze away from him and nodded toward the river. "Was that a beaver?"

He nodded, stepping to the side and looking back to where he'd knelt. The branch still sat partly in the water, but the beaver's head had disappeared.

"Do you have a snare hidden in the water there?" She couldn't see a pole like at the other trap he'd shown her, but it was probably hidden behind the bank.

Beaver Tail shook his head. "I had planned to set one, but my brave friend has gained my respect."

She raised her brows, studying his face to see if her ears had deceived her. "Really? But that branch…?"

He shrugged. "From his favorite tree."

Was he jesting? It sounded almost as though he knew that particular beaver and its preferences. But they'd just came to this area the night before, and from what the men had said, they'd all lived farther north. He couldn't have seen this specific animal before. Beaver Tail's lack of expression gave her no clues to his meaning.

He turned back in the direction she'd come from. "I've set all my snares. I'll show you where they are on the way back to camp."

A thrill slipped through her as she fell in step behind him. If anyone had told her a year ago she'd be following an Indian through the wilds of the Great Plains, learning about animal traps, she'd have never believed him.

~

*H*e couldn't have said why he offered this woman a tour of his snares. Maybe because she seemed so interested in them. Although that had never swayed him before.

Even before he'd been burned so fiercely by Ayadna, he'd mostly steered clear of the maidens in the camp. He simply didn't have a way with them the way some braves did. Maybe the ruckus with Ayadna had really been his fault, just like she'd said.

"This one is set for muskrat." He motioned toward a pocket trap at the edge of the water.

"What makes it just for muskrat?" She was leaning over the embankment, peering down at the snare he'd set with a thin layer of mud atop it.

"Mostly the lure I put inside the hole. It might catch raccoon or mink, too, but the muskrat won't be able to resist it." He hoped, anyway.

"What hole?" Now she dropped to her knees so she could lean farther over the edge. "Oh, I see it. How deep does that go into the ground?"

He dropped to his haunches beside her. "About the length of my arm. The bait is all the way at the back of the hole."

She glanced up at him, and something that looked suspiciously like respect shone in her eyes. "How did you learn all this?" If she kept looking at him that way, she might chip through the resistance he was doing his best to maintain. He couldn't let that happen.

He stood and took two steps back. "All of my people learn these things." He'd been one of the best when it came to setting snares, but his trapping and trading had barely kept his mother and sisters fed. When he'd snagged the attention of Ayadna, the daughter of the principal chief of their tribe, the trade goods her father offered would have been enough to finally provide everything his family needed. Even enough to see his sisters settled well with good braves.

But he'd not been enough for Ayadna. Of course, he hadn't.

Her father found her in the lodge of Running Cat, and the disgrace heaped on Beaver's own head at the broken betrothal was nothing compared to what his mother had suffered. She didn't deserve to be shunned by the other women in the camp, forced to draw water in the heat of the day when no one was around, left with only scraps from the summer harvest the women usually gathered together.

It was a wonder his mother had been able to win the attention of Hawk Flies, especially with no dowry to give. Maybe it was the man's advanced years and the loss of his former squaw, but at least he'd promised to provide well for Beaver's mother and sisters.

Leaving Beaver Tail free to finally escape his humiliation.

He forced himself back to the present, forced his focus back on the woman kneeling on the bank.

She stood, a graceful movement that would draw any man's gaze. "Your people are Blackfoot?" She moved toward the deer path they'd been following, and he fell into step beside her.

"Yes. Part of Ossinawaa's band. Near the river white men call Marias." Even speaking the name of Ayadna's father left a vile taste on his tongue.

She nodded. "I remember passing that river. The water was so cold as it joined the Missouri."

"It flows down from the snow in the mountains." He'd spent many summers among those peaks. Some of the happiest days he could remember—sometimes with a friend or two, sometimes alone.

Either way, he'd always been free to roam unfettered. The mountain wilderness renewed him, refilling his empty places with its unscathed beauty. A wild majesty he understood. That was one of the reasons he'd come on this journey. He'd desperately needed the freedom of the mountain country they'd soon be nearing.

Of course, that country was beautiful, but, if given the chance, its wildness would kill a man. Or a woman.

He slid a sideways glance to the woman beside him. She'd turned her attention to the trees on the other side of her. Maybe she was thinking of the peaks that lay beyond.

"I hope we get to see the mountains." Her tone held a wistfulness that made his chest ache.

He should warn her again of the dangers of entering that treacherous country with winter approaching, but he couldn't bring himself to quell the longing in her voice. The same feeling that stirred inside him.

If only they could head due west to the rocky cliffs now instead of southwest in the winding route to find Joel's brother. As dangerous as mountain country was, he could help her and her father navigate the perils. And if the others would come, too, there would be strength in numbers. As long as they could find enough food.

But Joel wouldn't hear of it, certainly. His brother was to have met them in Beaver Tail's camp in early spring, whether he found the horses he sought or not. When the man was a month late, Joel had paced. After the second month, they'd all four set out.

Maybe they'd meet Adam soon, then they could all travel north again through the mountains. It wasn't exactly the direct route back to his family's village, but the scenery would be worth the danger. And he was in no hurry to return home. The longer he could delay facing his people, the better. He'd have to go back eventually, would need to make sure Hawk Flies was providing for his mother and the two younger girls still in her lodge.

He forced the thought away, dragging his focus back to the present. Somehow they'd stopped walking, and Susanna was studying him, a worry line marring her pretty brow. "What's wrong?"

How had he let himself lose control so thoroughly? He struggled to wipe his face of any thoughts or emotions that showed there. "Naught." He gave his head a little shake to clear the last of the distractions from his mind, then started forward again.

Susanna fell into step beside him, and thankfully, she didn't press him again or try to fill the air with words. He'd noticed that about her. She didn't prattle on like his sisters or any other women he'd known.

That was a trait he appreciated about her. One of the many.

CHAPTER 10

*T*wo more days they rode, and by the end of the second, Susanna couldn't loosen the knot balling tighter in her chest with each coughing fit that consumed her father. It might be her imagination, but he seemed to be talking less also. Maybe speaking brought on the coughing, so he was trying to avoid them both.

Yet every time she rode alongside him to visit, his face shone with pleasure. He seemed to soak in the wild beauty around them like parched ground absorbing a gentle rain.

At least the heat from summer was fading into milder autumn days. Yet the land was so dry. She would have expected a grassland like this to experience more rain. They hadn't felt a drop for weeks now.

"What say we camp here?" Caleb, riding in the lead, reined his horse to a stop. "I haven't seen trees for a while, but this little hill will give us a break from the wind. We can use buffalo chips for the fire, and we're right here at the Missouri."

French shrugged. "Suits me."

The men had fine-tuned their process to set up camp so that

they had a fire roaring and everything ready for her to begin food preparations in less than a quarter hour. Those first few days when she'd tried to help, she'd found herself in the way every time she'd begun a task. And the men hadn't held back from telling her so—respectfully, of course.

Finally, Caleb had taken her by the elbow and pulled her aside. "We have all this taken care of, Miss Susanna." They'd agreed to use given names to make things easier, since they'd be traveling together for the foreseeable future. But Caleb couldn't seem to keep himself from adding the *miss* in front of hers, kind man that he was. If she'd had a little brother, she'd want him to be like Caleb. "You just see that you and your pa relax. Why don't you walk down by the river and stretch your, um…" His gaze darted down to her legs, then his entire face turned red, his ears flaming brighter than a hot fire. Some sweet mama had raised this boy right.

She fought the urge to stretch up to pinch his cheek. Her tired arms likely wouldn't reach that high, so she settled for resting a hand on his arm. "Thank you, Caleb. I'll take Pa to see the river. Shall I bring back water while I'm there?"

"That's Joel's job. Don't start doin' his work or he'll turn lazy on us." He shot the smaller man a cheeky grin.

She nodded and moved toward the water. Even as weary as she was, Caleb's kindness could bring on a smile.

From that day on, she'd done her best to stay out of the men's way as they set up camp. And with each day, she'd learned to appreciate their efforts a little more. Like a perfectly tuned rifle, each part performed his role exactly, working with the others to create a result both flawless and powerful. The main difference between these men and a rifle, though—their efforts didn't prove deadly to whatever lay in their path.

As she stepped over the hill to attend to personal matters, her mind shifted forward to her only real duty around the camp, other than seeing to Pa's comfort. The men seemed to enjoy her cooking, but she'd exhausted the short list of things she could make with the few ingredients they had.

She liked to save the cornmeal for the mornings, since corn gruel was warm and filling and tended to stay with a body for several hours. She'd made several variations on bean soup each evening, using the bear meat they'd be eating on for the next week, at least.

Maybe she could try mashing the beans into a sort of cake to fry with the steaks from the bear's backstraps. If only she had sugar to mix up a sweet treat. These men had been far kinder than she'd expected, and she'd like to do something special to thank them.

Alas, since no sugar was to be had, she'd have to look for another way to thank them.

The bean cakes cooked quickly, but the bear steaks took longer than she'd expected. At least the men didn't seem to mind eating half their meal lukewarm.

"Mademoiselle, you are a delight in every way." French brushed the crumbs from his hands as he straightened from devouring his meal. "It is my great pleasure that you and your pap accompany us."

She offered a teasing smile. "Perhaps not in every way, but at least I can please your belly."

He sent her a wink. "You do that for certain, but I have yet to find anything about you that doesn't charm me."

She turned away to hide her smile. Not long after meeting him, she'd learned not to believe half of French's flattery, but she could still enjoy it—innocent as his attentions were.

As she scraped bits of food stuck in the pan, a loud groan sounded behind her, and she spun. Caleb—already the size of a grizzly at full height—raised his hands in a massive stretch, making him as tall as the giants of Anak from the Bible. She had to fight to keep from shrinking away from him.

He dropped his arms and moved toward the pile of supplies.

"I'll go bring some water from the river. Anything else you need, Miss Susanna?" A gentle giant, to be sure.

"I've need of nothing, Caleb. Thank you." She could ask him to carry this pan to the water for her, but Beaver Tail always did so, mostly to keep watch against danger, she was fairly certain. They were camped only a dozen strides from the river's edge tonight, though. Maybe he wouldn't see the need to come with her. There really wouldn't be a need. He could sit in the comfort of the firelight and watch her.

But the thought of losing those moments with him sent an ache through her chest. He was starting to speak more now. Not that she minded his silence, as relaxing as it was. But it seemed an honor that he was comfortable enough with her to speak, too.

Once she'd gathered the dishes, she moved toward the river, doing her best not to look behind to see if anyone followed. She shouldn't act as if it mattered.

It didn't matter. She hadn't come to this country to flirt with a man, she'd come to grant her father's greatest wish. Her focus should be on Pa and ensuring his comfort. In truth, that task was almost impossible the way his body seemed to be destroying itself from the inside.

She'd dropped to her knees at the water's shallow edge before she sensed Beaver Tail behind her. The man was a wonder at walking without sound. One day, she'd have to ask him how he accomplished it. But why wait?

The thought brought a smile. Why not ask him now?

As she scrubbed sand over a plate, she glanced behind her. "How do you do that? Walk so quietly, I mean."

He stepped closer so he stood beside where she knelt. "It's simple. Walk toe-to-heel. All the children learn it in my village." This was the second time he'd spoken of the people from his home. She'd have to ask him more about the place and the people, but just now he was demonstrating the step he described.

She studied his motion, then set the plate aside and stood. Gingerly, she tried what he'd modeled. Her first step was awkward, putting her weight first on the ball of her foot, then easing down to her heel. She sent him a grimace. "You don't make it nearly so obvious as that."

One side of his mouth tipped in the moonlight. "You're walking on your toes. Just land lightly with a little rolling motion."

She tried it again, this time not so exaggerated.

He nodded. "Practice. The more you try, the more natural it will feel."

"You two dancin' out there?" The call came from the campfire and held the cheerful banter of Caleb's voice.

Heat flamed up her face as she moved back to her place with the dishes and dropped to her knees. What could she say to explain what they'd been doing?

"Just inspecting tracks." Beaver Tail beat her to the explanation, and somehow he managed to keep his voice as relaxed as ever.

A splash sounded from the water somewhere in the darkness. She glanced out as she scrubbed another plate with sand. The steady rustle of the river greeted her ears, along with the ever present chirp of crickets and the croak of a frog across the water.

"What tracks do you see?" Joel's voice sounded, closer than the camp. The whisper of his moccasins in the grass barely drifted to her.

She didn't turn to look at him but kept her ear tuned to what Beaver Tail might say. He'd started this topic. Now, he'd get to finish it.

"Deer, antelope, and buffalo. If there was more light, I'd

expect to see beaver and muskrat too. Maybe mink." Beaver Tail's voice turned away from her as he and Joel strolled downriver.

"Wish we'd see horse tracks." Joel's words came out with a sigh as the man stopped and turned to face the water. Her heart squeezed at the despondent slope of his shoulders against the backdrop of the moon.

"I'm surprised we haven't seen many riders. We're close to the land of the Shoshone."

"You think we're almost there?" The hope in Joel's voice drew her.

"We may start to meet braves soon. Finding the band your brother is with won't be so easy." Beaver Tail sounded thoughtful.

She scrubbed the last of the plates with sand, working at a stubborn spot of burned juice from the bear steak. Two years ago, she'd have never thought she'd be washing dishes in the muddy Missouri, nor boiling its water to use in cooking. Back home, they'd always had a well. But this grand adventure had taught her more skills than she could count.

Something moved just in front of the plate. She froze, staring at the water. Maybe the shift had been only the shadow of her body. She swiped the plate under the water to rinse the sand from it. A cold, slimy object brushed the back of her hand.

She screamed, jerking back from the water. As she moved, a dark form slithered where her hand had been.

A snake.

She screamed again, scrambling away from the river. Then she jumped to her feet and darted a few more steps back.

"What is it?" Beaver Tail jumped in front of her, his body tense as he faced the river, knife out and poised to throw.

"A snake." She'd never seen a water moccasin but had heard how painful and even deadly the bites could be.

Beaver Tail stepped closer to the water, peering into the murky depths. "Are you certain?"

Joel moved to his side, his own hunting knife drawn like a sword.

"Get away from it." The last thing she needed was for them both to be bitten. Snakes could slither and strike in the blink of an eye. She stepped forward just enough to grab an arm from each of them.

Beaver Tail glanced back at her, his brows lowering. "If it was a snake, it won't hurt you. It's more frightened of you than you are of it."

Her heart might very well pound out of her chest, but she struggled to pull her frayed nerves back together. "But it's poisonous. I've heard of the bite from a water snake killing people." Shouldn't he know this? Did they not have water snakes farther north where he'd lived?

He shook his head. "Maybe where you come from, but not water snakes around here. They're not good for much, but they're harmless."

She straightened, her gaze flicking back to the river. Could that be true? The bear species were different in this country, so maybe the snakes were as well.

His arm flexed under her grip, reminding her that she was still clutching him and Joel both. She dropped her hands.

"I wondered about the water snakes." Joel still studied the river. Like maybe a threat would spring from the water to attack. "We've seen plenty of rattlers out here though. I assume they're still poisonous?"

"For certain. That's the only snake I know of that can hurt a man." Beaver Tail slid her a look. "Or a woman."

She squared her shoulders. "My apologies for alarming you." But it took all the willpower she could muster to step forward and stack the dishes she'd washed. That last plate had to be rinsed again, but maybe it would be better to rinse it in the water she'd boiled for drinking. Mayhap all the dishes should be boiled in that same pot.

Without glancing at either man, she stood with her heavy load, then turned and marched back to camp.

She might have let a little feminine weakness show this time, but she wouldn't let it happen again.

CHAPTER 11

*H*aving so much time in the saddle to think had never bothered Beaver Tail before.

Yet now, he couldn't seem to get Susanna out of his thoughts.

The way French had flirted and winked at her the night before, and the secret smile that lit her face in response. She'd tried to hide it, but Beaver had been in the perfect position to see her pleasure as she turned away.

Caleb, of course, had charmed her with his earnest manners and the easy way he had of talking with any person he met. He'd had the same effect on the women in Beaver's village over the winter they'd spent there. What woman hadn't swooned after spending a day or two around that gentle giant? Of course Susanna would be no different.

And it even seemed she'd broken through Joel's crusty barrier. Why else would the man have come to investigate the night before when Beaver was showing her how to walk silently?

And why did Beaver care about any of this? He tightened his

jaw. They could all flirt and simper and act like fools fighting over her. He wanted none of it.

He nudged his horse forward, moving around the woman and her father toward the front of the line. He reined his horse next to Joel, who rode lead. "I'm going to scout ahead. See what game there is and check for Indian sign." Anything to get away from himself and the thoughts spinning in his mind. Not to mention the sight of the woman always in front of him.

Joel didn't even send him a curious look, just nodded. Either the man was too caught in his own worries or he didn't find Beaver Tail's actions odd. If the latter, good.

He kicked his gelding forward, maybe harder than he should have. As he gave the animal its head, the horse stretched out into a run, probably as grateful for the release as he was. They crested a rise, and the animal surged forward down the gentle slope.

Beaver ripped the leather tie from his hair, letting the wind flow through the strands with the freedom he craved. He bent low over the horse's neck so no part of him held the animal back. As one, they pounded through the high grass.

Ahead, a dark mass took shape. Buffalo. A herd so large they seemed to cover every part of the land.

He eased back on the reins, slowing a little so they wouldn't scare the herd. As the animals shifted, the dark blanket covering the land seemed to ripple like a cloth flapping in a gentle wind.

A shot split the air.

He ducked instinctively, reining his horse in as he scanned the landscape ahead. Was someone hunting? The animals were still far enough away that each was only a large spec, but he couldn't make out anything that looked like a man or horse among them. Nor could he find a stirring in the herd where one had fallen.

He'd better investigate to make sure whoever had fired that shot wasn't a threat before the others caught up.

Out in this open plain, there was no cover for him to ride through. Nothing to hide his approach. A steep cliff descended down to the river, so he couldn't even hug its watery edge.

He pushed his gelding into a lope, scanning the land in front of him for any sign of a person. A hill rose up to the right of the buffalo, hiding some of them from sight. That must be where the shooter stood. Maybe that meant he hadn't seen Beaver Tail.

Maybe he was friendly. Maybe only a Shoshone hunting party. But something in Beaver's gut warned of danger.

He closed the distance between himself and the rock at a steady lope, honing his focus on the area ahead but keeping his other senses tuned around him. It would be just like a Sioux war party to have men hiding in the tall grass, ready to leap out and strike him down the moment he neared. He had to scout out the source of the shot, to make sure he wasn't leading the others into danger. But it was up to him to make sure he wasn't ambushed.

No Sioux dogs had attacked by the time he reached the base of the hill. He slowed his horse to a walk, his finger on the front trigger of the rifle in his lap. Maybe he should dismount and creep forward on foot so he could be quieter. But he hated to be at a disadvantage against mounted braves, especially if they'd already seen him and were lying in wait.

He eased his horse forward, studying the buffalo that became more and more visible as he rounded the base of the hill.

When he reined the gelding around a boulder that jutted from the ground, a flash of silver was his first warning of the gun aimed at him.

A man sat atop a horse as golden as bright sunlight. At first glance, the stranger looked Indian, but as Beaver studied his features, he saw the man didn't have the sharp cheekbones of any of the tribes he knew of. The man's features were small and dark, somewhat like Joel's, although the two didn't really look alike.

Maybe this was Adam.

Beaver never took his eyes from the man. "By chance, are you Adam Vargas?"

A flash of confusion touched his dark eyes. He raised the rifle a little higher, tucking the butt deeper into his shoulder and closing one eye as he peered down the barrel. "What do you want?"

The man's words were draped in a thick accent. Not Indian, but a little like Joel's speech when he was angry. Maybe this fellow was from the same land his friend had hailed from as a boy. Spain, was it?

Beaver Tail kept his rifle in his lap, although every part of him itched to raise the gun and set this interloper in his place. Yet, if this was Joel's brother, he was friend, not foe.

He forced his breath to stay even. "I'm traveling with a friend, Joel Vargas, who's looking for his brother. Be you he?"

Again, the flash of confusion in the man's eyes, so quick Beaver would have missed it if he hadn't been watching. Then he seemed uncertain. Maybe trying to decide something. At last he spoke. "I am not, but I've met this Adam Vargas. A man who speaks my own tongue."

So they *were* from the same land. "Who are you then?"

Another pause, as if he was judging how much to tell. "Manuel Lucas. Where is this Vargas you speak of? The brother." He still pointed the rifle at Beaver. Obviously he didn't yet trust him as a friend.

The feeling was mutual.

"He is coming with a group behind me." Maybe he shouldn't have said anything about the others. He could have led this man away from the trail they traveled and kept them from possible danger. Maybe he still could. "What's your business in this place?"

The man raised one shoulder in a casual gesture. "Hunting. Gathering furs for trade."

"You are alone?" Beaver studied his expression to read the words he didn't speak.

The man bobbed his chin once. Then he lowered his gun. "I would meet the man Vargas. I can tell him of his brother."

Joel would like that. In fact, if Beaver Tail didn't bring this stranger to Joel, his friend may well express his frustration with fists. Joel was certainly worried about his brother.

But he hated to expose Susanna and her father to a possible threat, not until he knew this man's nature and intentions. Maybe he could bring Joel without the others.

Beaver gripped his reins. "I'll bring him to you here."

"I'll go with you." The man edged his horse forward, and if Beaver wasn't mistaken, he raised his rifle a little, for Beaver could now see the dark shadow inside the gun's barrel.

In truth, the powder residue showed clearly that the weapon was sorely in need of a cleaning. Wilkins would have a thing or two to say about it.

He kept the smile inside him. There were plenty of serious matters he needed to attend to. How could he keep this man from coming with him to where Susanna and Wilkins were? Did he *need* to keep the man away?

Joel, Caleb, and French would all be on their guard. Surely, with the four of them, they could keep this stranger from harming the two they'd promised to protect. He just had to stay on his guard so the man didn't get the upper hand on their ride back to the group.

He leveled the fellow with a hard stare. "I'll take you to speak with him, but you'll need to remove your finger from that rifle's trigger. You come in peace, or you don't come at all."

One side of the man's mouth tipped a tiny bit, and he gave another single nod. "Agreed."

Beaver Tail returned the nod, then, with all his senses on

alert, he turned his horse and rode beside Lucas across the open land. He could only hope he wasn't leading a wolf into his herd of innocent deer.

Susanna and her father trusted him. He couldn't let them down.

~

"*H*o, there." Joel's voice split the air.

Susanna's horse nearly bumped the animal in front of her as Pa veered his mount out of the line of horses that were all jerking to a halt.

"What is it?" She peered ahead, first right in front of Joel to see if his horse had surprised a rattler or other dangerous animal.

Nothing that she could see, but the man was staring off into the distance. The direction Beaver Tail had gone.

She followed his gaze. *There.* Two riders? As the figures grew larger, she made out twin silhouettes, both on horseback. One had to be Beaver Tail. He wouldn't let strangers meet them without him there to stand guard. She knew that without question.

But who was the other man? Joel's missing brother? Her heart leapt in her chest. Joel would be so pleased. But what would that mean for their party? Would the men turn back to Beaver Tail's town? Part of her wanted to go there, to meet the people who'd helped shape him.

But the rest of her craved a chance to see the majestic Rocky Mountains while Pa could still manage the trip. Could she and her father survive those treacherous peaks alone? She was less sure now than ever.

As the riders approached, the strong outline of Beaver Tail became clear, easing the knot she'd not even realized had formed in her chest. The second man had the same dark features as Joel, but the nearer they came, the less he resembled their friend.

When the two men stopped in front of their group, she studied the stranger. His eyes were set closer together—and narrowed as he scanned their group. The way they roamed over her—hovering on her face, then sliding down the length of her and back up—made her want to move her horse behind her father's.

But she wouldn't cower.

There seemed to be no recognition between Joel and the man. He must be a stranger.

Her gaze shifted to Beaver Tail. His look settled on her at the same instant, and a fierce determination locked in his eyes. Then he turned back to the stranger beside him. "This is Manuel Lucas." His nostrils flared, as though the name were distasteful to him. Then his gaze swung to Joel. "He's met Adam."

Joel sat up straighter. "Where is he? Is he well?"

Mr. Lucas nodded, a slow, singular action. "Last I saw him, he was riding west into the mountains with a band of Shoshone. Looking for what he called Palouse horses." The man eyed the rest of them, his gaze hovering on her once again. "You hail from the north or the east?"

The way he was looking at her, he might have meant the question for her alone. But Caleb spoke up, edging his horse in front of her. "We've come from a Blackfoot tribe north of here." He motioned toward Beaver Tail. "The town where his people live. We all spent the winter there."

He wasn't including her and Pa, of course, but Lucas wouldn't know that. Did Caleb make the generalization intentionally? Either way, she was happy not to be called out. The less she was brought to this man's attention, the better.

"And what of the lovely lady?" The stranger leaned sideways to see her around Caleb's bulk.

She didn't let herself move. Didn't shift to hide again. She could stand up to this man's impertinence as well as any man's.

"She and her father are riding with us. Under our protection." Beaver Tail's voice held an undertone of steel. He reined his horse over next to Caleb so he was facing the stranger—more of a shield for her.

Lucas raised his brows. "Good to hear. A lady needs protection in a dangerous land like this." Something in his tone crept over Susanna like a herd of fleas. Or maybe like these blasted mosquitos. If only she could swat this man away.

"What did my brother say to you? Did he tell why he was going farther into the mountains? Was he looking for Nez Perce Indians?"

The stranger shrugged. "I don't think he said."

"Surely he told you something more. Did the men he was with speak to you at all?" Joel had his back to her, but his tone made it clear he was growing suspicious of the man's lack of detail.

"Let's see." Lucas shifted his gaze to the sky, as though deep in thought. Then he leveled his gaze on Joel. "Something might come to me over a bottle of whiskey. Do you have any to share?"

"None." This time, French was the one to bark out the word as he reined his horse beside Joel's. "We none of us drink the rot gut." Now all four men had parked their horses side-by-side, like a shield protecting her and Pa. A sight she was more than thankful for just now.

"How did my brother look? Well? Any injuries?" Joel's hard tone didn't hide the desperation in his questions. Worry for his brother must be eating him from the inside out.

"I saw no wounds." Lucas slid a look at Beaver Tail. "He was riding with Indians though, so they could turn on him any time." The sneer was impossible to miss, as though he was leveling a direct charge against the man.

She held her breath as she watched the hard line of Beaver's jaw. Would he take the bait and attack this rude stranger? She'd like to take a swing at him herself, but keeping the peace was important. The last thing they needed was an enemy in a land already overrun with dangers.

"It's time you leave, Lucas." Joel's tone may have been steely before, but now his voice held a barely-restrained fury.

The man cocked his dark brows. "I meant no disrespect. Only that I haven't found that particular tribe very trustworthy." What was this man's game? She couldn't see him well over Caleb's shoulder. Did he still hold the rifle he'd been gripping as he and Beaver Tail rode up?

"We'd best be on our way. And you go along on yours." Even in a hard tone, Caleb's words sounded like something he'd say to a good friend. The man was simply too nice.

Lucas eyed him, then his gaze swung from one person to the next, skimming over Pa and resting only briefly on her. Then he nodded. "I'll take my leave, then."

He nudged his horse and maneuvered the animal around Beaver Tail. But instead of heading off on his merry way, the man aimed his mount at her. Before she could react, he leveled a venomous gaze on her. "It's a pleasure to make your acquaintance, *señorita*. I do hope we meet again."

"You won't." Beaver Tail spun his horse toward the man.

The action made Lucas's horse throw its head up and lurch backward. The man jerked on the reins to still the mount, tightening his grip on his rifle.

The gun exploded in a flash and a cloud of black smoke.

CHAPTER 12

Susanna screamed, pulling her horse away from the blast. *Dear God, don't let him have shot anyone.*

But even as she prayed, the sound of a man's cry registered in her ears. *No!*

She blinked to clear the acrid burn of gunpowder from her eyes. Who'd been hit? A single scan of the men made the answer all too clear.

Joel was leaning to his right, clutching his side even as he craned his neck to send a glare back to Manuel Lucas that should have slayed the man.

"Leave now, or your life is mine." Beaver Tail had his own rifle raised and aimed at Lucas's chest.

Shock blanketed the stranger's face, and his dark skin paled. At least the shot hadn't been intentional.

Lucas nodded, then eased his horse backward several steps before turning the animal. With a grunt, he kicked his mount into a lope.

Susanna turned her focus to Joel. He was almost doubled over now that the threat had been sent away. She slid from her horse and moved to his side. "How bad is it?"

Blood leaked over his hands. Not a good sign that it had already penetrated his shirt. But he was holding the side, not his back, so maybe the bullet had only struck flesh. If it missed a vital organ, he should heal.

If…

She'd heard a shot through the belly could be an awful way to die.

"I'm fine." Joel grunted, as though afraid to let the breath out of his chest.

"Get down off your horse." She took the animal's reins with one hand, then reached up to grasp Joel's upper arm with the other.

"I have the horse." Beaver Tail's quiet words barely penetrated her focus. But as soon as she absorbed them, she released the reins.

"Let me help him down." Caleb placed a beefy hand on her shoulder, easing her backwards. He'd be able to help Joel more, so she stepped out of the way.

"I can do it." Joel pushed Caleb's hand away, then gripped his saddle and raised his leg over the horse's rump. She couldn't see his face, but the pain from the act must have been awful.

When he slid to the ground, a groan slipped out, filled with enough pain to lodge in Susanna's chest. The moment his feet landed on the ground, he released the saddle and gripped his side, then stumbled toward the open ground in front of the horses. He dropped to his knees, then lay in the grass, curling around his injury.

Suzanna turned to ask her father to find their medical supplies, but he'd already dismounted and was rifling through the pack behind his saddle. Already pulling out what she'd need.

She dropped to her knees beside Joel. "I need to look at the wound."

Gripping the bottom of his shirt, she eased his hands away from his side. He unfolded a little, lying flat on his back. His breaths came in hard, deliberate inhales as he fought through his pain.

She lifted the fabric, heavy with blood, and the sight underneath made bile churn in her belly. Blood seeped from a hole near the outer edge of his side. She swallowed down the bitterness that threatened to rise in her throat and used a clean part of his hem to dab the crimson from his skin so she could better see the wound.

There was a chance the bullet had only plowed through flesh and muscle, not anything vital, but she had to know whether the ball was still lodged inside. "Can you turn a little so I can see if the bullet came out the back?"

Joel muttered words she didn't understand—and likely didn't want to know the meaning of—as she helped him ease onto his side enough for her to glimpse his back.

Yes. Blood leaked from a wound that matched that on his front. At least Joel wouldn't have to endure the pain of digging the bullet out. Pa would have been the one to handle that task, since he was so adept at working with tiny tools in tiny places. If he'd ever wanted to leave gunsmithing, he could have surely become a surgeon.

But now the binding of this wound was up to her since she'd learned nursing skills from her mother—at least what skills she could master by the age of twelve.

She had to stop the bleeding, and it would be best if she could wash away the gunpowder residue with a bit of alcohol. She glanced up at the men standing around her, eyes wide, every one of them. "Do we have whiskey or any other hard drink? I need to clean the wound."

French glanced at the other two men as he answered. "I spoke the truth. We none of us drink it." Then he looked at Pa as he shuffled to her side with the medical pack. "Do you have some I can retrieve?"

"No." She turned back to Joel and wiped her hands on a

clean part of the shirt. "I'll need water then. Pa, can you get a good-sized roll of bandage out of there? And some ground hot pepper." That should help quench the flowing blood.

Within minutes, she had the wounds washed out, dried pepper plastered to the holes on both his front and his back, and was ready to wrap bandages around him.

She glanced at Beaver Tail, who'd knelt beside her. "I need him to sit up so we can bandage him."

He nodded, then gripped Joel's shoulders and eased him upright. The injured man's face paled with the effort, and a vein in his neck jutted out. He looked as if he'd like to spew more of those Spanish words he'd been muttering, but the pain probably restricted anything from coming out—even breath.

As soon as Beaver Tail had him sitting, she set to work quickly. "Let's take this shirt off until it can be washed." Today wasn't as warm as other days, but there was plenty of afternoon sunshine to keep him from getting chilled.

With Beaver Tail on one side and her on the other, they soon had Joel's shirt stripped off and the bandage secured tightly around him.

She sat back on her heels and looked around. "Can we camp here for the night? He needs to rest, at least until the wounds stop bleeding."

French stepped closer. "Caleb went to scout out a good place by the river. Joel can go that far, *oui?*"

She nodded, then turned back to her patient. "Do you want to walk or ride?"

"Walk." He spoke through gritted teeth. After inhaling a deep breath, he rolled onto his hands and knees. Then, with Beaver gripping his upper arms, Joel eased up to his feet.

As she watched her patient limp toward the river, her gaze drifted to the man walking beside him, leading two horses with a third tethered behind.

Beaver Tail cut an impressive figure with his broad, muscled shoulders tapering down to a trim waist, his raven black hair fanning around his shoulders. But it was so much more than his striking physical features that had begun to draw her these past days.

He was a warrior, no doubt, but he used his strength for protection. His ever-present nearness was a way he showed respect—maybe even care—for those he called friends.

And as she watched him helping Joel, she couldn't stop a longing to be one of those friends. Someone who meant more to him than just a female he felt obliged to protect.

She wanted him to see more in her. To like what he saw.

But she had a feeling that with Beaver Tail, that would be no easy feat.

~

*B*eaver Tail regretted every unkind thought he'd harbored about Susanna's presence in their group.

She seemed to know exactly what to do for Joel, and she didn't hesitate to take charge of his care. A relief that all of them were thankful for, if the other men felt the way he did. And their expressions said they did.

Now, as he sat in their camp in the faint light the next morning's dawn, he let himself watch her. Susanna's face had turned fragile in her sleep, like the clear surface of still water. Dark shadows marred the pretty skin beneath her eyes, probably from the several times she'd been up tending Joel in the night.

The man hadn't slept well, shifting and mumbling through many of the dark hours. Pain would cause that, especially the deep agony of a belly shot.

Beaver shifted his focus to his friend. Joel's coloring seemed to have paled some, but that might only be the dusky filter of early morning. Surely the wound wasn't fatal.

Fear nipped in Beaver's chest, but he pushed it back. He'd

seen several men creased by a bullet in the side who'd healed quickly with no ill effect. Joel's wound was nearer his middle than a crease, but surely not so much that it'd struck something important.

The man shifted again, rolling his head with a moan. Clearly in pain.

Susanna stirred, probably awakened by Joel's activity. She sat upright, her hair rumpled in a way that made him want to stroke his fingers through its softness. When she looked around, her gaze landed on him, hooded with sleep and so pretty his insides stirred. This woman affected him in every way possible.

He nodded toward Joel, a topic that would surely take his mind off her allure. "How's he doing?"

She snapped to attention, turning her focus to her patient as she crawled to his side. When she pressed her hand to his forehead, her own brow puckered. "He's been warm through the night, but he's even more feverish now."

Beaver's chest tightened. He needed to do something to help. Rising to his knees, he reached for the pot. "I'll get some water. Is there anything else you need?"

Her gaze flicked to the fire he'd already kindled, then she shook her head. "Maybe once he drinks and eats, he'll be better. I'll make a tea to help with the pain."

He pushed to his feet, grabbed up the pot, and started for the river. He should have already gone for water so it was ready when she awoke, but he'd been too caught up in watching her sleep.

Maybe if he chose to think of Susanna like he did the others, he could ignore the effect she had on him. She was no man, that was for certain, but she could be a friend. He'd like her to be a friend. More than he wanted to admit.

When he brought the water back to her, he placed the pot to warm by the fire, then dropped to his knees by Joel's feet. "How can I help?"

She sent him a quick glance, and it looked as if she was trying to summon a smile. But the look didn't reach her weary eyes. "I need cold water, too. I'll make tea and corn gruel with what's heating, but I need some to cool him off with. His temperature's definitely rising."

Joel's eyelids lifted then, but only partway as his gaze caught on Beaver Tail. "I'm fine. We need to get saddled."

Beaver almost chuckled at the words. The way Joel had been pushing, he might actually try to ride today if they let him. "We'll stay put for today. Don't give the lady any trouble." He sent Joel a pointed look, and the man must have realized the futility of the effort.

His eyelids drifted shut on a long sigh.

Beaver grabbed the oilskin pail and headed back to the river. Susanna would have a gentler hand with Joel, so he'd start on the food. Together, they'd see their patient through the effects of his injury.

Just like any good friends would do.

CHAPTER 13

*S*he couldn't let him die.

Susanna squeezed water over Joel's front bullet wound, biting back a cringe at the mangled flesh rimmed in bright red. Why did men think it necessary to be so cruel to each other? Lucas may not have intended to shoot Joel, but if he'd not had his gun loaded and ready to fire, his finger on the trigger, this never would have happened.

She'd not expected Joel's fever to rise so high, nor the skin around the wound to look so inflamed. True, she'd not seen many bullet wounds. When she'd helped her mother all those years ago, she'd probably been shielded from the worst of the injuries and illnesses.

Was this normal? Maybe for a gunshot at such a close range. But did that mean he would heal once his body worked through the fever? Her instincts said something was wrong. Or maybe that was only her fears.

"What can I do now?" Beaver Tail's quiet words drifted from where he knelt on the other side of Joel.

Fear welled in her chest, rising into her throat so she had to swallow before she could speak. "I don't know."

His silence weighed heavier as she did her best not to look at him. She couldn't handle the worry or censure in his eyes. Surely he was thinking how none of this would have happened if she and her father hadn't been there. Or maybe if she hadn't been a woman. Lucas wouldn't have spared her a second glance if she'd been a man, and they both knew it.

"This isn't your fault, you know." His voice was low, gentle. And it nearly undid her.

She squeezed her eyes shut against the tears. Against the pain of her guilt. She wouldn't cry in this man's presence. Not in front of any of them.

With deep, steady breaths, she pulled herself back under control. He didn't speak, and she could imagine what he was thinking. Or really, she *couldn't* imagine. Had he seen the near collapse of her emotions? Or did he simply think she didn't know how to respond to his kindness?

She dared a glance up at his face—and her gaze collided with his intense focus. His eyes held her, called to her, drew her in. And as she sank deeper, weight pulled off her shoulders, the ache lifted from her chest. She could breathe again.

It was as though she'd taken shelter in his gaze.

She inhaled deeply and let herself relax. One corner of his mouth pulled up, and his eyes softened. He so rarely smiled, seeing the gentle look now sent a warmth through her like warm honey down an aching throat.

She couldn't let herself become used to this, though. Couldn't let his charm affect her into thinking she meant more to him than any fellow traveler would. Besides, she had a great deal more important things to worry over, like Pa's health—and now Joel.

Susanna pulled her gaze from Beaver Tail's and tried to concentrate on his injured friend. She forced her muddled mind to refocus on what needed to be done next. Joel's wound needed to be re-wrapped.

Her ministrations had started the blood flowing again, so she sprinkled more dried pepper, then studied the gash. What else could she put on it? Most of the medicinals she'd brought were for the lungs and other internal troubles. She hadn't thought to bring something to heal a gunshot wound. Although, knowing the wild land they were coming to, she should have considered it.

She couldn't do anything about the lack now, though.

"Can you turn him on his side so I can clean the back wound?" She didn't dare look up at Beaver Tail, just prepared a clean bandage for when she'd be ready to re-wrap him.

"You awake, Joel?" Beaver Tail's large hand settled on his friend's arm.

"Mmm." Joel didn't open his eyes, but the reaction was good. At least his high temperature hadn't rendered him delirious. Not yet, anyway.

After Beaver Tail shifted him onto his side, she worked at cleaning the wound. This one hadn't reddened as much, maybe because all the gunpowder had been wiped from the ball when it had struck the front.

The sound of heavy feet stomping through grass came from her left, and she glanced up to see Caleb and French, back from whatever they'd been doing with the horses. Something with their hooves, the men had said, although none of the animals were shod.

Caleb swiped a sleeve across his brow as he marched into camp, then plopped onto a branch they'd been using as a chair. "How's he doing?"

She worked for a smile but couldn't summon one. "I'm doing everything I know for him." She motioned for Beaver Tail to lay Joel down on his back again.

Caleb leaned forward, elbows on his knees. "You're not gonna die on us, are you, Joel? 'Cause that's not allowed. We gotta find your brother first."

A slight pull of one corner of Joel's mouth was the only sign he'd heard. Then his lips parted—chapped, swollen, and bright red as they were. "Not gonna die." His words came out in a rough croak, as if they'd been lying in the sun until parched and shriveled.

"Let's have a drink." She reached for the cup of water and held it to his lips, using her other hand to raise his head a little. He sipped, then took a second sip without her prodding. That was an improvement.

When she laid his head down, a long breath leaked out of him. "Wish it were stronger."

Caleb snorted. "Must be feeling better." Then he pushed up to his feet. "Where's your pa, Susanna. Reckon he'd like to play a game of cards?"

She nodded toward the river. "Reading by the water. I'm sure he'd love to play. Watch him, though. He plays a mean hand of five card draw." The words raised a host of happy memories that eased her worry. They'd spent so many contented hours playing the game, especially in the winter evenings when his eyes needed a break from the strain of his exacting work.

The big man raised his chin, surprised respect shining in his eyes. "Oh, ho. I appreciate the warning." He glanced at French, who'd been unusually quiet. "You playin' too, Frenchie?"

The man looked up, blinking as though coming back from another world in his mind. "Maybe in a few minutes."

Caleb shrugged and sauntered toward the river.

She reached into the medical pack and pulled out a lard mixture to put on Joel's chapped lips. After applying it, she placed the tin back in the satchel.

It was then that the silence sank into her awareness. She glanced up at the two men. They were watching her. Beaver Tail still knelt across from her on Joel's other side. French sat on a log. Both wore such sober expressions, it was as if they were already mourning the loss of their friend.

God, please don't let me fail them. Tears pricked her eyes, and she looked away, fumbling through the pack, pretending she was looking for something while she regained control of her emotions.

She needed something to distract them all. Something to get the men talking. She had plenty of questions, so that shouldn't be hard. "French, can I ask what your real name is?" She sent a glance his way to make sure the question didn't offend him.

He tipped his head, his familiar grin finally quirking his mouth. "I am Jean Jacques Baptiste, after the great violinist. Alas, there were two others named Jean Jacques in our boating party when I met these compatriots. I am honored to have stood out enough to be given such a singular nickname."

She couldn't help a chuckle. "Singular, indeed. Would you prefer to be called Jean or Jean Jacques? Or even..." It was easier to produce a smile this time. "...Monsieur Baptiste?"

He bobbed his chin like a royal acknowledging one of lesser rank. "The latter of course, mademoiselle." But the twinkle in his eye belied his words.

"Monsieur Baptiste it is."

He rose, seeming to push away his deep thoughts from moments before. With his arms overhead, he heaved a mighty stretch with a groan. "Guess I'll get in on the card game before it's too late."

As he sauntered away, she looked to Beaver Tail, and his gaze nearly drew her in again. She looked away quickly. "And what of you? Is Beaver Tail your given name?"

Silence was her answer at first for a few beats, and she worried she'd offended him. Then, he said, "My mother named me Ishtaay. But my father called me the English version, Beaver Tail."

She couldn't help but look up at him. "Your father spoke English?" That would explain why Beaver Tail spoke without much accent. Had he been exposed to white men before Beaver Tail's birth?

He met her gaze solidly. "My father was English. He moved from England with his parents, from near a place called Newgate, when he was coming of age. His family died on the voyage, so when he landed in the United States, he started west. He didn't stop riding that direction until he met my uncle. And then my mother."

His voice dipped quieter with those last words, but his face didn't betray any emotion, not through his entire speech, for it had been a speech—the most she'd ever heard from him at one time.

As his words absorbed into her mind, the picture she'd formed of him shifted, but not as much as she would have expected. She sent him a little smile. "I see now why you speak English with such minor accent."

He nodded. "My father left when I was five, but my uncle continued to speak the language with us."

So many questions she wanted to ask. His father left? What did that mean? And what of his uncle? He'd never mentioned the man before. But he hadn't mentioned other family either. She honed in on that last bit. "Us?"

"My mother, my three sisters, and me. The youngest not yet born." Was that a trace of bitterness creeping into his tone? It was hard to tell with the stoic expression on his face. That mask of indifference.

But of course he must be bitter if his father deserted them. Prying into that pain didn't feel right, but surely he wouldn't mind speaking of his sisters.

She tried to soften her own expression, to share a smile that would lighten his heaviness even a little. "I always wanted a sister. Or even a brother. What was it like to have three?"

Now his face took on some life, at least more than before.

His mouth turned down. "Trouble. Every one of them." But his eyes held a glimmer that could only be love.

She raised her brows. "They were younger than you?"

He lifted his own brows, a silent question in them.

A grin tugged at her lips. "I can tell by the way you speak of them. Your tone."

He cocked his head, his brows lowering. There was no doubt the question forefront in his mind.

She had to fight back a chuckle. "You're accustomed to being in charge, I can tell. You could only harbor such affection for them if they were younger than you and listened to your every word."

His lips pursed. Was he holding in a laugh of his own? Not this man, surely. "You think they listen to my every word? You've not met my sisters, then. They listen to naught but themselves."

Something in his words rang with more emotion than he'd probably meant to show. She'd have to inspect his meaning later when she was alone.

For now, she wanted to keep him talking. "I've known a few women like that." Most women, actually. "How old are your sisters?"

"The youngest is not yet ten and seven summers." If she wasn't born yet when their father left, and Beaver Tail had been five, that would put him around two-and-twenty years old. His smooth tawny face possessed a timeless strength, like he could be anywhere from twenty to five-and-thirty. It was a wonder he was so dark, being only half Indian. But spending all his time in the hot sun might account for some of that pigment.

Beaver Tail didn't look uncomfortable with her questions, at least not those about his sisters, so she pushed on. "Are any of them married or intended?" Did Indians become engaged and marry? She wasn't sure what their usual process was. Maybe each tribe was different.

"My oldest, Fox Running, is the squaw of a brave named He Who Sings. She will birth a child before I return." His brow furrowed. "Probably has already." That furrowed brow didn't leave, evidence of his worry, no doubt.

"Your mother's there to help her?" She couldn't imagine going through such an ordeal without a mother. Just one of the reasons she didn't plan to have children of her own. Or a husband. There was simply no need.

He nodded. "There are many women in the camp who will see to her."

She wanted to reach out to him. To place her hand on his arm, somehow communicate that she understood the pain, the longing he was trying to hide. But with Joel between them, she had to settle for letting her eyes speak to him. "I can imagine none would take the place of being able to present her child to her elder brother, the one she's always looked to for guidance and protection."

He looked away, the muscles in his jaw flexing. Now, even more, she wanted to reach out to him, to wrap her arms around him and comfort. Why did she think he needed comfort? One wouldn't suspect it from looking at him. Yet there was something. A deep part of her sensed it.

A cough sounded from the direction of the river, breaking through her thoughts. Shattering her focus like a bullet through thin glass.

She darted a look in that direction, although the underbrush concealed Pa and the others from view. The cough sounded again, this time continuing as the spell consumed him. With each thick, racking shudder, her muscles pulled tighter and tighter. How much pain he must be in.

Finally the outburst ended in a last, mucousy cough. He would be wiping his mouth with a handkerchief now, one so stained it had turned a spotted rusty brown, no matter how many times she'd scrubbed it. He'd try to hide the fresh crimson from the other men. And knowing Caleb and French, they'd look away to give him privacy.

Her heart ached with the awfulness of it all.

"Have you tried the root of a marshmallow plant?" Beaver's words broke through her painful thoughts.

She worked to shift her focus to his question. "I…I'm not certain. He's been to several doctors and tried all sorts of remedies. None seemed to help more than a few days before their effect faded." She glanced toward their pack. "The ground licorice root I put in his tea is the best I have for now. The other tonic that seemed to help was used up a few days ago."

Those frown lines wrinkled his brow again. She wanted to ask what was churning in his mind, but something held her back. Perhaps she didn't want to know.

Perhaps he was thinking how he'd better steer clear of her father, lest he catch whatever ailed him. He would be one of many who'd voiced or acted out that concern.

But for some reason, the thought of Beaver Tail holding such an opinion pressed an ache in her chest. One more knife wound piercing through the armor she tried so hard to maintain.

If her father didn't get better soon, her armor would be so chipped away she'd have nothing left to protect herself with.

CHAPTER 14

"I'm sure he's just out setting traps."

Susanna looked up into Caleb's earnest expression the next day and tried to let his kindness warm her. In truth, she was too exhausted to be warmed. Weary from worrying over Joel and Pa. And now, she couldn't seem to stop herself from worrying over Beaver Tail. He'd seemed so reserved after their conversation the day before. Either she'd offended him with all her prying questions, or hearing how bad her father's condition was had sent him retreating for protection.

Either way, he'd been gone since before they'd all awakened that morning, and he hadn't returned at all through the day. Now they were about to eat the evening meal, and he still hadn't shown himself.

She scooped a plate of beans and handed it to Caleb. "You're probably right." But they both knew Beaver Tail wouldn't be setting traps all day long. He hadn't taken his horse, so maybe he'd started with the snares and been hurt somewhere along the way.

Memories of the otter attack rushed through her, gripping her by the throat and squeezing until she could barely breathe.

"I'll eat a bite," Caleb said, "then go look for him."

She forced the panic aside, forced herself to focus on loading the spoon with beans, then pour them into another bowl. She nodded to Caleb but didn't dare take her focus off her work. "Thank you."

Part of her wanted to go too. Wanted to strike out and find him, to let him know she'd not meant to pry so deeply. If he didn't want to tell details of his life, she would ask nothing more. And if Pa's illness was the problem, she could assure him there was nothing contagious in the disease. After all, she'd been around him since the beginning, and she'd not contracted more than an occasional cold.

No matter what the problem was, Beaver could come back.

And if he'd tried to come and been injured somehow, well... He needed help. And she wanted to be the one to help him. It shouldn't matter to her, but it did.

There wasn't much talking in the group as they ate. Not the usual camaraderie between them that Pa had slipped into so easily, and not a companionable silence either. Tension hung thick around them, and when she'd finished her own small dish of food, she worked quickly to put away the supplies she'd used to prepare the meal. She would be ready as soon as Caleb was.

A whippoorwill sounded in the dark, jerking her attention up. That was the call the men used to alert each other when one was entering camp at night. Joel had shared that detail the second evening they were on the trail. Of course, there were real whippoorwills in this area too, so they'd have to wait and see if this was Beaver Tail, but her heart raced with the possibility.

She almost missed his entrance as the man materialized from the darkness, stepping into the firelight as though he floated.

"Beaver Tail." She had to keep herself from jumping to her feet and stepping toward him. She'd promised herself she wouldn't bother him, after all.

His gaze found hers and lingered there, his eyes saying so much. He'd thought of her that day. Maybe he'd even missed her. And he was sorry if he'd worried her.

Or maybe she was reading too much into what she saw there. Probably far too much.

His gaze shifted from hers, swinging around the camp, from one man to the next.

"It's about time you showed up, BT. You had the little lady worryin'." Caleb stuffed his last bite of beans in his mouth.

It took her a moment to process Caleb's words, then a wave of mortification swept through her. Part of her wanted to protest that she hadn't worried at all.

But that would be an untruth, so she turned back to the fire and busied herself scraping charred beans from the bottom of the pan. Caleb and French prattled on about how they'd been preparing to go looking for Beaver, even though they were plenty tired from their various duties that day—including the extra part that might have been Beaver's chores if he'd been around. The typical teasing the men often indulged in.

Beaver Tail didn't answer, although she could imagine the hint of a smile that sometimes played at his lips when he listened to their banter. She heard the crack of knees as he crouched next to Joel, then a low murmur that sounded like, "How are you, my friend?"

"Better." Joel's croak made her own throat hurt every time he spoke. His fever still troubled him, but it had seemed to lessen a little through the day. She could only pray it didn't spike again tonight, as fevers were wont to do.

A faint shuffling sounded behind her, then Beaver Tail appeared at her side. He dropped to his knees and unfolded a leather pouch.

Inside were a dozen or so plants, all the same species, with drooping leaves almost the size of her palm. The stems had been pulled from the ground with roots intact and covered with dirt.

"I'll clean them first, then you can cut the roots and stems and boil them in water to make a tea for your father. It will help clear his chest."

Her gaze darted up to his face. "You found these while you were out?"

He nodded. "I've seen some by the river before, but I didn't think I'd have to go so far to find more."

So he'd gone specifically to get these for Pa? And hadn't turned back until he'd found them. A wash of emotion flooded through her, surging up to sting her eyes. "Thank you."

She didn't look away this time. Wanted him to see the depth of her gratitude. Even if the plant didn't bring relief to her father, the fact that Beaver Tail had gone to such lengths to help meant more than she could express in words. He'd not rejected her and Pa. Instead, he'd reached out to offer aid.

She did finally drop her gaze when tears blurred her vision. No need to appear excessively weak.

"I'll wash them in the river. Do you need more water?"

The question pulled her from her emotional quagmire. "Yes, in this pot." She reached for the kettle she used for tea.

When he took the metal handle from her, the brush of his large warm hand against hers sent a skitter up her arm. She did her best not to let the reaction show.

Then he stood with the plants and the kettle, and, as silently as he'd appeared, faded into the dark of night.

~

"I can't tell you how much I 'preciate that new tea you brought, son. Think it might actually be helping." As if to give the lie to his words, Wilkins turned away from Beaver Tail and loosed a cough into his sleeve.

It didn't turn into a full coughing fit, though. Not like usual. And maybe the sound wasn't as thick and bubbly as it had been.

Beaver Tail glanced up from the moccasin he was mending and over to Susanna to see if she noticed the same.

She was studying her father like she often did when the man coughed. The worry marring her pretty face was clear. But a thoughtfulness narrowed her eyes, too.

He turned back to Wilkins with a nod. "I hope it helps, sir."

"Did I ever tell you about the doctor I once built a flintlock blunderbuss for?" Wilkins sank back against the tree behind him. "He specialized in surgeries, especially those of the throat. Real good with little details. I tried to tell him a 'buss wouldn't give him the aim he'd want when he was out hunting. But he said his vision was failing, so he needed something that would scatter enough shot to hit what he wanted it to." The man grinned and looked to be holding in a chuckle. Probably so the laugh didn't start a coughing fit.

Beaver Tail couldn't help sharing the good humor. There was something about Wilkins that made it impossible not to like the man. Made him want to open up. Even though Susanna sat nearby. "I haven't heard of a blunderbuss."

The twinkle in the older man's eyes deepened. "It's an old gun, not made new much anymore. Shoots like the muskets they used back in the war for independence." Wilkins tipped his head. "But I guess that wouldn't tell you much, would it? The barrel is flared at the end." He leaned forward and used his fingers to illustrate his words. "And it's used to fire lots of small shot instead of a single ball. It works for hunting small game in somewhat near range. Not so good for the big stuff."

He nodded toward his daughter. "Like Susanna's bear the other night. Wouldn't have done more than make it angry. Did I tell you it took three shots to bring that beast down? And that was with my strongest spiral-bore rifle. How are your scratches healing by the way, daughter?" This last bit was turned toward Susanna, and Beaver Tail couldn't help looking her way, too.

She ducked her chin, and her cheeks turned a pretty apple-red. "Much recovered." The words were mumbled, probably because of his presence there.

He couldn't keep his gaze from dropping to her leg where most of the damage seemed to have been. She'd stitched the wide arc the bear had torn in her leggings, but he still caught a limp anytime she stood after kneeling for a while. She seemed to be healing, though.

He pulled his focus from her, shifting toward the river where the other men had gone. "Joel seems much improved."

"He does." Relief brightened her voice. "When he woke without a fever this morning, he was finally able to eat on his own. He's getting his strength back quickly."

Once again, his gaze pulled to her like a mother bird to its nest of young. "You're a good healer. You have the patience for it."

A sadness shadowed her eyes, but she bobbed her chin. "I find I don't like nursing as well as I did when I was younger." The quick flick of her gaze toward her father revealed everything she couldn't say.

He could only imagine the challenge of caring for her father with his lung troubles. Or rather, he'd like to imagine it.

If only his own father had stuck around long enough, maybe Beaver would have had an opportunity to help him with something. Or at least get to know him.

❧

*P*art of Beaver Tail wanted to cheer Joel on as they rode the next morning. His friend was tough, no doubt. Even though sweat beaded his brow and his face hadn't

119

worn much color for several hours, Joel rode without complaining.

But the part of him that watched Susanna's nervous worry wanted to snatch Joel's reins and tell him to get off his horse and lie down. Maybe another day to recover was what the man needed. Susanna certainly seemed to think so, if her expressions could be believed.

They were moving into the rocky country of the lower mountains now, and the river flowed between steep cliffs on either side, making it impossible in some places for them to reach the water.

A beautiful sight to behold, though, with the rock face descending almost the length an arrow could shoot, the water far below looking so much smaller than it really was.

A gasp ahead grabbed his focus, tightening every part of him as he tensed for danger.

"Look." Susanna's voice held more than a little awe at the brown mass rippling just over the hill they were cresting.

Buffalo. Such a vast herd, they covered the land like a blanket with only a few holes worn through. This must be the same group he'd seen when he met Lucas.

Now that he thought about it, what had happened to the buffalo the man had shot that day? Beaver Tail hadn't actually seen an animal fall, but even a man who couldn't hit the broad side of a cliff wouldn't have missed his shot with the animals packed in so thick as they grazed. But Lucas hadn't taken time to dress his kill.

Anger churned in Beaver's gut. Any man who'd experienced a hungry winter knew better than to waste food like that. Not to mention the hide thick enough to save fingers and toes in a snowstorm.

French reined in their group at the top of the knoll as they all stared out over the sight before them.

Beaver had been riding in the rear, as usual, which gave him an easy view of Susanna at any time, but especially now as she watched the herd. But it was Wilkins who caught his attention.

The man's face curved into ripples of pleasure as he took in the vision before them. "That sure is a pretty sight." The words were just loud enough to hear, spoken in a whisper so full of awe, it birthed the same feeling in Beaver's chest.

But Wilkins's whisper ended in a wheeze, which turned into a cough, deep and croupy, snatching the air from the man and doubling him over. Cough after cough tore from deep inside, shaking his thin frame with a ferocity that looked as if it might knock the man over.

Susanna must have thought the same, for she nudged her horse alongside her father's, her hand hovering in the air but not touching his back. Beaver Tail signaled his horse along the man's other side.

Wilkins's bone-jarring coughs finally began to subside, turning into thick, chesty barks. At last, he heaved in a desperate gurgling breath, like a drowning man coming up for air.

His shoulders rose and dipped with each labored inhale, and his face had paled as white as new snow. He swayed, and if he hadn't been gripping the saddle, he may well have fallen off the side.

Beaver raised his voice loud enough for the group to hear him. "Time to let the horses rest. We can eat a bite too." Wilkins needed a break more than the animals, but he had a feeling the fellow wouldn't appreciate being called out.

The others could all read through his words, no doubt, and a tense quiet settled over the group as they dismounted. Joel, too, looked about to fall off his horse as he leaned forward to climb down. Maybe it would be best if they stayed in this spot longer than the length of a midday meal—a few hours at least.

He could pretend a need to ride ahead to inspect the buffalo herd while the group waited for him to return. If they'd needed food, he would take the opportunity to bring down one of the animals. But they still had plenty from the bear and his trapping, and they didn't have enough space to pack any more cured meat.

His glance slid to Susanna, who was helping her father sit under the only tree in the area. Maybe she'd like to ride with him to see the herd. But she'd probably rather stay near her father and Joel—the nurse with her patients.

And he shouldn't be looking for ways to spend extra time with her anyway.

CHAPTER 15

*B*eaver Tail waited until Susanna had finished passing out helpings of bean cake and meat to each of them, then he rose to his knees and glanced at French and Caleb. "I'm going to ride forward and see the herd. I'll make sure we have a safe route around them." Those two would likely see through his bluff.

Joel too, if he had his wits about him. But just then, the man was lying on his back with an arm over his eyes, chewing slowly as if the task took great effort. Wilkins was slumped against the tree, sipping water and nibbling on a bean cake. If the fatigue on his face were any indication, he'd be stretched out like Joel within a few minutes. Good.

Beaver Tail stood and turned to catch his horse, which he'd turned loose to graze with its saddle on.

"Can I ride with you?"

Susanna's voice froze him mid-step. He turned back to her, his heart beating faster than her simple words should have effected.

Her eyes were always pretty—that was one of the first things he'd noticed about her that day on the river's edge—but now they were rounded and pleading, and the hope in them pressed like a weight on his chest. He glanced at her father just to escape the longing her gaze drew from him.

"I suppose I should stay here," she said. "Forget I asked."

His focus shot back to her face, which she'd turned to her father. She must have interpreted Beaver's look toward the man to mean he was asking if she worried about leaving her father in his ill state. Maybe he had meant that, but the thought of Susanna not going with him sent a surge of desperation through his chest.

Before he could stop himself, he looked to Caleb. "You can see to anything that's needed here, right?"

Caleb nodded, then sent Susanna one of his charming grins. "You ride out an' enjoy yourself, ma'am. A big herd of buffalo like this one is a sight to behold. We'll all just sit here an' enjoy the breeze." He swiped his sleeve across his brow as though he'd worked up a sweat.

Beaver had to bite back a snort. The man did know how to play things up for a woman.

But Susanna didn't seem affected by his charm. Instead, she turned to Beaver with uncertainty in her gaze.

He reached out for her. It wasn't until he already had his hand extended that he wondered why he'd done it. He wasn't standing close enough that she could actually slip her fingers in his. But this woman seemed to make his body act before his mind had time to stop himself.

The thought scared him more than he wanted to face right now.

But he'd already put himself out there, so he kept his hand extended. After a long moment—maybe not as long as the silence felt—she nodded, then pushed to her feet.

*S*omething felt different.

Susanna breathed in fresh air as a breeze brushed her face. The day wasn't overwarm, but the wind held a freedom she hadn't tasted in so long, she could barely remember the feeling.

Beaver Tail rode beside her, their horses covering ground in an easy jog. She wasn't sure what had possessed her to ask to come along. Well, if she were honest, the impulse had probably been triggered by more than one thing. But she didn't want to be honest with herself just now. Didn't want to think through anything rationally.

She just wanted to taste the freedom lingering in the air. Wanted to be a little reckless.

With that thought prodding her, she glanced sideways. "Can we move faster?"

Surprise flashed through his eyes. Then, he pushed his horse into a lope.

She should have known he wouldn't waste time with words.

She kicked her gelding into a faster run than his to make up the ground they'd just lost, then let the horse speed by Beaver's mount. His gelding stretched out to pull even with them again. She could push her horse harder and maybe even win the race, but winning wasn't so important.

Just letting herself run, releasing the weights that had been holding her down, crushing her beneath their mass—this was what she'd needed. This foretaste of heaven. In that wonderful place, there would be no coughing or illness. No gunshots, accidental or otherwise. No sickness taking mothers from little girls who needed them.

Everything would be right in that world.

For just a moment, she could imagine she'd already reached that land. That paradise was here in the vast untamed wilderness. With this man keeping pace beside her.

When they neared the buffalo, she sat back and reined the mare down to a trot, then a walk. Beaver did the same, keeping stride beside her. He had the unique ability to move in tandem with her, as though he could read her thoughts and fade into her shadow. Words weren't necessary with him.

The horses pricked their ears as they walked to the edge of the herd, stopping only a couple of strides from the nearest beasts. From a distance, they'd looked like a dark rolling blanket, all a single chocolate brown. But standing this close, she could see the nuances in their thick, layered coats. Some still had chunks of lighter winter coats covering the shorter, dark layer of summer hair. And their heads—massive wooly things that made the animals look twice as frightening, especially with sharp horns poking through on either side.

These creatures were large enough to plow her down if she weren't on horseback.

"Have you ever been wounded by a buffalo?" She glanced sideways at Beaver Tail and caught the flicker of his cheek as he stared straight ahead.

"I've never given them the chance." He turned and met her gaze. "I've never moved among them without my horse."

His gaze was so deep, so rich and luring, his words barely registered as his eyes held hers, cradling her in a warmth she would have loved to wrap herself in all day. His arms would likely be even more wonderful.

But that wouldn't be. Not the way he jerked his gaze away, leaving her alone and defenseless as she tried to pull her emotions back to safety.

She turned to the buffalo and nudged her horse forward. Motion. She needed to move. Needed to do something impetuous for once. And Beaver had said these wouldn't hurt a horse, right?

The gelding hesitated when Susanna reined her between the first two buffalo—on one side a cow with her calf tucked close, and on the other a mid-sized buffalo, maybe a yearling or a two-year-old, if these animals grew at the same rate as cattle.

Susanna nudged the horse forward, and it picked its way through the herd. The buffalo nearest her raised their heads to stare, and with those creatures eyeing them with lowered horns, she could see why the horse hesitated. But they pushed their way through, and most of the herd proved gentle, and even somewhat afraid of this intruder to their peaceful grazing.

Beaver Tail waded through the beasts just behind her. The ever present shadow. And she couldn't deny the sense of security his presence provided. She had the pistol she kept tucked in her waistband in case any of the animals charged, but she'd rather not have to use it. Would the smaller caliber gun even affect these massive creatures? Surely it would be enough at close range.

Unless all that matted hair stopped the bullet before it could penetrate the flesh. She eyed one particularly wooly beast that stared back at her, its dark eyes almost covered by the hair curled tight over its face. A flap of extra skin hung below its jowls, a feature most of the other buffalo didn't share.

"He's one of the bulls. A young one, from the looks of him."

She had to force herself not to tense at Beaver's quiet words. In the world of cattle, bulls were much fiercer than mild-mannered cows. "Is he dangerous?" She shouldn't have pushed her horse through all these unknown animals. Even though she was feeling reckless, it wasn't fair to put the horse in harm's way.

"More unpredictable than the others. I've never seen them attack, but probably best not to push him."

She looked back at Beaver Tail, and the gravity in his expression made her midsection churn. She never should have brought this gentle gelding into the herd, and now, they needed to work their way back out posthaste.

"Turn and ride past me. I'll stay until you're out of the herd so he doesn't think we're running and come after us." Beaver's voice held a quiet strength, a tone that inspired confidence in his abilities.

She should let him retreat and keep herself as the guardian until he and his gelding had exited the herd. But she hated to put her horse in danger, too. And Beaver would know better how to conduct himself to keep the buffalo from reacting.

She turned and followed his instructions, careful not to meet his gaze as she rode past him. Their legs brushed in the close confines of the surrounding buffalo. Her focus jerked to his face against her better judgement.

He didn't spare her a glance, just stared straight ahead, his jaw carved from stone. He must blame her for putting them in danger. Why hadn't he stopped her before she entered the herd? He'd let her go in, only staying nearby as that ever-present shadow.

Of course, his rifle lay across his lap, ready for any sign of danger. Ready to protect.

$\sim$

*B*eaver Tail could barely contain his frustration with himself. He shouldn't have let Susanna ride along with him from the beginning.

Spending time with a woman always got him in trouble. He knew better than to think this time would be any different. Back at the camp, when she'd held him with those mesmerizing eyes, he'd let his foolish hope lead when he should have used his head and told her to stay in safety with the others.

The bull buffalo growled, a deep guttural sound powerful enough to reach far across the plain. The buffalo around them raised their heads, a restless energy shifting through the herd. Beaver's gelding shuffled backward, loosing a nervous snort as it bobbed its head.

Beaver glanced behind him to see where Susanna was. She and her mount had almost reached the edge of the herd.

When he turned back to the bull buffalo, the animal was pawing the ground. Not good.

Another fierce rumble echoed from the beast, louder than before, and Beaver spun his horse to retreat. The animal might charge any second. He'd seen bull buffaloes face off in battle, and the power they wielded could mortally wound his horse. Or him, if he were thrown from his gelding and exposed to the beast's wrath.

The milling buffalo had closed off the gap Susanna opened as she rode out. Cows bellowed and calves answered in pitiful bleats. A group about twenty strides away began to scuffle, one cow attempting to climb over another in an effort to reach its calf.

The bull growled again, and the sound echoed like thunder. But no. That wasn't the reverberation from the bull. Hundreds of hooves began to thud over the ground as the herd shifted around him.

No. Maybe if he stayed still, the bull would quiet down. The herd wouldn't stampede.

But like water rushing around stones in a riverbed, the buffalo moved toward Susanna, sliding around her, picking up speed. She turned to Beaver Tail with a look on her face that was pure fear.

As the buffalo broke into a jog, then a lope, Susanna's mare whinnied, and his own mount responded with a high-pitched neigh. He gripped his reins tighter as his horse danced a nervous shuffle, then he freed one hand to raise a palm to Susanna. *Stay still.* He didn't dare yell loud enough to be heard above the thunder of hooves.

But she seemed to understand his meaning. She looked like fear had frozen every part of her, but she held her horse still, even though the mare pawed and jerked at the reins to escape the animals clambering around it.

Soon the herd would pass and they'd be safe. Thankfully, the buffalo in back of the herd hadn't reached a full run like those in the front had now. The bull must be somewhere in the midst, driving his herd forward.

But...no. Realization slammed over him. The stampede was running straight for the rest of their group. Susanna's father. Joel. Would any of them see the herd coming? Could they get out of the way in time?

Just once, he wished there was truly a Great Spirit who could step in and control the uncontrollable. An all-powerful being who could pluck his friends out of the path of the buffalo. And while he was at it, maybe that being could heal Susanna's father.

But there was no such spirit, and if Beaver Tail could have any hope of helping the others, he'd have to get there in time.

As the stragglers loped around him, he dug his heels into his gelding's side and turned the animal toward the edge of the herd closest to the river. The buffalo were smart enough to give a little room between their running and the edge of the cliff leading down to the water. He could use that space to get ahead of the animals. Maybe he could get to the others in time.

Weaving around the calves who darted in front of him was frustrating, but he kept his horse at a run slow enough to dodge the obstacles. If his horse stumbled over one of them and went down, there was no way he'd reach the men. He couldn't risk it.

His mind raced ahead, remembering the image of Joel lying on the ground, Wilkins looking so pale and weak, he probably couldn't get out of the way of the buffalo even if he were given warning.

He'd need help.

Would Caleb and French have the presence of mind to get

the weaker ones out of the way? Surely they would. All the men were capable—in mind, if not in body at the present.

He'd covered half the distance when a glance sideways caught the blur of a horse and rider behind him.

Susanna. Of course, he should have expected her to ride hot on his heels. She would be there when her father needed her, or she'd die trying.

He couldn't let that last part happen.

CHAPTER 16

*A*head, the cliff edge had eroded farther than at other places, narrowing the space Beaver Tail could ride through. He'd have to slow down and nudge the buffalo out of the way. The animals had increased their speed, fear hurdling them forward in a frantic, thundering wave.

As he neared the spot, he reined his gelding in. The animal fought the hold at first, but finally eased down to a trot as the buffalo thundered past. The space between the crumbled cliff edge and the animals wasn't wide enough to support a horse. And the way the buffalo tore by, the animals wouldn't pay enough attention to make them slow. Maybe he should try jumping the opening. But it stretched farther than the length of his horse, and he couldn't count on the gelding making the leap.

And Susanna. He couldn't let her try such a feat. Couldn't even let her think it was an option. Of course, she certainly wouldn't stop here and leave her father to whatever fate befell him. The front of the herd had probably already reached the men. With all the dust the animals raised, it was hard to tell.

But his friends might need help still, and the sooner Beaver reached them, the sooner he could give aid.

When he reached the narrow place, he reined his gelding to a stop. Within seconds, Susanna pulled her own mount in behind him.

"I'm going to push my horse into the herd. When there's enough room, move quickly past this place." He motioned toward the cliff's edge.

"The buffalo will run you down. They're so panicked they can't see anything." They were both yelling over the din from the herd, and Susanna's shoulders heaved as she struggled for air.

They didn't have time to waste arguing, and there wasn't another way for her to pass through in relative safety. He moved his horse a few lengths before the shortened edge, then pushed his heel against the animal's side to shift it into the path of the buffalo. The horse didn't budge, for there was no way to push over the wall of rushing animals. He'd have to move them first.

He spun to face the oncoming animals, then waved a hand in the air. "Yah!" Using his highest pitch, he broke into the war whoop he'd been taught a dozen years ago. "Yah, yah, yah!"

The piercing cry worked. The buffalo shied away from him, and he pushed his horse into the path they'd taken just seconds before. He had to keep up the cry, so he couldn't turn to make sure Susanna was following orders, but he had to trust she was.

When he'd given enough time for her to get past the narrow spot, he spun his horse and dug in his heels, spurring the animal into a run so they weren't trampled once the buffalo veered back into a straight line.

Susanna galloped ahead of him, her horse charging in a full run as they closed the distance between them and the camp. He pushed his gelding hard, but Susanna still led him by a distance.

He could see a form ahead—the tree they'd sat beside. The buffalo blocked his view of anything underneath its branches. But then a motion near the cliff caught his attention. A cluster of men and animals. Were they all there? He couldn't tell.

As he neared, the figures grew clearer. The man kneeling must be Joel. Behind him stood French with two horses. Further back in the row, Caleb's tall head reached above the others, and several horse bodies shifted around.

Since the men weren't frantic, did he dare hope Wilkins was somewhere there, safe?

Susanna reached the group and flew from her horse. "Where's my father?"

He couldn't understand the men's response, but she charged past them, moving dangerously close to the stampeding buffalo as she maneuvered around the men. Beaver Tail finally reached them and pulled his horse to a stop, slipping to the ground in the same movement.

"Is anyone hurt?" He didn't stop to check each of the men as he followed the same path Susanna had, just waited for a spoken response.

"We all got out of the way in time." Caleb's voice rose above the buffalo's thundering.

Thank the heavens above. He reached Susanna, who knelt beside her father at the cliff's edge.

He was coughing, probably from the dust that hung thick in the air. Even though the man had turned away from the cloud, it was impossible not to breathe the mess. He might find a little better breathing if he could stand so he was higher off the ground, but the way the coughing wracked every part of his body, he didn't look able to rise.

The buffalo behind them were thinning now, and the last fragments of the herd would soon be trotting by. The old and weak, exactly the kind wolves sought. Thankfully, no wolf howls had sounded in recent nights.

As the noises around them quieted, Wilkins's cough hadn't yet lessened. It tore from him in gasping bursts, as though his insides were working their hardest to spew out of him. The man surely couldn't breathe with the coughs gripping his body so fully, and with each blow, he seemed to lean farther toward the edge of the cliff. If he lost control of his body, he'd topple.

Beaver dropped to his knees beside the man, opposite where Susanna knelt. He gripped Wilkins's arm, just in case his body gave way beneath him. Should he thump the man's back? Susanna wasn't doing that, and Wilkins seemed so frail, even a gentle pat seemed like it might break something within.

At last, the coughing slowed, allowing short breaths in between. Each inhale sounded loud and rasping in the quiet around them—the aftermath of the stampede. Something inside Wilkins's chest gurgled as he worked to take more breaths. The man was truly ill—more than a bit of marshmallow root could remedy.

Finally, the cough subsided completely, and Wilkins seemed to wilt.

"Come lie down, Pa. Rest a few minutes." Susanna's voice was so gentle, it surely soothed some of the pain shadowing his face.

Wilkins nodded, then shifted backward on his knees. He looked over at his daughter and patted her leg with such a loving expression, pain struck in Beaver's chest. He'd never seen such a bond as what linked this man and his daughter. He was glad Susanna had this connection with her father, but if Beaver wasn't careful, watching them would crack the cover he'd long ago tightened over his own longings.

"Here is water for you." French appeared beside them and held out a canteen to Wilkins. The older man took it, yet seemed too exhausted to raise the flask to his lips. Susanna cupped her hand around her father's and lifted it for him.

"The ground is a dusty mess around that tree where we were, what with all those hooves marching through. Might be best just to stretch out right here." Caleb kicked aside a clump of dirt to clear a smooth spot where Wilkins could lie.

After another drink of water, Susanna helped her father

recline. Beaver stayed by the man's other side in case he was needed, but father and daughter worked together as if they'd accomplished the task often.

Beaver glanced around the area. The day was only half over, but it might be best if they stayed until tomorrow morning. Wilkins couldn't sit a horse in his weakened state, and Joel hadn't risen from where he knelt, either.

Both needed rest.

He cut his gaze to French, who met his look with a knowing nod. "I'll take the horses to unsaddle and let them graze. I'll unpack supplies for the night, oui?"

"Oui." Beaver nodded.

Susanna swung around to stare at him, her gaze almost frightened. "Are you certain?"

He tried to read in her expression what troubled her so much. Did she think her father was able to continue on? Why would she want to push him? Maybe she worried they weren't safe in this place.

He glanced around once more, just to make sure there wasn't a danger he'd missed. All was remarkably quiet, save the murmur of the river far below. On this plain, there was no way an enemy could approach undetected. They would be as safe here as anywhere.

Turning back to Susanna, he met her gaze. "It's good to stay here the rest of the day. Tomorrow we can move on."

She still looked worried, but she nodded, then shifted her focus back to her father.

Something about her expression felt off to him. Seemed he'd not discovered the root of her concern. It shouldn't matter to him. As long as she and her father were safe and they didn't stop him from accomplishing what he needed to, this woman's thoughts shouldn't cause him worry.

And yet worry he did.

~

*S*usanna picked her way through the darkness, across ground churned by thousands of hooves. The horses nickered softly ahead of her in response to the man she sought. As much as she wanted to avoid the topic, she needed him to know how grateful she was that he'd allowed Pa to rest this afternoon.

Yet she didn't want to hold them back. And the last thing she wanted was for them to ride away without her and Pa. The thought of being left behind—alone, with Pa's condition worsening so quickly—frightened her more than anything.

Well...not more than anything. Not more than the worst possible thing.

But she couldn't dwell on the thought of losing her father. She had to do whatever it took to stay with these men. Their protection and help had become more valuable than she'd ever imagined. And Pa seemed to relish their company.

When she reached the horses, she couldn't see Beaver Tail, yet she knew he was there. He would make himself known when he was ready.

She rubbed each horse she came to, spending a few extra moments with her gelding. This sweet horse had been an able partner during their time on the trail, especially today during the ordeal with the buffalo.

Susanna's gut churned as the memories flooded through her. What an impulsive chit she'd been. One more thing she needed to offer Beaver Tail—an apology.

"Your father is sleeping?" The man shifted from her thoughts into a shadowy form at the mare's head. His sudden presence should have startled her, but it seemed as natural as breathing.

"Finally. He drank three cups of the tea with marshmallow root and licorice before the coughing fits stopped." Getting so much dust in his lungs had kept Pa coughing all afternoon. One more awful result of her foolishness.

"He needs the rest." Beaver Tail's voice held a gentleness she hadn't heard often. A tenderness she wanted to soak into.

But his words were the opening she needed. She inhaled a strengthening breath. "Thank you for calling a halt so my father could recover, but we don't want to hold up the journey. We'll be ready to ride out with you all in the morning."

She steeled herself for his reply, but silence was her only answer. That and the chirping of crickets, the chomping of horse teeth in grass, the distant flowing of the Missouri River—all the sounds that normally soothed her. Yet her body tensed more the longer his silence stretched.

"Your father isn't the only one who needed to rest this day. Joel wasn't ready for a full day's ride either. We can wait to see how they both fare at the sun's rise. Maybe it's best to stay in this place another day."

No. She'd seen Joel's impatience so many times already. He'd force himself to ride on tomorrow morning no matter how weak he felt.

And if her father wasn't able to keep up, she and Pa would be left behind. As kind as these men had been, they had their own lives to live. Their own mission to accomplish.

She shook her head. "My father will be well enough in the morning. I'm sure of it." While she was at it, she should go ahead and finish what had to be said. "Also, I need to apologize for starting the stampede earlier. Riding into that herd was foolish and reckless. I shouldn't—" Her voice broke as memory of what her actions had wrought poured over her. How much longer would the dust from all those hooves hover in the air? Pa struggled to breathe under normal conditions. The last thing she'd wanted was to make his struggle worse.

"There's never knowing what causes a stampede, but I doubt

you riding into the herd made them run." His words were quiet. Confident.

If only she could feel as confident.

Beaver Tail was silent again, and she could feel his scrutiny, even in the darkness, as though he could read through her defenses, could see her fears and flaws underneath. Could see the desperate little girl she was trying so hard to cover up.

"What is it you're afraid of?" His voice was gentle, yet probing.

Maybe he hadn't seen everything inside her yet, but he was getting close. He'd realize it all soon enough, so she might as well tell him. At least this way, she could present her fears in a way that didn't make her sound fully helpless.

She swallowed to clear her throat. "You all have been such a help with my father's weakness. Your protection has been"—she struggled to find a word strong enough—"very appreciated." That didn't say the half of it, but she pressed on. "I don't want you to feel like we're slowing you down. I know Joel is eager to find his brother. You all are."

There. He would read between her words and understand it all, but at least she'd not sounded like the helpless little girl she felt like so often these days.

Night shadows darkened his face so she couldn't read his thoughts. He took a step nearer, and his presence loomed large before her. She could reach out and touch him if she wanted. And part of her did—a very small part. The only part that was still brave and strong.

She fought the urge to wrap her arms around herself. To find strength in that tiny protection.

"Susanna, we won't leave you. You have my word. Whatever I can do for your father's comfort, I'll do it. And for your safety." He took another step toward her, and his words seemed to loosen something inside her. How could she have doubted him after all the protection he'd offered them already? In that moment, she knew her fears had been unfounded. Of course Beaver wouldn't leave her. This protector would never abandon her and her father.

She stepped into his arms. Arms she'd not even seen open to her. But they wrapped around her now, tightening in a hold so secure—so safe—she wanted to stay in this place forever.

CHAPTER 17

*B*eaver Tail couldn't remember an action ever feeling so right as this one, holding this woman in his arms.

This touch went against everything his past had taught him. Was opposite to what his mind said was wise. But something inside had pushed him toward her. Had opened his arms to receive her.

If there was a Great Spirit, then Beaver Tail might have believed he or she had prompted him. No matter the reason, holding Susanna as she clung to him had somehow drawn a warmth through him stronger than he'd ever experienced. He'd never felt such a fullness. Such a completeness.

She melded to him, her breaths rising and falling between them. He could feel the beating of her heart, and she must have been able to sense the racing of his own.

When she pulled back, he wasn't ready to let her go. Thankfully, she didn't retreat far, only enough so she could look up at him. He kept his hold tight around her back.

Her striking beauty made his chest clench, with the sliver of moon shimmering in her eyes. Eyes that always captured him, yet now they possessed a power to hold him in an unyielding grip.

She didn't speak. A good thing, for words would have ruined the moment. What passed between them, what shifted inside him, was more powerful than words could ever express. The fact that Susanna understood, that she didn't try to fill the space with talk, made him appreciate her even more.

As his eyes roamed her face, every feature strong yet fragile, an urge planted deep inside him. The urge to protect was nothing new, yet there was more. A desire to cherish, to show her how special she was.

He kept one hand around her back, but raised the other to cradle her cheek. So soft she was, especially under his rough palm. And her eyes...they drew him nearer. Pulled him closer. Close enough to feel the warmth of her breath on his chin.

He dropped his forehead to hers. He wanted to kiss her. He wanted to simply relish her nearness. To savor this sweetness he'd never thought possible.

But the longer he held her so close, the stronger his first desire grew. Would she even want his kiss? With their brows joined, the softness of her under his skin, he could do nothing to frighten her. Only cherish.

He pulled back and met her eyes. Searched them. Her gaze dropped to his lips, giving her answer in a way that sluiced through him.

His lungs ceased working as he lowered his mouth, ever so slowly. The anticipation of her lips tightened everything inside him. Just before his mouth met hers, he paused to savor her once more. The warmth of her breath, the tiny catch of air as she swallowed, her jaw working under his hand. Everything about her was perfect.

He closed the distance, brushing her mouth with his, tasting her sweetness. Her lips were a little rough from long days in the sun, and that protective urge welled up within him. He caressed them with his own, savoring each touch.

Her response was strong yet unschooled, and it made him want to protect her even more. Even from himself. He moved slowly, not pushing too deep. Until she threaded her fingers through his hair, cupping her hands around his neck, pulling him closer.

The touch loosed desire inside him, and he deepened the kiss. She was more than he'd ever dreamed of. Her touch, her taste, like the sweetest drink. And he gulped her in.

Yet a pulse in the back of his mind forced its way forward. Protect—at any cost. He softened his touch, tightening his hold on his desire. Loosening his hold on her waist. Caressing her mouth. Taking her breaths inside him as fuel for his own body.

This woman... She undid him, yet made him want to be better. Made him want to be the man she needed.

When desire threatened to take over again, he drew back completely. Separating their lips, pulling away enough to drink in her beauty with his eyes.

Her own eyes were wide, and with a shadow cast over them, he couldn't see her expression. But from the way her chest heaved, the way she stayed soft under his hand at her waist, he could imagine how their pretty brown color had darkened. And her swollen lips...

If he didn't rein in his eyes and thoughts, he'd be pulling her tight again, pushing his restraint aside.

A sadness swept through her, an emotion he felt as much as he saw in the scant light illuminating her features.

She tucked her lips in. "I shouldn't have done that."

Pain pierced his chest. The last thing he wanted was for her to feel regret. Not when this new closeness had opened a freedom he'd not known possible.

He stroked his thumb along her cheekbone, memorizing the lines of her with his fingers. "Don't back away." It was his heart's cry, but the words came out so paltry. So desperate. He'd never been able to say what he really meant with words.

Her chest rose as she inhaled a breath. Her body trembled a little with the effort. "My father. I can't… My focus needs to be on him."

Understanding crept through him. She wasn't rejecting him. Wasn't denying the intense connection between them. She simply didn't think she could open herself to him when so much of her internal strength was being poured out for her father.

And in that second, he knew with certainty she expected her father to pass away. Maybe they'd been told such by the healers they'd sought out before. Or maybe it was an inner knowing. But this was the reality she struggled under.

With an ache searing through the center of his chest, he pulled her to him, wrapping his arms around her, tucking her head under his chin. She clung to him, gripping his shirt with a desperation he could feel in every part of him. Perhaps he shouldn't kiss her again, but he would be there for her. He would protect her from the outside and do his best to shore up her insides.

Together, they would face what lay before them.

$\approx$

Susanna kneaded the dough as best she could, using the pan as a worksurface. She'd expected that cooking over an open fire would be the most challenging part of making biscuits out here in the wilderness, but finding a decent place to work was almost as hard. She was probably touched in the head to think she could bake out here, but she had just enough flour left to make a batch of Pa's favorite treat. Although without yeast, they'd probably end up as hard clumps.

If the batch was too awful, maybe she wouldn't share them with anyone but her father. No sense in making the others think she didn't know her way around a kitchen. She'd handled cooking for her and Pa since she was twelve, and she'd ruined more than one pan of biscuits since then, too. Her father, of course, always ate whatever she set before him. He'd even taught her to see the humor in attempts that didn't end so well.

Would Beaver Tail be able to find the amusement in cooking gone ill? At the moment, she wasn't even sure *she* would be able to accomplish that feat. Her emotions were in such a turmoil, especially when it came to that man.

His kiss had been...there weren't words to describe the incredible feeling of being so cherished. Her innermost self had come back to life, and she hadn't even realized how parched and shriveled she'd become.

She'd never wanted a man before, not the way she desired Beaver Tail. It wasn't just his handsome appearance, with features perfectly formed and so striking, her heart ached every time she looked at him. But what attracted her to him was so much more than outward appearance. He was strong and capable—and when he'd held her, she'd felt the warmth of his safety. Of his strength. For the first time in so long, she'd not been the one with the weight of responsibility smothering her.

Yet she did have responsibilities, and hiding from them would do no good for anyone. Her father was dying, whether she wanted to face it or not. His weakness and almost constant coughing today only proved how quickly he was withering. She had to focus all her efforts on making Pa comfortable. On easing his pain.

On bringing what pleasure she could to his final days.

She didn't have the energy to worry about anything or anyone else. Not even Beaver Tail.

"This is the last of the wood that'll do any good for burning." Caleb kept his voice low as he crept into camp and eased the load down in a pile near the fire. He glanced over at her father. "Glad to see he's finally sleepin'. That cough is awful enough, I feel the pain right along with him." He grimaced with the words, then took off his hat and swiped a sleeve across his brow. "French is gatherin' up buffalo chips to finish off what we'll need to burn tonight."

His gaze landed on the dough she was cutting into circles. "Lands, is that what I think it is? Tell me those are biscuits."

The pleasure in his voice almost pulled a smile from her. "I hope they turn out. I don't have yeast, and it'll be a trick to bake them over this open fire."

"You tell me what you need, Miss Susanna, and I'll get it or make it or whatever I have to do. I never have tasted anything so good as my mama's biscuits, God rest her. I've craved them every day since she left this earth."

She sent him a glance. "I'm sure they were wonderful, but please don't get your hopes up too high about these."

"You know what? I think French still has some honey tucked away from that hive we found right after we started out. That'd make 'em taste just like Mama's did." He spun as if he planned to sprint out and find the man to make certain. Then he paused and looked back at her. "You need anythin' else, Miss Susanna? Water maybe?"

Now he did pull a smile from her. There was something about this overgrown boy she couldn't help but love. "Not a thing."

And he was off. Not in a sprint, but his long legs covered the ground in huge strides.

A thought caught her before he'd gone far. She straightened and called after him, "Where's Joel?"

He turned and walked backwards as he pointed along the river's edge. "Out seein' the sights."

And probably walking off his impatience with another day in camp. Joel hadn't argued the need to wait another day, but he'd been awfully quiet after Beaver Tail made the announcement.

She'd seen the two men talking by the horses a few minutes later, and Joel didn't seem quite as terse after that. She could only pray he wouldn't grow angry or bitter over the delay.

His own wounds had looked much better when she'd changed the bandage that morning. The fresh bleeding that started after yesterday's ride had stopped, and the inflamed skin around the edges seemed to be settling.

If only Pa's sickness could heal so easily.

She placed the last of the biscuit rounds in the makeshift rock oven she'd created, then used a flat stick to heap red coals over the unit. As she brushed the dust from her hands, the sound of Pa's coughing broke the quiet.

His voice had faded to a whisper from so much irritation in his throat, and his coughs were equally raspy. Even as she turned to see what she could do to help him, part of her wanted to look away so she didn't have to watch him struggle. A very selfish part of her.

How frail his body had become. As he lay on his side, his frame convulsing in deep hacks, blood trickled from his mouth like spit. She had to swallow down the bitter taste of her own bile as she crawled to his side.

The coughs finally ceased, and she wrung a wet cloth from the dish beside him to wipe his forehead. He sent her a grateful look but didn't seem to have enough strength to lift his head from where it lay on his arm. His eyelids drifted shut.

She'd given him the last of the tea from the marshmallow root earlier, but, thankfully, Beaver Tail had gone to look for more. *Lord, let him find it.*

She had nothing left to give her father. Nothing that would make him more comfortable. All the medicines she'd brought had been used up—quicker than she'd expected, since he'd needed more as his symptoms worsened. Maybe they should have stayed back in Illinois, where they had access to medicines to ease his pain. But he'd never have experienced this spectacular country. Which choice would truly have been better for him?

There was no reason to ponder the question at this point. All she could hope was that Beaver Tail would find the herb he sought and return quickly.

And maybe, just maybe, he'd take her in his arms when he came, and she could soak in a bit of his strength. That wouldn't hurt anything, would it?

CHAPTER 18

The moment Susanna heard the whippoorwill just outside the circle of firelight, she knew it was Beaver Tail. As he stepped from the darkness, she studied him, trying to place exactly what was different. His gaze met hers, soaking through her, warming her. Distracting her.

A question touched his eyes, and she knew without hearing the words he was asking how her father fared.

She let her gaze drift to Pa, more to stem the attack of tears than anything. She couldn't let herself weaken like this. It was exactly the reason she had to push all thoughts of Beaver Tail away. She couldn't open up to him—to anyone—right now. It would only weaken her when she had to be strong.

He stepped forward, holding up a leather satchel. "I found more marshmallow root." He crouched beside her and opened the bag's flap. "I also found some slippery elm. I've seen them both used for a cough like your father's."

Joy surged inside her. "Thank you." Something new to try. Maybe this would help even more than the marshmallow plant.

While the men talked of their activities from the day and munched on the last of the biscuits—which had turned out better than she'd expected—she chopped the bark from the elm and tied it in a cloth to boil. She'd kept water heating for the past hour in preparation for Beaver's return.

She slipped a sideways glance his way as he knelt beside his pack. He seemed fine. Right now, he focused on French while the man told the tale of a covey of pheasant he'd surprised, but Beaver's eyes flicked her way, and the corner of his mouth lifted. Just the tiniest glance, but it sent a warmth flooding through her chest. He had the power to affect her more than anyone she'd ever known.

He rose and stepped toward Joel, a leather-wrapped bundle in his hand. In that instant, her mind registered two things at once. His step faltered, and a blank expression settled over his face, impossible to read. Almost like a mask he'd put in place to cover something. Something like *pain*.

"You're hurt." She turned to face him fully.

He froze, that blank expression cracking for an instant. Enough to reveal a glimpse of surprise in his eyes. She was right. He'd been trying to hide an injury.

She pushed to her feet, a sliver of fear sliding through her. Not Beaver Tail. She couldn't take one more person she cared about getting hurt. "What happened?"

She scanned the length of him. Nothing looked amiss, although his leggings were plenty dirty. Which foot had he limped on? His left maybe.

"It's naught to worry over." His voice maintained a steady, soothing cadence.

The sound had the opposite effect. If he thought he could cover an injury just to pacify her... If he thought she was a wilting flower who couldn't handle the hard truth... He'd see shortly just how much she could handle.

"You'd better tell her, son." Pa's words drifted from where he lay on his bedroll. His voice was weak but stronger than he'd sounded all day. And maybe with a little mirth in his tone.

"She'll not let you rest until she satisfies her need to set things to right."

Beaver Tail straightened, the gesture so slight she might have imagined it. But she didn't imagine the defiant set of his chin. He kept such a tight rein on his reactions, she'd thought him impossible to read those first few days. Like a statue, and just as handsome as the sketch she'd seen in a magazine of Michelangelo's *David*.

But now she knew better. She simply hadn't been looking deep enough.

As he met her gaze with slightly raised brows, she returned the look. Maybe his injury was in a place he didn't want to expose. And she probably should be careful in tending a man not her relative. Especially a man who affected her so strongly.

But she had to know for sure he wasn't hurt badly. If he had an open wound that might fester, he could lose a leg, or even his life.

She couldn't let that happen. Pushing down the fear that clawed up her throat, she stepped toward him. "At least tell me what happened. Is it a knife wound? Did you fall on the rocks?"

His head tilted as he studied her, but he still didn't say anything. And didn't look like he planned to. Stubborn man.

She'd have to uncover the answers herself. Closing the distance between them, she bent and reached for the bottom of his leggings, which covered the leg he'd limped on.

He gripped her shoulders, stopping her before she could touch the leather. Then he pulled her up to standing again, and she raised her gaze to meet his. She opened her mouth to ask again, but the piercing in his gaze made her pause.

Yet, even though he could see all the way to her core, there was a gentleness in his eyes. "It's only a snakebite. Nothing to be concerned over."

Snakebite. The word squeezed her chest so it was hard to

breathe. She gripped his arm. "What kind of snake? Where did it bite you?"

He'd said rattlers were the only venomous snakes in this area, and they'd seen more than a few these last several days, mostly in groups, sunning themselves on rocks near the river. But hadn't he said the marshmallow root grew near the river?

Oh, God. She gripped his arm tighter. The venom from a rattlesnake could kill a man. She might lose Beaver Tail before she even lost Pa. *Lord, no.*

Beaver Tail must have sensed her rising panic, for he released her shoulders and dropped to one knee. "It's nothing. The snake bit through my legging and moccasin, so it barely left a mark."

He made quick work of loosening the leggings on his tall moccasins, pulling them down far enough that he could work up the hem of his buckskin trousers. Shadows from the flickering firelight made his skin look like a darker copper than she suspected it really was.

She crouched beside him to see the exposed place better. The swelling in his lower calf was impossible to miss, especially compared to the lean muscle around the area. Twin red marks broke the skin in the center of the raised part, but it was the dark bruising spreading away from the punctures that made her suck in a breath.

No wonder he limped.

Looking up, she met his gaze. "How long ago did this happen?"

He shrugged. "Before I started back."

She raised her brows at his hedging. "An hour? Two?" Maybe he wasn't accustomed to measuring time in minutes and hours. "Was the sun starting to set yet?"

"It had just touched the mountains." He began to work his hem back down, but she grabbed his wrist.

"Wait. Let me think if I have anything we can poultice it

with." What had their neighbor used the time their youngest son was bitten? Eggs and gunpowder, and maybe some whiskey mixed in. She didn't have eggs or whiskey. Would the gunpowder work on its own?

Maybe a simple healing salve would be best. Beaver's leg wasn't as swollen as that poor boy's had been. The lad's ankle had grown to almost the size of his head.

"Stay put." She moved back to the medicine pack and pulled out the salve, then hesitated over her bandages. Should she wrap the wound? Beaver Tail might object, but he'd probably humor her if she pressed. At least a cloth tied around the leg would keep the ointment in place.

After gathering what she needed, she turned back to Beaver Tail and set to work.

～

"Sit down and rest your leg in front of you."

Beaver fought a smile at the determination marking Susanna's pretty face. But he did what she commanded, stretching both legs in front of him. In truth, his wound didn't need tending. He'd been bitten before and seen many more rattler bites on others.

The animal's venom had been mostly absorbed by his leathers as the fangs pierced them, so all he had to worry over was a constant throbbing and a little swelling. They would pass soon enough.

He was much more concerned about the woman now bent over his leg. The last thing he wanted was to bring more hardship on her, or give her one more thing to fret about. That was why he'd hidden the wound to begin with—or at least attempted to.

Her savviness was one more thing he liked about her. But not when it brought her pain.

153

"Susanna." He couldn't help but reach out and finger the braid that had slipped over her shoulder. With the others sitting nearby, resuming the conversation his entrance had interrupted, he wouldn't do more than touch this tip of hair. Even though his fingers itched to pull her to him. But if he chased that thought, he'd run into a host of trouble.

"Yes?" She'd applied the salve and now wrapped a cloth around his leg. She didn't look up from her work. Instead, her pretty brow furrowed with her focus.

He'd been about to tell her again not to worry about him, but that would be a waste of words. Maybe instead, he could distract her from her fears. "I saw my beaver friend again. He Who Is Brave."

She raised her head, curiosity brightening her features. "Not the same one you fed that other time. Do beavers roam this far?"

"I wouldn't have thought it, but he has patches of light brown circling each of his front legs up near the shoulders. An unusual marking. He was still brave this time, taking the aspen branches I offered."

She'd straightened as he spoke, and now a gentle smile curved her mouth. "You've made a friend." She tipped her head, her eyes growing curious. "Do you think this is his home? Is there enough wood here for him to build a dam?"

"Not to sustain him through the winter. But there'll be more as we move deeper into the mountains."

Merriment danced in her eyes. "Maybe he'll continue as our traveling companion then."

She turned back to his leg and tied a knot in the bandage. "There. Now stay still so your blood doesn't carry the venom through your body. I'm sure your walk back already accomplished that, but we should still be careful."

He didn't like the thought of being tied down, but he'd sit for a while if it eased her mind.

In truth, he'd willingly do a great deal more for her than sit still. He'd never thought to feel this way about a woman. But he'd not thought he'd meet a woman like Susanna.

~

Susanna watched the man standing alone by the edge of the cliff. She'd never seen so much loneliness bound in a single figure. Outlined by the morning sun, he looked like the only man for miles around—or at least, he looked as if he felt that way. The pain in Joel's form made her own heart ache.

"He's not angry about stayin' another day, ya know." Caleb's voice accompanied the sound of his footsteps as he moved beside her. "I mean, he would like to head out and find Adam, but he understands why we need to wait."

She looked over—or rather, *up* at him. "Are you certain?"

He nodded, but she wasn't sure she believed him. Caleb was just kind enough to say something like this to make her feel better.

In truth, Pa's health hadn't improved. If anything, he'd worsened through the night. He hadn't risen that morning except to relieve himself, and merely moving from his bed pallet had caused him pain. Pa had lost so much weight, she probably could have lifted him herself, but Caleb and French had been there to aid him.

Maybe if she could get him to eat more, he would regain his strength. He claimed his belly wouldn't hold anything other than the little bits he picked up.

At least the men had all accepted their staying in this place another day. Even Joel had nodded, although his silence worried her more than if he'd spoken his thoughts on the matter.

Now, he stood at the edge of the cliff, staring down into the river, and she couldn't seem to focus on anything other than his lonely form.

"Do you think he would mind if I went to talk to him?" Maybe there wasn't a way to ease his angst, but she could at least thank the man for this sacrifice.

Caleb shrugged. "Go ahead. I imagine he'd like a pretty lady seeking him out." He cut her a sideways grin. "Even if Beaver Tail has already staked his claim on you."

Heat flared up her neck, making her want to duck like a turtle into its shell. "Staked his claim?" She tried for a light tone, something teasing.

"Yep." He sent her a wink, which made everything worse.

She'd best move away from Caleb before her ears turned crimson and gave her away completely. She cleared her throat to gather her wits. "I'm going to talk with Joel."

A chuckle drifted behind her as she marched forward.

CHAPTER 19

Susanna had to pick her way to Joel through the grass and prickly pear, what little was left after the buffalo stampede anyway. If they didn't get rain soon, the tromped vegetation might not grow back until spring.

Joel surely heard her coming, but he didn't acknowledge her until she stopped beside him. He glanced at her, then turned back to face the vast canyon below, where the river ran through like a wide snake.

The thought of a snake immediately brought Beaver Tail to the front of her mind. In truth, he was always somewhere in her thoughts. But she pushed back the image of him sitting by the fire the night before, distracting her from her worries with the story of his beaver friend.

Just now, she needed to focus on the hurting man beside her. This was a good reminder that she wasn't the only person in the world who had pressing worries.

After they'd stood for a moment in quiet, she finally broke the silence. "I'm sorry we've delayed you another day. But I thank you for allowing my father a chance to recover his strength."

As though to punctuate her words, a deep croaking cough sounded from their camp. It didn't last nearly as long as some of the other coughing spells. Pa probably didn't have the strength a long episode required.

When the sound died away, Joel turned to her. "I'm sorry he's suffering so."

She met his gaze, and the earnestness in his dark eyes caught her by surprise. No anger flashed in their depths, only deep sincerity.

He turned back toward the river with a sigh that seemed to leak out of his soul. "I'm not upset about the delay. I need to find my brother, but it's already been this long. Another few days can't make much difference."

Something about the desolation in his voice belied his words. Did he think his brother had died or would never be found? If that was what he truly believed, he may not want to talk about his fears.

She well knew that feeling. She still couldn't bring herself to speak or even think much about Pa's fate, especially now that his days seemed so numbered. It was easier to dwell on the good times. Those periods when life had been normal.

Maybe that would help Joel, too. "Were you and your brother born in the States?"

He shook his head. "Andalusia."

"That's in southern Spain?" It had been quite a while since she'd seen a world map.

"The land of beautiful horses." A fondness curved his lips upward. "We both had horses in our blood, but Adam really loved them. The animals from our homeland are majestic. Big creatures with long flowing manes and exquisite pedigrees. Known all over the world for their beauty and abilities."

He let out a huff. "When we met a Mandan chief on the way up the Missouri who told us of the unusual horses of the Shoshone and Pierced Nose Indians, Adam could barely contain himself. A couple of the braves were taking a more direct route to trade with those Indians, and he begged us to go with them. To see the great horses the Mandan spoke of with spots all over their bodies and superior abilities in speed and endurance."

Joel slid a sideways glance her way. "Adam never could turn down the chance to see a new special horse." Then he stared forward again. "I should have agreed. Even though winter was coming fast and we were pushing hard to reach Beaver Tail's camp before the snow grew bad, I knew how much he wanted to go with those braves. I knew he'd not let it rest."

A long silence settled over him. She'd been told the outcome of the story. Adam had gone to find the tribes with their unusual horses. But she had a feeling there was more to the brothers' parting than a simple farewell.

She should leave it alone, but she still found herself asking, "Adam decided to go with the Mandan braves on his own?"

Joel's mouth tightened to a thin line before he finally spoke. "He left in the night. I found a note beside me that said he and the braves he was traveling with expected to reach the Shoshone before the first snow. He'd winter with them and find the horses the Mandan told us about. When spring came, he'd follow the Missouri north to find us at Beaver Tail's camp."

She gave a single nod. "Sounds reasonable." If a person were comfortable traveling with men he'd just met, to a band of Indians he had no way of knowing were friendly. With a hard winter coming fast. Adam must have quite an adventurous streak—and no fear.

Joel slid her another glance. "That's what I told myself. Adam was older than I and always did what he wanted. I've never been able to stop him when he got an idea in his head. And frankly, this time, I didn't want to go along." The look that passed through his dark eyes held so much regret, her chest ached.

She wanted to reach out and touch him, but that didn't feel right. So instead, she offered a sad smile. "Everyone needs a chance to follow their dreams." After all, that was why she and Pa had traveled a thousand miles to this majestic wilderness.

And that was why she was almost certain she'd never go back east.

~

"I think it's time you leave us. Ride on and finish the journey you'd planned." Susanna squared her shoulders as she eyed each man in turn.

"We can't do that, Miss Susanna." Caleb wiped a sleeve across his brow, even though the day wasn't hot. In fact, the morning was cold enough she'd donned the wool coat she'd purchased just before they left home. "No man in his right mind would leave you and your pa alone out here. Not with—" His words cut off as his gaze darted to where Pa lay, far enough away that he couldn't hear their conversation.

His ears turned pink as he looked back at her. "Not with winter coming on and your pa's health not so good."

He'd been going to say something about Pa being on his deathbed, she was fairly certain. She was grateful he'd stopped himself, though. Finally, she was able to admit to herself that her father's days were numbered. Maybe only a few weeks. She swallowed down the lump that tried to climb her throat. She simply wasn't ready to speak of the subject aloud.

She spread her stance and raised her gaze to meet Caleb's head-on. His eyes were gentle, but she couldn't let her defenses slip. "We'll manage. We're holding you back, and there's no reason the four of you should delay any longer."

Inhaling a breath, she leveled her voice. "I can't thank you enough for your help. All of you." She couldn't bring herself to look at Beaver Tail. There was too much chance the thought of losing him would break her down. She couldn't allow it.

"Mademoiselle, please. It is not safe for you. Your papa."

French stepped forward and took her hand, then pressed his other hand over hers. "We cannot leave. We will wait for your papa to recover." He shot a look at Joel. "It is the only thing to do."

"He's right." Joel's face had been impossible to read—and still was. "We don't feel right about leaving you behind. We'll wait a few more days for your pa to recover."

The burn rose up in her throat again. These men were so kind. Truly, God had blessed her and Pa when He'd led Beaver Tail to them. She'd never imagined how important he'd become to her during that first chance sighting of him on the fateful day when they'd reached the falls of the Missouri.

But as much of a blessing as their help had been these past weeks, she couldn't hold them back any longer. It wasn't fair. She and Pa weren't their kin, had only known them a short time. These men didn't owe them anything. In fact, the situation was quite the opposite. The simple cooking she'd done wouldn't come near paying for the horses, protection, and supplies these men had shared.

The time had come for it to end, and reasoning with them clearly wasn't working. She straightened her shoulders, squared her stance, and raised her chin. "Leave. Please. I'm asking you." She didn't meet any of their gazes. She wouldn't have been able to hold her determination if she saw pity, or even hurt, in their eyes.

No one responded, at least not right away.

"Susanna." Beaver Tail stepped forward as he spoke, and the tenderness in his voice, the way he said her name, nearly cracked her armor.

She sucked in a breath, and may have closed her eyes, as she struggled to find her composure.

He took another step toward her, and she held out a hand to halt him. "No. This is best." She still couldn't bring herself to look at him. That would be the end.

"Tell ya what." Caleb spoke up, drawing her attention to him. "How 'bout we fellas talk amongst ourselves for a while."

She wasn't sure how that would help. They'd probably just agree that they all agreed. Or maybe this would give Joel the chance to say what he really thought. Maybe he'd make the others see that she meant her words.

Turning to Joel, she gave him a pleading look. His face had that unreadable look again.

Finally, she nodded, then took a step back. "I'll go check on Pa."

Then she could go back to scraping hides. Most of them had been working at the task the day before and that morning. Both because Beaver Tail had a stack of furs that needed to be worked, and also to keep them from losing their sanity with nothing to occupy their time.

When she returned to camp, Pa was finally sleeping, only the occasional cough breaking through his heavy breathing. So she set to work on the hides.

She did her best not to look up at the men while they talked, and she managed the feat except for a couple glances. But she'd almost scraped a hole in an otter skin by the time Caleb separated from the group and headed her way. With a glance at Pa to make sure he still slept, she rose and strode to meet him.

"We've made a decision, Miss Susanna." When he reached her, he turned, and the two of them walked together to rejoin the others.

For the first time, she let herself look at Beaver Tail. He had that emotionless expression he sometimes wore, but as she neared, she could see the glimmer of hurt in his eyes. Did he think she was sending him away—sending them all away— because she cared nothing about him?

In fact, her reason was so much the opposite. His presence made her think and feel things she couldn't bear to think and feel right now. She may never be whole again—at least her heart felt that way right now—and he deserved so much better.

When they reached the men, she braced her hands across her chest and prepared for what they would say. She would reinforce her earlier request—demand they leave if she had to.

"Miss Susanna." Apparently, Caleb had been elected as the spokesperson of the group. She turned to face his earnest expression. "We all talked and we decided Joel an' French are gonna go on ahead. They'll look for Adam again, and they'll leave us markers along the way so we can follow as soon as you're ready."

His eyes held a sadness she didn't want to interpret. And why hadn't he said *as soon as you and your pa are ready?* She pushed the worry away.

"So you and Beaver would stay with us?" As she spoke, her gaze wandered to Beaver Tail of its own accord. His eyes glimmered with intensity, as though he held his breath waiting for her response. The relief that swept through her at the thought of him staying was a sensation she shouldn't let herself feel.

But she couldn't stop it. Dratted tears welled in her eyes, and even when she tried to swallow them down, they still clouded her vision. She tried for a smile. "If that's what you all want to do."

"It is what we want." Beaver Tail stepped close and touched her upper arm. Then with a gentleness she'd never have thought he possessed, he pulled her to his chest.

She gripped his shirt, and there was no use trying to fight off the tears anymore. The emotions roiling inside her were too strong to hold back.

When she wiped her sleeve across her eyes, she no longer saw the other men around them. They'd wandered back to camp. *Bless them.* With no one else to see her meltdown, she let herself sink into Beaver's strong arms.

CHAPTER 20

$\mathcal{H}$e was doing the right thing, there was no doubt in Beaver Tail's mind. But watching Joel and French ride out that afternoon was harder than he'd expected.

When the horses had ridden only twenty or so strides, French turned to send them a white-toothed grin and a final wave.

From beside Beaver, Susanna returned the gesture, and he had to resist the urge to slip his hand around her waist. He was where he needed to be, by her side during her pa's final days. Caleb would be encouragement to her as well, especially since they shared the same beliefs about their God.

Beaver glanced over Susanna's head to where the big man stood on her other side. Caleb met his gaze with a nod. It was up to them now.

While they watched, French and Joel became only specks in the distance.

"Well." Caleb clapped his hands together. "Reckon it might be best if we set up some kinda shelter. Just in case we get a gully washer. BT, think one of us could shimmy up that tree an' cut a few branches?"

Beaver raised a brow at him. Rains could strike with little warning on these plains, but that hadn't happened out here in a very long time. As for climbing the tree, they both knew Caleb's bulk would knock the thing over if he tried to climb it. Good thing Beaver had spent many hours climbing trees in his youth.

He touched Susanna's arm as he turned to her. "Choose where you want the shelter built. Under the tree might be best, or closer to the water."

She darted a quick glance at him as she sniffed. From the looks of her red-rimmed eyes, the task would be a welcome distraction.

With his hatchet tucked at his waist, Beaver Tail jumped to reach the bottom limb, then struggled to pull himself up. Not an easy feat, and for a moment, he wasn't sure he would make it on the first try. Hopefully, Susanna wasn't watching.

He finally climbed up to the branches that would make the best lodge poles, and, within a half hour, they had enough limbs cut. With only one tree in the area, the shelter would have to be small, but he would make certain it was large enough for two to sleep underneath, should a rainstorm strike at night. He and Caleb wouldn't melt from a little rain, as unlikely as it was. And the tree would provide some shelter for them too, since Susanna had chosen to place their camp under the awning of its branches.

As Beaver climbed down, Caleb was already cutting the smaller branches from each limb, piling them in stacks according to how each would be used. Most were too green to burn but would help insulate the shelter.

Susanna stepped in to help, but Caleb shooed her off. "You just go do whatever else you need to, Miss Susanna. Or sit yourself down by the river and enjoy the view. I'll bet that Pa of your'n would like to hear somethin' from the Bible."

She stepped back and wrapped her arms around herself, her gaze roaming from Caleb to Beaver. He dropped down from the tree and brushed the bark from his hands. He'd managed the job with only a few scratches on his wrists and the backs of his hands.

He sent her a reassuring look. "It won't take us long." He'd built many a shelter on his longer hunting trips, a few of them with Caleb.

She looked so forlorn standing there, still wrapped in her coat. The fabric of it was thick but wouldn't keep her warm when winter hit in force. He had a couple wolf pelts that would make a proper coat for her. She needed moccasins too.

Eventually, maybe she'd let him make a full dress and leggings, like the women from his camp wore. That would be easier than trying to find a trader who carried clothes like she wore. But maybe she didn't want to dress like the Blackfeet women. If she preferred white women's clothes, he'd go whatever distance he needed to for whatever she wanted.

She was a beauty, no doubt, but it was the deeper part of who she was that drew him, that stirred him like no other woman ever had. Not even Ayadna.

Funny, he hadn't thought of his former intended or the tumult she'd created for days now. He could almost be thankful for those events now, if they hadn't so badly affected his family. That had been the final reason he'd left with these friends, and if he'd never ventured on this journey, he'd never have met Susanna.

She was looking at him with brows raised, her pretty face expectant. Had she asked him a question while he'd been lost in his thoughts? Surely not. He never lost himself.

But the sweet tipping of Susanna's lips and the sparkle in her eye showed he'd clearly missed something. She was so pretty, he didn't know English words enough to express how much she lit a fire inside him.

With deliberate steps, he strode toward her, locking her in his gaze so she wouldn't be able to look away even if she wanted. Her sweet mouth was his aim, and a good kissing was the perfect thing to cover his lapse.

Her eyes widened, and, as he neared, she took a little step back, even as her gaze danced. If she'd looked at all like she didn't want his kiss, he'd have stopped. But her pretty mouth tugged in a grin that beckoned him.

When he reached her, he slipped one hand behind her back and pulled her to him. Their gazes never parted as she tipped her face up to his.

Then her eyelids lowered, and he swooped in to claim his goal.

Sweet victory. And if the way she melted in his arms was any sign, she didn't mind conceding. She melded her lips to his, and he took his time, relishing the feel of her.

Way too soon, she pulled back. Her eyes opened, and she blinked twice before the haze cleared from them. A pink flush appled her cheeks as she glanced at Caleb. She pressed her hands to Beaver's chest and tried to push back, but he wasn't about to let her go. He didn't care if Caleb might be looking on.

"Beaver." She glanced up at him, the red now spreading from her cheeks to her ears. He wanted to lean in and nibble on one of those ears, but he restrained himself.

He couldn't help a chuckle, though, and he glanced over his shoulder. The man was chopping away at little branches on a limb, humming a tune as though he wasn't at all aware of the pair of them. Of course, he was turned at an angle where he could easily lift his gaze and watch them without breaking his rhythm.

Beaver turned back to Susanna. He lowered his face near hers again. "He's not watching." He spoke in a whisper only she could hear. "And even if he were, he's not worth worrying over."

He rested his forehead on hers, then touched her nose with his own. Her mouth curved in another smile, and her warm breath fanned his face. When her hands on his chest gripped his shirt, he closed the last of the space between them.

He shifted so his back was to Caleb, Susanna hidden in front of him. Just for good measure.

~

Susanna rested her head on Beaver Tail's shoulder as they sat on the edge of the cliff, legs dangling above the river far below. She soaked in his strength, the warmth of his arm wrapped around her, tucking her closer to him.

A week had passed since Joel and French rode away. Pa's cough remained about the same—although, in truth, how much worse could it get? Each spell doubled him over, wracking his body with every cough, spraying blood with each shudder.

But the coughing episodes weren't growing any closer together. For that she was thankful.

All the new symptoms that had cropped up could be due to other things. The pain in his back might be merely from lying on his bed pallet for so many days straight. And the same for the trouble he seemed to have in walking when he stood to relieve himself.

That morning, she'd caught a glimpse of his stockinged feet when he was airing his boots after a damp night. His ankles had swollen as large as her upper legs. Maybe that was from lying still so long, too. If only she knew what would help him.

Maybe a walk from camp to the river would be good for him. A distance of only about thirty strides. Surely he could manage the effort, even though just a few steps to the back of the tree seemed to exhaust him.

She would go help Pa in a few minutes. After a little longer in this peaceful setting, with this beacon of strength beside her.

"Beaver." She wasn't sure why she spoke his name. She didn't have anything in particular to ask him. She just...needed him. Needed something that would make her world right again.

He pulled her closer, leaning in to brush a kiss on her hair. "Whatever happens, we'll face it together." Did he mean all four of them? Or that he'd be by her side through whatever came? Both probably.

Caleb, too, had been a good friend. Like now, he sat reading the Psalms to her father. She'd not known until a few days ago that Caleb had been ordained as a reverend back in Oklahoma. He'd served in a little church there for less than a year before heading west with Adam and Joel. Why he'd left so quickly, he hadn't said.

But his presence had come to mean a lot to Pa. They spent hours together each day, with Caleb reading the Bible aloud or talking about something he'd learned in his Bible training that related to a passage. Pa couldn't talk much without a coughing fit, but Caleb was kind enough to fill the void himself.

"I think I'll see if my father can walk out here." A breeze brushed her face. Even though it brought a fresh gust of cold, the caress of the wind tasted like freedom. "What do you think Joel and French are doing right now?" Her mouth had a mind of its own today. She'd not even been thinking about those two until the thought slipped out in words.

"Riding, I imagine." Was that a hint of longing in Beaver's voice? She wasn't sure without seeing his face.

She leaned back to see his expression. "Do you think they've found Adam?"

His brow lowered as a faint line creased his forehead. "I think not yet. Joel said the Mandan braves spoke of the horses with the Shoshone, but...I have only heard of them with the Pierced Noses. Nez Perce, I think the white men call them."

"You think they'll have to ride a long way to reach those people?"

"Into the mountains. The Pierced Noses live among the

peaks and valleys where they hunt antelope and mountain sheep."

Her heart lifted inside her. They may very well get to journey into the depths of the mountains after all, even with winter coming on. Surely Joel wouldn't hold back in search of his brother.

But what was she thinking. Her chest twisted. Pa wouldn't be able to travel that far. And she wouldn't be leaving him. Not as long as he could draw a single breath, and she couldn't imagine leaving him even after that.

In truth, the thought of beyond scared her so much she'd not allowed herself to think it. She was supposed to go back to the States. To her father's cousin in Boston. A man she'd never met, but the only family she would have left. He'd offered to take her in, to help her in whatever endeavor she wished to pursue.

She'd always thought that would be nursing, but in truth, tending those who were ill had lost any glory it once held. The act of nursing came naturally to her, but it was the fear of losing her patient, fear of that heart-rending pain, that she hated. Never would she be able to willingly put herself in that position. Not even to relieve the suffering of others.

She simply wasn't strong enough.

Beaver Tail squeezed her waist, as though he knew she needed to come out of her thoughts. "I'll help bring your father to the river." He pressed another kiss to her hair, and the tender act made her want to nestle deeper into his hold. There was no way she could go back to the States. She couldn't imagine leaving this man.

Still, she forced herself to pull back. To straighten and stand. "I hope he can walk on his own. I think the effort is what his body needs."

But she was wrong.

Pa only managed a few steps before coughing doubled him over. Those awful convulsions almost rent her own chest in two. Her father would have collapsed to his knees if Beaver hadn't gripped him under his arms.

Once the episode finally waned, she met Beaver's questioning gaze. As much as the act felt like defeat, she nodded toward the bed pallet. She couldn't put Pa through this suffering.

As he straightened and wiped the dripping blood from his mouth, she stepped close to him and wrapped an arm around his waist. "Let's get you back to your bed."

He met her gaze, and he seemed to find strength from somewhere deep within. "I want to see the river." Even though his voice rasped and a tremble laced his words, he'd used the tone that was so familiar. The one that embodied determination.

Somehow, they would make it to the edge of the cliff. Together.

Tucking herself under his arm, they limped forward. He leaned much of his weight on her, but he was so light, she might have been able to pick him up and carry him. *Oh, Pa.*

When they reached the edge of the cliff, Beaver Tail helped ease Pa down to sit. From the rasp of each breath, even sitting up seemed to be a challenge. She settled beside him as Beaver Tail retreated back to their camp—probably to give her time alone with her father. The man always seemed to know what she needed.

Several minutes passed without a word, only the heavy labor of Pa's breathing. She wanted to speak, but everything she could think to say brought the sting of tears to her eyes. Would this be the last time she sat like this with Pa, enjoying the view of the majestic wilderness God created for him?

"I'm glad we came here, Susy." Pa shifted his hand to drape it over her knee, like he'd done so many times when she was a girl. His tanned skin was wrinkled and spotted, maybe from age or perhaps the sun. Or possibly from his sickness.

She laid her hand atop his. "I am too, Pa." She would never

be able to go back to the States. Not after having tasted the wild freedom of this place. Not after having met Beaver Tail. She swallowed down the lump clogging her throat.

Pa looked over at her, offering a welcome distraction as she met his gaze. His blue eyes that used to be such a clear navy now shimmered cloudy like those of an old man—far older than his five decades. But when his voice emerged, its raspy tenor vibrated with that determination again. "Let's go to the mountains, Susanna."

CHAPTER 21

*S*usanna wasn't sure she'd heard her father right, but the sparkle breaking through his cloudy gaze told her she had.

The weight on her chest pressed harder, sending a pain all the way through her. "Pa." He'd never make it even an hour on horseback. And Beaver Tail said it would be another hard day or two of riding to reach the edge of the real mountain country.

He squeezed her leg. "I can make it. I need to. It's…important to me, Susy." When she was little, before her mother passed, she'd hated that nickname. But during those dark days—and every day after—hearing the pet name in Pa's voice wrapped a bit of his love around her like a hug. Now, she could feel its effects swaying her.

She twisted to look at the distant mountains behind them. "There. You can see them from here." He wouldn't give in to that, of course. But he would appreciate the attempt at humor.

He chuckled, but the sound turned into a cough that echoed across the canyon below. She clutched his arm to keep him from falling forward, and somehow, he was able to stifle the cough before it turned into a full episode.

Wheezing in harsh breaths, he gripped her knee with more strength than she'd have thought he still possessed. At last, he regained enough air to speak. "Please. Susanna. I want to...try it." Each word seemed to take more out of him. How would he ever make it in the saddle?

Yet everything in her wanted to help him accomplish this last goal. The mountains were what he'd always talked about. What he'd really wanted to see from the moment he first dreamed of this trip.

And she knew well how he felt. That same yearning pulled inside her.

She forced out the breath clogged in her chest, blowing a long exhale. "I'll talk to Beaver about it."

Again, her father turned to her. "I like that young man, Susy."

She met his gaze, a smile threatening her mouth as his words soaked through her. In his look was something even more than that simple statement. A hope.

Hope seemed too much for her to reach just now, but she let the smile spread as far as her weary face could muster. "I do too, Pa."

~

"I'm worried this knot won't hold. The leather's too stiff."

Beaver Tail looked up from his own tie to see where Caleb motioned. "I'll work on it." He could soften the buckskin to make the knot pull tight. No matter what, they couldn't let a corner of the sling fall and injure Susanna's father.

"I'll strap down the rest of the packs." Caleb turned away to gather the satchels, starting up a whistle as he worked.

He couldn't blame the man for being eager to ride out again. Beaver had been itching to move, too. It would be different if there was something productive he could do here. He'd worked all his furs to the next stages, and watching Susanna's grief as her father deteriorated a little more each day made him feel impotent.

At least this way, they were helping Wilkins accomplish his last request. When Susanna had come to Beaver the day before to ask if he could think of a way for them to take her father into the heart of the mountains, he'd finally had something to work at. A problem he could actually solve.

After massaging bear fat into the stiff leather to soften it, then tying a strong knot in that corner of the sling, he stepped back to examine his work.

His two horses carrying the contraption were the best they had for the job, his own mount and the spotted gelding Susanna had been riding. The one she called Horse. The sling mounted between them was tied to the saddles at its four corners, and poles at the front and back would keep the animals spaced the same distance apart. This should allow Wilkins to lie down while they traveled so he wouldn't have to expend energy to stay upright in the saddle.

Hopefully, they'd be able to travel long enough each afternoon to reach the base of the first cliffs within two days. And then another day or two to climb the mountain. Could Wilkins hold out that long?

Beaver's gaze swung toward the camp, to where the man was, even now, bent over in a coughing fit. Each wheeze was so weak, it didn't seem like he could bear up under the pain much longer. Maybe not more than a few days.

An ache started in Beaver's chest and radiated through him. They had to accomplish this last wish. For the gentle man struggling to draw each breath. For Susanna. He knew what it was like not to have a father, but he couldn't imagine the pain of knowing his pa, of being as close as the two of them were, and knowing that soon the man would be ripped from his life.

At least Beaver had been too young to understand the pain when his father had walked away.

After the supplies were fully loaded, Susanna held the two horses hitched to the sling while he and Caleb assisted Wilkins to the animals. He could tell Susanna itched to help as they lifted her father onto his new bed, but she had her hands full keeping the horses steady.

Beaver eyed the knots holding the sling in place as the spotted gelding shifted. What was he thinking putting this man's life at risk in this contraption? If either of the horses spooked and bolted, the leather would give way. Not even the best knots could hold up to the force of these massive creatures.

The horses had settled now, but his spirit was torn inside him. Did they dare take a chance? He met Susanna's gaze. She seemed to read his thoughts, for her expression turned determined, maybe even a bit pleading. *We have to try this,* her eyes said.

He inhaled a breath to steady himself, then released the spent air. They could try. But if the danger seemed too great for her father, Beaver would put a stop to the journey.

Within a few minutes on the trail, the horses had settled into a steady walk. Even after such a long break, these animals were seasoned enough to save their energy. Wilkins rode quietly most of the morning, staring out at the landscape in front of them during much of the ride. But when the coughing fits took over, they seemed to steal what little energy he had left. After each bout, he would lie lifeless, eyes closed and face as pale as the white fur of the wolf hide beneath him.

As much as the sight made Beaver's chest ache, he could only imagine how much it pained Susanna.

But neither she nor her father called a halt. Beaver finally stopped them at midday to rest the horses. He'd been holding off because of the challenge of getting Wilkins in and out of the sling without hurting the man's frail body, but the set-up needed to be readjusted anyway. A stop would help them all.

Beaver took the horses to graze while Caleb put together a cold meal and Susanna helped her father settle on a blanket spread over the grass. Quiet fell over their group as they ate. There simply wasn't much that could be said to break through the sadness permeating this leg of the journey. They were starting to ride through rocky land with more trees and hills and boulders—the foothills. Wilkins just needed to hang on a few more days, and they'd reach the mountains he craved so deeply.

Beaver glanced at the man, who lay with his eyes closed and his chest rattling through every inhale. He couldn't tell if Wilkins slept or not, what with the effort he had to expend for each breath. *Just a few more days. Hold on. Please.*

"I'm going for a walk." Susanna pushed to her feet and spun away from them. Her action was so quick, so unexpected when she'd been sitting quietly staring into the distance the moment before. She must be fighting her own fears. Or maybe tears. He should go after her, be there in case she needed him. Shouldn't he?

Beaver glanced at Caleb. The man met his gaze with a shrug, but the wrinkle in his brow belied the casual motion. "I think sometimes women like to cry. My ma always seemed better after she went off an' cried a while."

Would getting the tears out help Susanna? If only Beaver knew. If only he were better at reading women. If there really was a God above, like Caleb and Wilkins had been speaking of so much these past days, couldn't that God be merciful and give Beaver a bit more understanding when it came to a woman's mind?

Susanna's mind especially.

Caleb rose and wiped his hands down the sides of his pants.

"I'll get these things packed up. I don't reckon' we need to rush on, but I can get this part done, at least."

Slinging the pack of food over his shoulder, Caleb sauntered down the hill toward where the horses grazed. The brittle grass crunched under his feet, the barren effects of the rainless summer. At least winter's snow would bring water for the land and refill the rivers.

"Beaver." Wilkins's raspy voice barely carried over the short distance between them.

Beaver Tail's body tensed as he moved to the man's side. Surely these weren't his final moments. "Yes?" He was close enough to hear the gurgle of each labored inhale and exhale as Wilkins struggled for every breath.

"There's something...I need to know." He had to pause partway through to take another painful breath. His chest barely rose with the effort.

Beaver shifted closer. "What is it?" He would tell the man anything he wanted to know if his words could relieve the suffering Wilkins endured every moment.

The older man fumbled his hand along the ground toward Beaver. It took a moment before he realized Wilkins was reaching for him. Other than Susanna, no one touched him.

But he couldn't let the man expend needless energy, so he reached out and allowed Wilkins to place his hand over Beavers. The hand was light atop his, but its bony grip held stronger than Beaver expected. Just like a father's.

"Son."

Beaver raised his gaze back to Wilkins's.

The cloudy blue of the older man's eyes cleared as he focused on Beaver Tail. "Have you met my God?"

The words weren't at all what he'd expected. Not the deathbed wishes most men imparted. But they sank a weight through Beaver, the same tug that had been pulling at him for weeks now. He cleared his throat. Wilkins probably wanted him to say yes, but he had to speak the truth. "I don't know Him."

He'd never wanted a god to bow to. Never thought one actually existed. Only when he met Caleb had he started to hear of the God Wilkins now spoke of. He may have had some moments recently when he wished an all-powerful being were real, but he still couldn't credit it. How could he believe in something he'd never seen?

"He wants to know you. He cares...about you...and has the best...planned for you. If only you...put your life in...His hands." Each word was so hard for Wilkins, yet he pushed himself through to the last, then let his eyes drift shut as his body heaved in strangled breaths.

Put your life in His hands. Even if Wilkins's God did exist, Beaver would never be able to give over control of his life, not even to an all-powerful being. Even if that God had the best planned for him, as Wilkins had worked so hard to tell him.

Yet he didn't want to bring this man any more pain than he already suffered, so he held his tongue.

The older man lifted one of his eyelids enough to peer at Beaver through a narrow slit. He must have read Beaver's response, for he groaned a little with his next exhale.

His hand squeezed Beaver's. "I was prayin' you would...be the man for...my Susanna." He stopped to cough, but thankfully, a full fit didn't overtake him. "But I can't give her...to a man who...doesn't know...our God. She'd never be...happy." His last words faded to a rough whisper.

The import of the words pierced through Beaver like a hundred arrows. *I can't give her to a man who doesn't know our God.* This man thought Beaver wasn't worthy simply because he didn't believe in a being he couldn't see? Anger surged through him until Wilkins's final words echoed in his mind. *She'd never be happy.*

Like a punch to his gut, the statement knocked the breath from him, leeching the ire from inside—and all his strength too.

He'd already begun to picture Susanna by his side, even after her father passed, making the rest of the journey with them, keeping him warm on the cold winter nights in the mountains. He'd pictured taking her back to his camp, presenting her to his mother. His sisters.

Bile rose up in his throat, but he swallowed it down and let the anger return. Susanna wouldn't want him, just like Ayadna hadn't. And all because he didn't fit the perfect model she expected of him.

He turned away from Wilkins, pushed to his feet, and marched down the hill toward Caleb and the horses. Too bad he couldn't leap aboard his gelding and let the freedom of the wind ease his fury.

CHAPTER 22

Something wasn't right with Beaver Tail.

Susanna could feel the weight of his irritation in the air between them as they rode on after their midday rest. A glance at him showed his jaw locked, the tendons pulsing as he rode. That same tension radiated through her neck and shoulders. She didn't have the energy to focus on whatever was bothering him, no matter how much she'd like to ease his frustration.

Not when her father lay dying in the sling beside her. She'd finally come to terms with death's nearness. She'd had to. He'd barely opened his eyes since they hoisted him back on the sling, and each breath seemed to be farther apart.

Were they doing the right thing pushing on to the mountains? If he only had a day or two left, she should spend it by his side. Speaking to him, reading to him, letting him feel the intensity of her love. Not mounted on a horse. But this was what he'd asked for.

Hold on, Pa. Don't leave me yet. Please.

A motion ahead of them jerked her focus forward. Caleb threw his hand out as though to halt them, but he didn't stop.

Rounding the hill ahead of them was an Indian. Two of them. Nay, a whole group.

Her heart surged, and she tightened her grip on her reins as she glanced at Beaver Tail. Should they halt? The two of them had to signal their horses together to keep the animals side-by-side, lest they rip the sling off their saddles and injure Pa.

Beaver's gaze was locked on the men riding toward them. His body wore a mask of relaxed calm, but she could sense his tension.

So he wouldn't stop. Not yet. She kept part of her focus on watching for a signal from the man beside her as she glanced ahead.

The party were all men, some decked with feathers—a decoration she'd never seen Beaver wear. One of the men near the front wore a smear of black across his cheeks and nose. War paint?

Each man had bow and arrows slung either on his back or fastened to his horse. Did that mean they were a war party? The pressure in her chest tightened. What would they do if these men attacked? With Pa in the sling, they wouldn't be able to run. *Dear God, help us.*

The Indians were only ten or twelve horse lengths away and advancing at a steady walk. She glanced sideways at Beaver and kept her voice low enough for only their little group to hear. "Should we stop and move Pa to my saddle?" He might not be able to sit up by himself, but she could hold him upright.

Beaver Tail gave his head the slightest of shakes, then he spoke loud enough for Caleb to hear in front of them. "Wait."

She inhaled a strengthening breath, then exhaled her nervousness and settled her face into the bravest expression she could muster.

The oncoming men stopped with only a couple horse lengths between them. One of the horses danced as its rider edged forward. The man spoke, gesturing with his hands in dramatic movements. He wore his hair in two long braids, with feathers hanging from both sides, and looked to be a decade or so older than Beaver Tail.

His language came out in a series of guttural sounds, occasionally pitching high before dropping low again—nothing she could understand. She glanced at Beaver, whose gaze was honed on the man with a fierce intensity, as though he was trying to understand the language. Could he?

Beaver couldn't ride forward without her also moving up, but Caleb had shifted sideways so Beaver could see and be seen by the strangers.

When the leader stopped speaking, Caleb glanced over at Beaver. "You know what he said?"

Beaver nodded, but never took his eyes from the Indians ahead. "They're a Shoshone hunting party looking for buffalo. He asked who we are."

Then he spoke to the strangers in a high-low cadence that was almost musical in its rhythm. Like the other man, he used his hands in sweeping gestures. In all the many hours they'd spent together, especially this past week, she'd never heard him speak in his Indian tongue. Why had she never asked to hear his language? Why had she never asked him to teach her?

As he spoke, she couldn't help but watch him. He was so handsome, this man. And with the unfamiliar language rolling from his tongue, part of him seemed almost exotic, yet also intensely personal. As if she were part of him. As if she'd always known him, somewhere deep inside.

When he stopped speaking, she shifted her focus to the Indians. The one who'd spoken turned to look at those behind him, and the rumble of voices sounded as they talked amongst themselves. They seemed to reach a consensus, and the leader turned back to Beaver.

When he spoke, the sounds were different than those Beaver Tail had used. The cadence unlike the rolling rhythm she could have listened to for hours. Maybe they were speaking in different languages? Perhaps the hand gestures were the main way they made themselves understood.

After the stranger finished, Beaver Tail responded, and she focused hard on both his words and his hand movements. She couldn't make sense of either, at least not from this side view.

The two went back and forth a couple more times, then Beaver gave a decisive nod. "Stay still as they pass." He spoke low, just loud enough for their group to hear.

She gripped her horse's reins and had to force herself not to pull back on them. The group of braves moved forward again, riding past them on Beaver's side. Several of the men stared at her as they rode by, two even turning to leer at her after they passed.

Beaver Tail sat straight as a lodgepole pine, twisting to watch them with his chin raised. She couldn't see his face, but she could feel an animosity in the air that hadn't been there moments before. Because of the stares she'd garnered? Probably not.

When the Indians had moved out of sight behind a cluster of trees and a low hill, Beaver turned back to them, his focus honing on her. His gaze roamed her face, perhaps ensuring she was unharmed.

"He sounded like he had a lot to say." Caleb broke the heavy silence. "Anything useful?"

Beaver flicked a glance at him. "Said they met a few braves from the eastern tribes, a white man with them. They were pushing west in search of spotted horses."

"When?" Eagerness filled Caleb's voice as he turned his horse to better see Beaver. "Were Joel and French with 'em?"

Beaver shook his head. "They saw them in early spring when they came down from the mountains for the first hunt. They haven't seen two white men riding alone."

Another layer of worry pressed Susanna's chest. "What does

that mean? Are we not on the same trail Joel and French took?" Hadn't Beaver been following the marks they'd left? He'd shown her two of them earlier in the day—trees with a large J cut into the trunks.

He turned his focus to her, and his gaze softened on her like a warm blanket, easing her fears. "We are following the path our two have taken. These Shoshone have come a different route."

His words held no hint of doubt, and she nodded, easing out a breath. "Did they say anything else?"

He shook his head again. Then he looked down at her father. "Should we keep riding or stop for the night?"

She followed his gaze. Pa's eyes were still closed, as they'd been every time she looked at him since their midday stop. His brow was drawn low, forming deep creases of pain, and his mouth parted just enough to let his gurgling breaths through. Should they stop?

His lips closed, then opened again. "Keep going." The words came out barely louder than a whisper, but he'd spoken his mind.

As she swallowed down the lump clogging her throat, she looked up at Beaver. The pain in his gaze mirrored her own heart, but she nodded. They would keep going.

~

*B*eaver Tail stood at the edge of the rock, staring out over the valley below as the murky light of dawn brightened the distant sky. This would be their second day on the trail, and they would most likely reach the true mountains today.

As long as there were no delays. From the sound of the labored breathing drifting from the man sleeping not far behind him, a delay was certainly possible.

Maybe Wilkins would be too exhausted from the day before

to travel today. Riding up and down through the rocky foothills the day before hadn't been easy on him. Even if he was, the man wouldn't let anything hold him back. He'd soaked in every view, his joy in even the lower heights they'd climbed evident, despite the effort each word required.

I can't give her to a man who doesn't know our God. She'd never be happy.

Wilkins's honesty had taunted him all through the night, which was the reason he now stood staring out into the faint dawn. More than anything, he wanted Susanna to be happy. Even more than he wanted her to be with him. Why couldn't he have both?

He was willing to hear more about this God. If Wilkins and Susanna and Caleb—people he respected—believed so fully in Him, maybe He was, indeed, real. Beaver lifted his gaze to the darkness of the overhead sky. Scattered clouds concealed the stars that might have glittered their final moments. Was a God looking down on him, even now? What did He think of Beaver?

A pang tightened his chest. Was he judging him for all the ways he'd fallen short through the years? Especially with Ayadna. That atrocity had been his biggest blunder. A new wave of pain soaked through him. If he were to have a future with Susanna, he'd need to tell of her Ayadna. He'd need to tell her why he left his family.

A murmuring sounded from the camp behind him. Caleb's heavy steps marched out toward the horses. He could hear the raspy whisper of Susanna's father, and her sweet lilt as she answered, but he didn't strain to make out their words. They had a right to a private moment together.

Then her soft tread sounded behind him, and he braced himself for the impact she always affected inside him. He turned to her, took in the way the dim light softened the weary features of her face. For a long moment, she just looked at him, and he drank her in.

Everything in him wanted to pull her close, to ease away at least a little of her strain. Whether that took a kiss or just holding her, maybe rubbing circles over her back. Maybe even letting her cry as long as she needed.

But something held him back. Perhaps it was her manner. A brittleness about her, as if she were afraid to give way to any emotion, for then she'd succumb to it all—and might not recover. He knew that fear of breaking down. And he could respect it. There would be time for tears and holding later. For now, his presence was the best gift he could offer.

"Pa wants to speak with you." Her delicate throat worked as she swallowed. Then she turned away, stepping gingerly down the hillside where they'd camped. Probably headed down to the creek below, although she hadn't taken anything to carry water in. Time alone would help her most. Hopefully.

Beaver turned and moved to Wilkins's side, trying to hone his thoughts for the coming conversation. The man surely wanted to continue their talk from the day before. Beaver dropped to his knees beside him.

Wilkins barely raised the furs covering him, and only his head and one hand peeked out at the top. His body must be struggling to keep him warm. He opened his eyes a little, and the pain on his face eased as he took in Beaver. The softness in his gaze formed a knot of emotion in Beaver's throat.

"Son." His voice came out in a thick rasp, but the sound didn't change the impact the word had in Beaver's chest.

Wilkins had called him this before, and each time, it swept through him like a torrent of water. Had he ever been called *son* by a man? Especially a man he respected as much as this one. In truth, he wished he *was* this man's son. Whether by birth or by marriage. If only they had more time.

Wilkins shifted the fur covering, working his arm out from underneath. The movement took effort, based on the look on his face, and Beaver reached to help him. Wilkins caught

Beaver's hand in his own and squeezed it. Seemed that had been his intent all along.

The contact—the fatherly touch from this man he respected —thickened the lump in his throat. He couldn't speak if he wanted to.

"I hope you've been…thinking about…what I said." He paused to take in a gurgling breath between every few words.

Beaver nodded. He couldn't stop thinking about it.

Wilkins pushed on, even though talking seemed to take all he had left. "I'll be going on…to heaven…soon. To meet…our God. I hope I'll…see you there…one day."

See him again? He'd heard of heaven. The place it was said people went who followed this God. A yearning started inside him. Maybe it had already been there, but the intensity of Beaver's desire seemed to expand with every breath.

What would it be like to know what would happen after he died? To have the hope of another world—a good world. A world where he would be reunited with others who'd gone before him. Like this man.

Wilkins had closed his eyes again. He raised the lids partway. Waiting for Beaver's response.

He couldn't promise to be in this heaven. He wasn't even certain the place existed. And he respected Wilkins too much to lie to him, even to ease his worries as he lay dying. So he offered as much hope as he could. "Perhaps."

Wilkins's eyes drifted shut again, but his hand squeezed Beaver's. "You've been…a blessing…son."

Beaver didn't move as Wilkins struggled through each breath. Beaver's body was almost numb, yet his mind churned. The words had felt like good-bye. *Don't let him leave yet.*

Just one more day. If Beaver could have just one more day with this man, maybe that would be enough.

CHAPTER 23

*T*hey were climbing a mountain now, a true cliff with precipices jutting out in several places as they wound upward. With every step of the horse's hooves, Susanna's heart weighed heavier.

Pa was holding on until they reached the top, she was almost certain. Then he would stop fighting for every breath. If there was any way she could fight for him, she would do it. She'd gladly give her breath to him if it would keep him with her longer.

But that wasn't fair to Pa, not when pain tormented him. He'd been hurting longer than he'd let on, if the deep lines etching his face were to be believed. She had to let him go to the better place the Lord had prepared for him.

Midway through the afternoon, Caleb raised his hand to signal a halt. "It doesn't look like we can go any farther on horseback." He looked back at Beaver Tail. "Think we can carry him?"

Beaver nodded, and she didn't have to see his eyes to know the grief she'd find there. They were all grieving, yet this wasn't the time for sadness. These were the last precious hours they'd have with her father, and she meant to make the most of them.

While the men untied the litter, she took Pa's hand in hers, cradling the gaunt fingers. "We're almost there." He didn't open his eyes, but his hand squeezed hers. She could almost feel his arms wrapped around her in the hug he would give her if he could.

She fought the burn of tears. Not yet. She couldn't cry yet.

When they had the ties unfastened, Beaver turned a gentle gaze on her. She released her father's hand and sniffed back her emotion. "Go on. I'll settle the horses and catch up." She needed a job to do. Something to occupy her thoughts.

He nodded, then the two men started forward on the game trail they'd been following.

She made quick work of unsaddling the horses. Only a few sprigs of grass grew on this part of the mountain, but some shrubby trees poked out of the rocky ground. She tied the animals so they would stay close, then left everything there except a canteen and one of the packs she'd wrapped food in. Pa might not need this, but she'd have it handy just in case.

She jogged up the trail as long as she could, then walked to catch her breath, then jogged again. The stitch in her side brought a welcome distraction. Ahead, she saw the men, walking in tandem with her father's sling carried between them. Beaver wasn't as tall as Caleb—few men were—but his broad shoulders tapered to a lean waist, catching her notice as he always did. Yet even that distraction didn't last long as her focus honed on the furs draped between the men.

As she ran the last bit of distance between them, panic clawed in her throat. What if Pa had passed already while she'd been tending the horses? What had she been thinking to leave him, even for a few minutes?

Beaver glanced back as she neared, and he must have seen the fear on her face, for he and Caleb both stopped.

"Pa." She grabbed Beaver Tail's arm when she reached him, panting to catch her breath from her sprint.

Pa's hand lifted from the furs, and the movement sent such a wash of relief through her, if she hadn't been clutching Beaver, she would have gone to her knees.

She took her father's hand, then inhaled a steadying breath. Beaver raised his brows in question and she nodded. "Go ahead."

The last of the climb passed far too quickly, and as much as she tried to prepare herself, when they reached the precipice, she wanted to turn and run back the way they'd come. She wasn't ready to reach the end.

The sight before them stretched in endless majesty. Mountains rose up on either side of them, and below flowed the Missouri River, smaller here than the mighty waters they'd followed for months.

"Pa." She rubbed her thumb over the leathery lines covering the back of his hand. "You should see this."

His eyes opened wider than they had in days. He stared up at the sky above, then around, like a new baby discovering the world. Then his gaze found hers. "Sit me up." Although his voice still rasped, the sound came stronger than the rough whisper he'd been using. As though these mountains infused strength into his failing body.

The men lowered him onto a smooth boulder, and Beaver helped her sit him upright. He couldn't sit upright on his own, so Beaver positioned himself behind Pa to support him. That allowed her to sit beside her father, gripping his hand in hers.

Pa laid his head on her shoulder—it was probably too difficult for him to hold it up on his own—and she savored the extra touch. She rested her cheek on the top of his hair. He bore the scent of his disease, a smell that would always turn her stomach, yet there was also the unmistakable fragrance that was her father. That aroma she'd known since her earliest memories, the one so precious it now made her eyes burn.

"It's beautiful, Susy." Even though his voice had weakened again, the awe in her father's tone returned her focus to the view before them.

"It is. As magnificent as I thought it would be."

"Even better." He took in two gurgling breaths. "I only wish your mama could be here with us."

Now she had to fight harder to keep her tears at bay.

Pa seemed to realize it, for he gave her hand a gentle squeeze. "I can't wait to see her again."

She had to sniff before she could speak. "I know, Pa."

"We won't be far, honey." He moved his other hand atop hers. "Don't ever forget...how much we love you. And how proud...we both are. You and your mama...are the best gifts...I could ever...imagine." He was wearing down, his words fading with each labored breath.

She stroked his hand with her thumb again. "I love you, Pa."

They sat that way for a long time, her mind wandering through all the memories she loved. Working alongside him in his gunsmithing shop. Handing him tools and listening to him talk about gun locks and cock screws and rifled bores. The passion that would fill his voice as he spoke of the work he loved had drawn her more than anything.

In the summer evenings they would sometimes go exploring around their little farm, spotting wild animals and seeking out unusual burrows or oddly shaped trees. The land always offered up something, and Pa would often thumb through his books once they'd returned to the cabin, finding answers to satisfy his curious mind.

She gave his hand another gentle squeeze. He didn't squeeze back. In fact, his hand was limp.

Panic surged through her and she jerked her head up to see

his face. "Pa?" His breathing no longer gurgled, and realization sank over her with a smothering hold. "No."

A warm hand settled on her shoulder. Beaver Tail.

As tears spilled down her cheeks, she sank back against him. Laying her head on her father's again, she let herself be cradled with the two men she loved.

For once, she didn't try to be strong.

$$\sim$$

*B*eaver Tail couldn't remember ever crying, but tears fell now.

Tears for the loss of this good man. A man he'd come to respect, to love. For the second time in his life, he'd lost a father.

Yet, his pain was nothing to Susanna's. The weight of her grief clawed at him. She'd become his heart, and this rending in her spirit made his own chest squeeze so tight, the pain felt as though he were tearing in two.

For a long time, he held them both. Letting her grieve. Grieving with her.

Then her breathing eased. Grew steadier. Maybe she'd finally succumbed to sleep, and that would help her more than anything he could offer. Not only must her body be exhausted, what with awakening often through the night to care for her father. Her spirit must be weary beyond words. This would take longer to heal, but rest would help.

Beaver lifted his head from where he'd tucked it over Susanna's. Caleb shifted to his side. The man must have been waiting, ready to help whenever needed. Beaver nodded toward Wilkins, and Caleb stepped in and took the man, easing him away from Susanna, then laying the lifeless body on the ground nearby.

Beaver couldn't help but follow the body with his gaze. Was it true that his spirit had gone to Heaven? Beaver had spent so many years rejecting his people's belief of a Great Spirit, the idea of accepting this idea of an all-powerful God and a place where the spirit of a person went after death twisted his mind into a painful knot.

He couldn't untie the strands now, not with his insides so raw. But he could care for Susanna. She would be his focus as long as she needed him.

As much as he wanted to tuck her into himself and hold her for hours, she would rest better snuggled in her bedroll. He motioned Caleb closer and spoke in a low whisper. "Her bedding."

The man nodded. "I'll bring all our things up."

Good. That would give him a little more time with Susanna while Caleb hiked down to where they'd left the horses.

He pulled her onto his lap, tucking her head in the crook of his neck, and did his best to give her what comfort he could.

~

The next day passed in a blur for Susanna. Maybe it was more than a single day.

Each time she awoke, the weight on her chest immediately brought back the immensity of her loss. The skin on her eyes pulled tight from all the tears, and her head ached.

Beaver Tail stayed close, always there with a cup of cool water. He offered food, but her stomach roiled at even the thought. She simply couldn't manage it right now.

She would have to pull out of this stupor soon. But not yet. She didn't have the strength for it yet.

Her second day without her father, she knew she had to get up. Pa's body still lay wrapped in the furs, waiting to be laid to rest. And as patient as Beaver and Caleb were being, they couldn't stay camped on the side of this mountain forever, suspended in time.

Winter would be on them within weeks, or maybe only days, if the fiercely cold nights were any indication.

After she'd stumbled downhill for a few moments of privacy, she returned to the camp the men had set up. The mountain protected them on two sides, keeping the almost-constant wind from blowing out their fire.

Caleb looked up at her approach from his place by the fire. Beaver sat a short distance away, stitching buckskins. Both men studied her.

"You ready for a bowl of corn mush, Miss Susanna?" Caleb stirred the mixture in the pot nearest the flame.

She nodded. "Thank you." Her voice rasped as she forced her raw throat to work. She still felt half-asleep, her mind numb and her eyes not willing to focus, but she dropped down to sit beside the fire. Maybe its warmth would wake her fully, bring her back to this world. As much as she didn't want to face it, she would have to make a new life without her father.

Her gaze wandered to Beaver Tail. He looked up from his work as though he could feel her watching. The softness in his eyes reminded her of Pa, and the burn of tears rushed in again. She blinked them back, then allowed her eyelids to drift shut as she turned back to the fire. She inhaled a long breath, let the woodsmoke fill her senses. Let the turmoil inside her ease.

One step at a time. First, she would break her fast with corn mush. Then she'd ask the men if they could bury her father here. Though his spirit was in heaven worshipping the God he loved, she couldn't imagine a more perfect place for his body to rest than these mountains he'd loved so much.

CHAPTER 24

"Where to now?"

Both men were looking at her, waiting for her to answer the question, and Susanna's heart clutched almost too tight to let the words out. Did they think she should go back east like Pa had planned? Find the cousin he'd arranged for her to live with and build a new life in Boston? The thought twisted sourly in her gut.

After tasting the freedom of this beautiful country, the wild adventure of each new day in this land, how could she possibly go back to ordered, mundane living among people who thought civilization was the best life had to offer? Especially living in a city. She and Pa had visited larger towns, especially as they searched for his cure. But she'd never been forced to live so closed in, surrounded by people and industry and noise—constant noise.

She met Beaver's gaze. The decision was an easy one. Not even a choice, really. "We need to find Joel and French, right? And Adam." As long as she was with these men, she would be safe. She would have a purpose.

Maybe another path would make itself clear to her at some point, but for now, this seemed right.

Beaver studied her, looking deeper than her eyes. She opened herself to his gaze. In truth, she didn't have the strength to hide anything.

The Adam's apple at his throat worked, and his mouth parted. The pain in his eyes deepened, and at last he expelled a ragged breath.

He turned to Caleb with a single nod. "All right."

～

*B*eaver Tail glanced over at Susanna as they rode. Did each step of this journey bring back painful memories for her the way it did for him? Winding down this mountain, he could almost hear each gurgling breath Wilkins had fought for.

Such a remarkable man. Even in the few weeks Beaver had known him, he'd been impressed by the man's wit and intelligence, his attention to detail, his abilities with guns. And underneath it all, the caring streak he wove into every interaction. Every look. Every touch.

How could he not respect such a man? And how could he not give serious consideration to the faith that had been so important to him? Especially if that faith was also important to Susanna. He'd had a few questions to ask Caleb when they were alone.

He slid Susanna another glance, and the weary slope of her shoulders pressed hard on him. *God, if You're real, take Susanna's grief and give her comfort.* He wanted to be the one to do that himself, but he was a mere human, and the weight of her pain was too much for any one person to overcome. He would help shoulder as much as he could, though.

They traveled much more quickly down the mountain than

they had up, and where the trail separated, they turned westward. As best he could tell, this was the direction the Shoshone had said Adam and his group were headed.

He'd have to watch for markings from French and Joel to make sure they'd turned this way as well after skirting the mountain's base.

They made camp by the Missouri River that ran between the mountains, peaks rising on both sides like mighty sentinels. Majestic towers he'd love to explore if he had more time. He understood why Wilkins had longed to come to this land.

Caleb offered to set out the meal for them, a simple fare of dried meat and roots he cooked over a fire. Beaver Tail made quick work of settling the horses. Should he make a shelter for Susanna, too? The sky was clear and bright, stars sparkling in the early darkness. No sign of rain, even though the crispy grass longed for moisture.

Still, Susanna deserved to be cared for and protected, cherished in every way he could. A shelter for her to sleep under was the least he could do.

He glanced to where she stood by the river's edge, staring down into the water. Loneliness draped her figure, separating her from everything around her. His chest ached with the pain of it. He could ease her loneliness, make sure she knew she would never be alone, not unless she wanted it.

Now the ache in his chest felt like a knife blade. Would she turn him away? Now that her father wasn't there for her to worry over, now that she was free to make a choice for herself, would she find him unworthy? Ayadna had, but Susanna wasn't like her. She wasn't like anyone. He'd never felt so connected to another being as he did with Susanna.

Never loved anyone as he did her.

Maybe this wasn't the right time, but someday, somehow, he would find a way to tell her that. When she was ready.

His feet moved toward her before his mind had a chance to

direct them. Should he step up behind her and slip his arms around her like he wanted to? Maybe she needed a friend more than anything right now.

He stepped beside her, soaking in her quiet, the steady murmur of the water rushing before them. Settling into the connection between them.

A splash in the water caught his attention. A flash of brown, then it was gone. He studied the spot, straining to hear any unusual sounds. He'd let his awareness dull these past days of sadness, but no more.

The brown resurfaced in the water, a spot about the size of his palm. As awareness sank through him, his mouth threatened to pull into a smile. Surely this wasn't the same beaver.

He glanced toward the trees to their left. That aspen would be tasty. He touched Susanna's elbow and pointed out at the creature.

She squinted at the brown patch.

He crept toward the aspen and found a small branch that still contained a few leaves. Then he eased back to the edge of the river. The beaver still watched them, about two arm lengths away from the bank. Beaver Tail would have to stretch, but he could probably reach the leaves to the creature.

Motioning for Susanna to come closer, he bent low so he made a less formidable figure for the animal. She gripped his arm as she crouched beside him, and the warmth of her touch distracted his focus.

He couldn't help a glance at her, so pretty in the moonlight as she stared toward the beaver. He turned his attention back to the animal, too.

Reaching out the aspen branch, he rested the spindly twigs with their few leaves on the water. The beaver didn't move, and Beaver Tail could barely make out wide eyes staring at them. Bristles of its damp fur spiked in waterlogged sections. His little sisters would have called the creature cute.

Little by little, it crept nearer, raising its head out of the water just enough to show its nose. Then its mouth and a flash of white teeth as the animal took a leaf in its mouth.

A rush of exaltation surged through Beaver Tail, but he worked hard to keep his body still. The animal's head shifted slightly as it chewed, then it reached for another leaf. When it moved, patches of light brown fur showed at the base of its head near the shoulders.

For long moments they crouched there, watching the beaver eat while it kept a steady eye on them. After a few more leaves, the animal seemed to have its fill. With a little splash, it slipped backward, disappearing under the water. The flowing river smoothed out the ripples the creature had caused, leaving no sign the beaver had been there at all.

Susanna released an audible breath, and her grip tightened on his arm as she stood. He rose to join her, turning to meet her pretty gaze. Those wide eyes tightened his chest, making him want to slip an arm around her waist and pull her close.

"Do you think that was the same one we saw before? It couldn't be, could it? Would he have come so far?" She looked at him as though he had all the answers.

In truth, he could barely breathe under that look, much less think. He forced his mind to form words that made sense. "It doesn't seem likely, but I've never known a beaver to be so brave toward people. And he bore the same light brown markings on his shoulders." The corners of his mouth pulled as the name he'd given the animal came back to him. "He Who Is Brave."

Susanna's face softened, losing some of the angst that had molded her features for days. Her eyes almost smiled, like she'd forgotten—just for a moment—the weight of her sadness. "He is a brave little fella. And cute."

She glanced back toward the water, looking for the beaver

again maybe. The motion exposed the creamy skin of her neck, the fragile line of her. The sweet vulnerability.

He couldn't hold himself back any longer. He stepped nearer, slipping a hand around her waist.

The action didn't seem to surprise her. She leaned into him, resting her head against his chest. Fitting perfectly under his chin.

He wrapped both arms around her and breathed her in. This feeling of wholeness was stronger than anything he'd imagined. He'd never thought a woman could stake such a claim on his heart. Never believed he'd need another to complete him.

The question was, could he be the man she needed? He had to come to a decision about the God she believed in. *I can't give her to a man who doesn't know our God. She'd never be happy.* Wilkins words still rang in his ears, and there was a powerful truth in them.

He would wait until she was ready, 'til the hardest of her grieving had passed. Yet even then, he couldn't ask Susanna to become his unless he knew he could be what she needed.

In every way.

⁓

*A*nother day. Susanna's weary limbs ached as she climbed down from her gelding the next evening.

Caleb appeared at her horse's head and gripped the reins. "I'll take him, Miss Susanna. You just sit yourself down and rest awhile."

The usual twinkle in his eye had dulled these past days, and he tended to look at her with a sadness bordering on pity. She didn't like being pitied, but that was probably a normal emotion. Knowing what to say when someone lost part of their world was harder than some realized.

In truth, how could any words ease the pain? Yet she had to

go on. Even though her heart and mind and spirit balked at the thought, she was pushing her body through the actions of each day.

She untied her bedroll and her personal satchel from behind her saddle, then turned to where Beaver Tail was already setting up camp. They'd followed the river all day, which had involved skirting the base of one mountain and climbing partway up another.

Even riding on horseback, the day had been exhausting.

Beaver was bent over, pulling parcels from their food pack, when she dropped her own bundles nearby. He shifted his gaze to her and straightened. "I'll get wood for the fire. Sit and rest." He turned and strode toward a copse of pines.

Sit and rest. The same thing Caleb had said. Did they both think she was such a weakling? She might look exhausted, but she would do her part around camp. Maybe she hadn't carried her load during those first two days after Pa's passing, but she would now. No matter how much the work took out of her.

She dropped to her knees and started unwrapping the food bundles she'd need to prepare the evening meal. She couldn't afford for the men to think of her as a weight that only slowed them down.

Surely Beaver Tail wouldn't think of her that way. Not the man she'd come to know...and love. Yes, in her deepest heart, love had curled and wound itself like a beautiful ivy, waiting for the moment when it could break through to the sunlight.

Her emotions were in such turmoil now. But, Lord willing, soon she'd be able to open her heart to this man who'd been waiting so patiently, always there for her, even in her darkest days.

Except...had he ever come to accept her faith? Pa had cautioned her against giving her heart to him. Said Beaver didn't believe, although he'd been talking with him of the hope waiting for them in heaven. Surely Caleb had laid out the truth of God's love, too. Had Beaver given his heart to the One who stood waiting? Would he speak of it to her if he had?

Shame niggled in her chest. She should have also shared her faith with him. Spoken of the God who meant more to her than anything in her life with the man who was coming to mean almost as much. *Lord, forgive me. Draw him to You.*

For once, she wished God hadn't given his creation free will to choose whether they would come to Him or not.

Lord. She didn't have the words to express the angst building in her chest. But God knew, and she let her spirit speak with her Creator as she moved through the motions of making a warm meal for them.

The icy wind tugged at her coat, blowing through even the thick layer of wool, numbing her hands and ears as she worked. Had winter finally arrived? She might need another layer of protection if they stayed long in the mountain country. Another coat, gloves, some kind of hat to cover her head, and a scarf. How could she come by such clothing out here?

Maybe using furs, if Beaver Tail would help her catch the right animals and work the hides. She wanted to learn the art he'd plied so easily on their journey, in the evenings and quiet days when they'd been waiting for Pa.

She'd watched him, even helped scrape some hides. But there was much more she'd not yet learned. He seemed to handle each type of pelt a little differently. A master who understood the nuances of each project.

Beaver Tail returned with an armload of wood and dropped to his knees. She handed him some tinder and the bow and stick he used to kindle fires and couldn't help watching as he scooped the tinder into a pile, then worked the stick and bow until the place they joined began to smoke.

The lean muscle in his wrists flexed, and she could even see the bunching of his arms and shoulders through his buckskin coat. Her fingers craved to reach out and touch him, to feel his strength under her hand. To be cradled by that strength.

She inhaled a breath to steady herself. A walk to the river might be in order, especially since she needed water for the evening meal anyway. But more than anything, she needed to clear her mind.

Put a little space between her and this man before she lost what little control of her heart she had left.

CHAPTER 25

*B*eaver Tail hadn't felt this nervous since he'd faced off with a mountain cat last spring. He pulled the buckskin from the pack he'd left near the horses and smoothed the leather over his arm. The texture was as soft as he could make it from the furs he had with him. He'd done his best work with the stitching. He could only hope he'd fitted the size right. If not, would she be insulted? He could remake whatever he needed to.

Maybe he should just start over. Tell her what he wanted to make for her and get her input on sizes. Would she prefer that over the surprise of an ill-fitting gift?

If only he could read women better.

The last thing he wanted was to anger Susanna like he had Ayadna. He was relieved that he'd lost her, now that he looked back, although a knot still formed in his belly when he thought of what his family had suffered.

But Susanna…she truly mattered. He couldn't lose her.

"Beaver, I was telling Caleb—" Susanna's voice clipped short as he spun to face her.

He must look guilty. In the shadowy darkness of this cloudy

night, he couldn't see her expression well. But she stood motionless. Soundless.

He raised his chin, forcing a composure he didn't feel. "You were telling Caleb...?" He'd merely twisted his body to look at her, while he still knelt in front of his pack. He couldn't stand or turn completely without revealing the buckskins draped over his arm.

Her intake of breath was audible across the three strides between them. "I was telling him I saw a mark on a pine tree farther up the river when I went for a walk. I think it's the J that Joel and French were leaving."

Hope surged through him. He'd been worried he'd lost them completely.

"The cliffs are low enough to allow horses to cross near there, so maybe that's why we haven't seen their tracks for a while. Maybe they came across the river and now they're moving west again."

He nodded. "I'll look at first light." He might miss something important if he examined the mark and the area around it in the dark.

Her gaze dropped to his pack. Now was the time. He might as well finish what he'd started.

Pushing to his feet, he turned to her, exposing what he held. "I made you better clothing. For the winter."

He extended the bundle to her. "If they don't fit, let me know, and I can alter them. Or make new." His face burned hot like he was standing over a campfire.

"You did?" Was that happiness in her voice? Or simply curiosity? She stepped forward to take the clothing, and her fingers brushed across the top of his. "When did you have time for this?"

The urge to twist his hand and catch hold of her gripped him, but he refrained. Instead he focused on her face. "In the evenings, mostly after you already slept."

As her fingers sank into the buckskin, her eyes widened. "It's so soft."

She lifted the top piece, a long tunic like his sisters wore that would keep her warm and still allow her freedom of movement. He'd fringed the bottom so water and snow would flick off but hadn't added any other decoration. Maybe he'd offer to if she seemed open to the idea.

A smile lit her face as she held the tunic up to her shoulders. "Beaver, it's beautiful."

She was beautiful. Even with the thick shadows, he could imagine what she would look like in the garment, every graceful curve of her. With her sun-tanned skin, she would almost pass for an Indian maiden. But the brown of her hair gave her a uniqueness he loved much more than if she were just another woman from his village.

She raised her gaze to his, her eyes shimmering. "Thank you." Her voice caught on the words. "They're just want I needed. What I wanted."

His throat closed so he could barely speak. She wanted clothes like the Indian women wore? He could imagine her among his people, walking to the river with his sisters, cooking alongside his mother. They would love her, with her fierce determination and strength, and the care she offered so freely to those who gained her trust.

The thought sent a surge of warmth through him.

So much that he almost missed when she took a step closer to him. Then her nearness seemed to fill the air around him, making his chest struggle to breathe. Everything in him wanted to reach out, pull her closer, and press his mouth to hers. To inhale her sweet kiss, feel the connection with her he'd been craving—dreaming of—since that last time.

She tilted her head, and the shadows shifted away from her eyes. Was that longing?

Her look cleared away the last of his self-control. He closed the distance between them in a single step, gripping her arms and pulling her close. She stepped into his embrace, and he wrapped her in his arms. He had to stop himself from holding too tight. In truth, he may not ever be able to release her, now that his arms felt the warm softness of her.

He lowered his face, hovering just before touching his forehead to hers. Her warm breath caressed him, and just her nearness made his chest quiver. This woman had become his heart, the best part of him. He would do anything for her.

With their foreheads touching, he brushed her nose with his, nuzzling her, cherishing her. She brought her hands up to cradle his face, and her touch lit a fire inside him.

He worked hard to bank the inferno, for Susanna was too special to risk burning. He tipped his head and gently lowered his mouth to hers. Brushing her lips. Treasuring the taste and feel of her.

After this kiss, he may never be the same.

~

"Miss Susanna. Wake up. There's a fire."

Rough hands shook Susanna, pulling her from the clutches of sleep. Why was Caleb worried about their campfire?

She forced her eyes open. Darkness hung thick around them, and the smoke from their fire must be wafting in her direction, for the stench was strong enough to gag.

Caleb was throwing packs over his shoulders, loading his massive back with most of their things. What in the world?

Her groggy mind struggled to make sense, to focus on the words he was muttering.

Then he spun to her. "The grass is on fire. We have to get out of here."

Like a smack to her cheek, the words jolted her into full awareness. She bolted upright, spun to look outside their camp.

A little distance upriver—maybe thirty strides—fire lit the sky. Thick smoke billowed from the flame as it licked trees and grass in its path.

"I can't find Beaver, but we have to get out of here." Caleb scooped up another bundle, looping the strap around his neck, then tucked his rifle under his right arm. "Grab what you can and run to the horses."

She was already on her feet, fighting one of the blankets tangled in her legs. Her body wasn't cooperating with what her mind demanded.

Finally she freed herself, then she scooped up her bedding. She spun and grabbed the pot from beside the fire, then dumped its water over the coals. No sense adding to the coming flames.

Then, the full meaning of Caleb's words smacked her.

She spun to him. "Where's Beaver?" Where could he be in the middle of the night?

"I don't know. When I woke, he was gone and the fire was twice as far away. It's moving fast. Maybe he's getting the horses free. Start running, and we'll meet him there."

She glanced at the flames again. They had closed at least a third of the distance between them. "Maybe he went to try to slow the fire." Fear clutched her chest with the thought. *God, don't let him be in that inferno.*

That was also the direction of the marking she'd told him about last evening. Had he gone to investigate while they slept, then been caught by the fire?

The blaze cut a wide swath between the base of the mountain and the cliff down to the river. If Beaver was anywhere near it, he'd not survive unless he jumped off the ledge into the water.

God, protect him.

"Susanna!" Caleb's bark jerked her from her fears, and she spun toward him.

She started toward the horses, which were, thankfully, in the opposite direction from the fire. Running in the new buckskins Beaver made her was easier than her other clothes, even the men's trousers. Yet the bundles in her arms made her gait awkward, especially with the heavy pot in one hand. Caleb had the worst of it though, loaded with almost all of their supplies, and he kept a steady trot beside her. Almost like a herding dog, nudging her along. They'd left Beaver Tail's furs behind. How much would he grieve their loss?

By the time they reached the horses, the fire was already nipping at the trees near their camp.

The animals were frantic, jerking and pulling at the ropes that tethered them, wide eyes flashing. All four horses were there, including Beaver Tail's gelding. Wherever he'd gone, he left on foot.

Surely he hadn't gone to the fire. He would have warned them before he left, and there was no way he could stop a blaze that massive, so surely he wouldn't have tried. He couldn't even get near it without melting from the intense heat.

Her clothing was already pasted to her body with sweat, and thick beads ran down her face as she worked to slice through the tether straps.

"Throw the saddles on the horses and cinch them just enough to keep the packs from falling off. We don't have time for more." Caleb had to yell over the crackling roar of the fire.

He was right, saddling the horses securely enough that they could ride would take too long. For now, they could make better time on foot if the horses carried the awkward packs. Her stomach churned as she worked the leathers, scrambling to move with the fear-crazed horses. Should they go on without knowing where Beaver was? They didn't have a choice.

She turned to squint at the mountain. The fire lit the night, but there were enough shadows from smoke that she couldn't tell if there was a way Beaver could have climbed the rocky cliff to escape the blaze. Maybe.

Lord, protect him. Help, God, please!

She couldn't lose Beaver, too. Not now. Not ever.

But she couldn't slow Caleb and the horses down either. She was just finishing with her second horse when Caleb dragged his two closer to her. "You ready?"

She pulled the cinch strap in place, then dropped the stirrup and grabbed a better hold on the ropes of her gelding and Beaver's. "Let's go."

She wasn't ready, but she wouldn't hold them back any longer. Beaver was in God's hands, and she'd have to trust Him. *Take care of him, Lord. Please.*

They ran.

Dragging the horses behind them, they ran until Susanna was almost doubled over from the stitch in her side. Her chest felt like a horse had stomped on it, and every breath she struggled for reeked of smoke.

"Let's go down in the water here." Caleb slowed to a walk and motioned toward the river. A steep animal trail sloped diagonally down the cliff. Goats could descend it with no problem. Deer, most likely. But horses?

She looked back at the fire. A distance behind them now, but it raged forward with incredible speed, engulfing everything in its path. With a dry summer and almost no rain for weeks now, the landscape was primed to spread the fire with fury.

"We need to get across the river. I'll go down first." Caleb started toward the track. "Hold my pack horse until I get Josie down."

She took the animal's rope and positioned herself to encourage Caleb's mare to follow him down the slope. The horse was just as amiable as her master under normal conditions, but this fire had her panicked just like the others. Still, it took the mare less than a minute to skitter down the steep path.

Caleb came back up for his pack gelding, and the horse didn't take much urging to follow. He was probably accustomed to trailing Josie wherever she went.

"Now hand me your gelding." Caleb was breathing hard as he climbed back up the trail.

Susanna had bonded with this gentle horse and wanted to take him down herself. But they didn't have time for a discussion. She handed Caleb the rope and gave the gelding a pat on the shoulder. "Be good for him."

The spotted horse took a bit longer to work up the courage to descend than the other two had, and Susanna couldn't help eyeing the fire while they encouraged him. How could the blaze move so quickly?

If they didn't get into the water in the next couple minutes, the fire might be close enough to scorch them, as much heat as the flames were putting out.

She drew back and gave the horse her hardest whack. "Get down, boy."

The horse must have felt her urgency, for he leaped down the incline, reaching the ground below in two rabbit-like hops.

"Let me have him." Caleb's breathing was almost louder than his words as he climbed back up and reached for Beaver's gelding.

This horse was the most spirited of them all, and without Beaver there to calm him, he might give them trouble.

"Hey, boy. Let's get to safety."

While Caleb took the rope's end down the path, she led the horse to the edge.

He nickered and bobbed his head, his feet dancing nervously.

"Move on." She tugged his halter forward and gave him a firm pat just behind his front leg.

The horse started down the hill, picking his way nimbly over the rocky incline.

Thank you, Lord.

She followed, and when she reached the bottom, Caleb was already tightening the girth on his mare. "We should ride now since we're going into the water."

He was right, but they didn't have time to mount up.

Heat pierced her layers, searing her skin as she struggled with her cinch strap. Her fingers wouldn't do as she commanded, especially with the horse fidgeting.

Finally she had it tight enough. She dropped the stirrup in place, fit her foot in it, and swung up. "Come on."

Caleb was just landing in the saddle as she kicked her mare forward into the water.

CHAPTER 26

*S*usanna stared at the scorched remains in the early dawn light. Beaver Tail couldn't be gone. It wasn't possible.

God wouldn't strip her of the last thing she loved. First her mother. Then their home. Then Pa. Now He'd taken Beaver Tail.

Why not her too? Why did He leave her behind in this desolate wilderness? This blackened land of charred hopes and dreams.

Her body was numb, too numb even to climb down from her horse. Part of her wanted to keep riding, to hold out hope that they'd find Beaver Tail. They'd tracked upriver to the fording place where she had told him about the mark on the tree. Caleb said the fire-blackened land across the river would still be too hot for the horses' hooves, so they hadn't crossed.

In truth, if Beaver Tail was in that barren mass of coals, only his seared body remained. And she couldn't stand the thought. Even now, her mind conjured images that made her stomach churn.

She wrapped her hands around herself, pushing down the bile, letting her body remember the feel of Beaver's strong arms around her. Her eyes burned, but the tears didn't surface. Even her tears were too numb to work properly.

"Let's stop here a while. Eat and let the horses rest." Caleb's deep voice rumbled gently in the barren silence of the landscape. He must be exhausted too. And grieving. He'd known Beaver Tail much longer than she had.

Yet, the ache pierced her chest like a knife blade slicing her heart. How could God take him away?

She let Caleb help her down from the horse. Let him coax her to lie on the fur he stretched over the ground. Part of her felt as though she were watching the scene from outside herself. She curled on her side, folded her hands under her head. Her grainy eyes resisted closing, but she forced them. If only sleep would push away the awfulness. Push away the empty desolation.

She made herself lie still, motionless, waiting for sleep to finally come and swallow her in its dark clutches.

～

Susanna jolted awake, her eyes popping wide as her heart throbbed. The terror of the fire reaching burning hands to clutch at her, flashed through her mind. Only a dream, yet she could still feel her desperation to reach Beaver Tail. The fire held her back, absorbing her in its searing midst, even as Beaver was pulled away by some unseen hand.

She pressed a palm to her chest to still her racing heart.

Beaver. Where could he be? Surely he hadn't actually died. It didn't seem possible. He was so strong and virile, full of more ability to outsmart a raging fire than anyone else she knew.

A glance around showed the afternoon was melding into

evening. On his bed pallet nearby, Caleb snored in a steady rhythm. He must be exhausted from the night. She'd not made things any easier on him either, as comatose as she'd been before she finally fell into the awful dream.

Her pulse picked up speed again as the image of the fire wrapping itself around her flooded her mind. In the dream, she'd been the one engulfed, not Beaver Tail. Maybe that meant he was still alive.

She pushed the blanket aside and rose to her feet. Her legs didn't want to hold her, so she stood still for a moment to let them adjust to her weight. She should take this opportunity to study their surroundings.

This side of the river, which hadn't burned, formed a wider valley than on the opposite bank, but the land was mostly barren of trees. Tall aspens and cottonwoods grew in the distance upriver.

Across the water, the scene stretched much bleaker. The fire had ravaged the strip of land between the mountain cliffs and the river, burning grass and brush and tree alike. The blackened forms left behind stood like grotesque skeletons, reminders of last night's horror.

She swallowed to wet her parched throat. She had to go over there and look for Beaver. If he'd somehow survived, maybe tucked in the crevice of a rock, he might be badly injured. Finding him might possibly save his life.

And the hope of that possibility gave her something to cling to.

Turning, she strode toward the horses. Caleb had tied them out to graze, a task she should have helped with. God had placed such a good heart in that man. Some woman would get a gem if he ever found someone good enough for him.

That wouldn't be her, not when she'd already given her heart to Beaver Tail. She'd never met a man she could see herself marrying before him. There was no way she could ever feel this intensity of love for anyone else. And if she'd lost him now…

Oh, God.

The stab of pain nearly doubled her over. She wrapped her arms around her belly and fought down the sob. She couldn't have lost him. Not Beaver. *God, he's all I had left.*

You have Me. The thought sprung so clearly into her mind. Not like words, but a fully formed thought that overshadowed everything else.

Her legs grew weak beneath her. The way her mind spun, her body didn't have strength to manage standing too. She *did* have God. No matter how much she wanted Beaver Tail too, could her Heavenly Father be enough?

Conviction wove through her, pressing hard in her chest. She'd always told herself the Lord was most important to her. Had reminded herself when they struck out for their westward journey that when Pa's illness finally took him, she'd still be safe in her Heavenly Father's care.

Yet, somewhere along the way, she'd forgotten to remind herself. Maybe it was when she'd begun to put so much faith in Beaver Tail. He'd been her rock through these last days. There when she wanted him, giving her space when she needed it, and wrapping her in his strength when she had none left.

Had Beaver become more necessary to her than God, her Creator and Sustainer? The Heavenly Father who held her life in His hand and promised to give her hope and a future. The Lord Who also held Beaver's life in His hand, as He'd now proved.

She bowed her head, dropping her chin to her chest as pain flowed through her. "I'm sorry, Lord." The words seeped out in a whisper, her heart crying to the Father. "You are all I need. In You I place my trust." God truly was her only hope. If only she'd realized that before He'd sacrificed Beaver Tail to remind her.

Tears trickled down her cheeks for the first time since the

fire. Grief for Beaver Tail, for her wayward heart, for the pain she'd caused them all. And maybe a little relief that God hadn't left her too. She wasn't alone, although part of her still felt the desolation of life without the man she loved so dearly. How would she survive losing him?

With God's strength, she'd have to make it one day at a time.

She let herself cry for several minutes, then forced the emotions back down. No matter how impossible it seemed that Beaver Tail might be alive, she still needed to search for him. She wiped her face with her sleeve, and the cloth came away streaked with black. She must look a sight.

Pushing to her feet, she glanced around her. Back at their camp, Caleb still slept, his massive body stretched out under several furs stitched together.

A motion in the distance caught her attention. Was that an animal? Her muscles tensed. Another bear? She hadn't grabbed her gun when she started out for the horses.

Turning, she took long strides back toward camp, but kept her focus on the figure. Actually, there were two figures.

Elk? No, men on horses. Or people on horses, at least. She should know better than to automatically assume they were men.

They were too far away for her to recognize them, but Beaver Tail had no horse, so neither of the figures could be him. Indians? She should be armed when she met them, just in case.

When she reached the camp, she dug for her rifle. It wasn't with her pack. A glance over her shoulder showed the strangers drawing closer.

"Caleb, wake up." She moved near enough to shake his shoulder. He jerked mid-snore, then his eyes flew wide and he stared up at her.

"People are coming. I can't find my rifle." She'd packed Pa's gun carefully in his satchel. She hadn't planned to ever use it, but she hadn't planned to be in this situation either.

As she dropped to her knees beside the pack that contained her father's things, Caleb lumbered to his feet. "I don't believe it."

His voice held a wonder that made her jerk around. He stared off at the horsemen, and she followed his gaze. Was there something familiar about them?

"I think its French an' Joel. At least, French an' someone."

She scrambled to her feet and squinted to see better. Her eyes still burned from smoke, and the skin around them pulled tight from her tears. But as she strained to make out the details of each form, one of the figures took on French's fine-boned outline. The other man was so bulky, he couldn't be Joel.

Caleb was already striding toward them, his rifle in his hand. It would take too long to find her father's gun and take time to load it. She glanced at their pile of supplies once more, but saw no glimpse of a smooth wooden stock or long metal barrel. She'd have to rely on Caleb's weapon for safety. Surely French wouldn't be riding with someone he didn't trust, would he?

She ran to catch up with Caleb and was breathing hard as she settled in beside his extended strides. Even though she lengthened her own step, his long legs required her to add a running stride every few paces.

"That's Joel, too, but he's got someone in front of him." Caleb's words brought her focus up from keeping pace with him to hone in on the strangers.

One of the horses did carry two people. No wonder the outline had looked so bulky.

As she stared, a numbing awareness sank through her. Beaver? Did he have Beaver braced in the saddle in front of him? The man's head was tilted backward, leaning against Joel, so she couldn't see his face. But the outline of his shoulders was a view she loved. A memory forever stored in her heart.

She broke into a run, joy and fear tangling in her chest to

drive her forward. They'd found him. He must be alive. He had to be.

Running took most of her strength and focus, so she was only vaguely aware of French spurring his horse into a lope to meet her. Joel stayed at a steady walk though. Why didn't he run too? She had to see Beaver Tail.

French reined in when he reached her, and she shot a glance at his face before returning her focus to Beaver. "Is he alive?" She heaved to catch her breath from running.

"He's alive but hurt."

Alive. Joy surged through her, and as much as she wanted to find out what had happened, getting to Beaver was more important than anything else. She had to touch him, to feel with her own hands that warm lifeblood pulsed through him. To do whatever it took to help him recover.

She broke into a run, closing the thirty or so strides that separated them. Her heart thundered in her chest, making each breath ache as she sucked in air. Nothing mattered. No amount of pain would slow her down from reaching Beaver Tail.

He was alive.

At last she neared them, and she honed her focus on Beaver as she slowed to walk the final steps. He lay back against Joel, his head on the man's shoulder as though he was unconscious. She couldn't see his face, only his neck and the strong set of his chin. Soot darkened his leggings and tunic. Or was that water? Maybe both.

Joel pulled to a stop beside her, and she reached out to lay a hand on Beaver's leg. The grimy feel of wet buckskin met her touch. Her heart pressed so hard, each beat pulsed in her ears. Was he truly alive? She couldn't tell for sure without seeing his face.

"Beaver?" The voice didn't sound like hers as she pushed the word through her raw throat.

He didn't respond, and she darted a glance at Joel.

Weary lines etched under his eyes. "He took in a lot of smoke and water. We think he might have hit his head on a rock. Let's get him to your camp and lay him down."

Yes, he needed to lay down. Then she could get a better assessment of his injuries. She reached up for Beaver's hand, which dangled loosely at his side. Warm. *Thank you, Lord.* But his hand stayed limp as she gave it a gentle squeeze, and the fear inside her grew a few notches stronger. She could still lose him.

CHAPTER 27

*W*ith effort, she forced herself to release his hand. To step back and allow Joel to nudge the horse into a walk. She needed to get to camp ahead of them to ready a place for Beaver Tail.

She pushed into a run again, but the bark of her name drew her up short.

"Here, ride with me." French pulled his foot from the stirrup and motioned at the saddle in front of him.

That would be faster. She climbed into the tiny space he opened up. The saddle's seat wasn't big enough for them both, but several packs were tied behind him, so there was no other room.

She gripped the horse's mane as he pushed the animal into a lope. They passed Joel and Beaver, and the moment French pulled up at the camp, she swung her leg over the horse's neck and leaped to the ground.

Her blankets would be fine for Beaver to lie on, but she straightened them, then turned to find their medical supplies and a canteen. Only a little bit of water sloshed inside the flask.

She'd have to send one of the men to the river for more once they settled Beaver.

Murmurs from Caleb and Joel drew nearer, and she turned to watch as they closed the final short distance to camp. Beaver Tail still lay lifeless against Joel. Had the blow to his head caused his unconsciousness? Her spirit churned inside her, bile roiling in her belly.

Caleb and French lowered Beaver from the saddle and carried him to the blankets she'd readied. Beaver's head didn't hang as limp as it might have. Maybe he was regaining consciousness. Or trying to.

The men stepped away from him, and she dropped to her knees beside the man she loved. The man she'd thought to never see again—at least, not alive.

She stroked the hair from his forehead, taking in his soot-smeared face. The raven-black hair, so thick and rich before, hung in tangled tendrils around his cheeks and neck.

His skin was cool to the touch. And no wonder with his leathers so wet still. She reached for the extra blankets and pulled them over him, but they would only become soaked themselves. She glanced up at the men standing around her. "We need to get him out of his wet things."

French nodded. "We'll do it."

She turned back to Beaver Tail and let her eyes linger on his face, absorbing the strong features that had drawn her admiration that first day—and every day since. She stroked his forehead again. "I won't be far away, my love." She tried to speak low enough that the men didn't hear. Beaver Tail probably couldn't hear anyway. She wanted to lean forward and press a kiss to his forehead, but the men were watching. Waiting.

Drawing back, she stood and stepped farther away. "Please be careful with him. His head."

"Yes, ma'am." Caleb patted her shoulder as she passed by him.

This would be a good time for her to refill the canteen and wet some cloths to clean the soot from Beaver's face and hands. She hadn't seen any injuries yet, but she'd know better after the men changed him.

She took her time at the river, letting her gaze wander over the blackened landscape across the water. Where had the men found Beaver? How had he traveled so far away from their camp? And what had caused the injuries? She should have questioned them before leaving them alone.

But Beaver's comfort came first. She would satisfy her curiosity later.

For now, she could only lift a shaky praise to the Father. But she couldn't help following it with a plea. *Let him recover fully, Lord. Please.*

~

*P*ain radiated through Beaver's head, pounding so hard he could barely feel the ache spreading through the rest of his body. Could barely feel the soothing touch.

He should open his eyes, but he couldn't summon the strength to make his body work. Instead, he focused on steady breathing. A long, slow breath in, and then, he eased the air back out. Another breath, slowly, deeply, filling his lungs. Filling his body with life.

The life-giving air God had created. Made to sustain the people He'd also created. This new understanding felt like an awakening. His mind had been closed in a dark lodge during the first part of his life and could now see the wide world around him, illuminated by bright sunshine.

Not even the agony in his skull could dim the wonder of this new awareness. The reality he'd come to terms with as he fought to escape the fire's blaze. The unmistakable peace that had taken root since then.

As the life-giving air flowed through his body, the pain in his head eased a little. Enough that his mind registered the cool cloth wiping his face. Then the warm touch. A soothing caress.

His body yearned to draw nearer, to lean into that hand. He worked to open his eyes. To see the woman he longed for. The only person who could bring his senses to life like this.

He was only able to manage thin slits, but that was enough to see her blurry outline over him. The light pierced his eyes, sending a fresh round of pain. Forcing his lids closed again.

But touching Susanna, feeling her softness with his own hand, would be worth whatever effort required to make his body work. He focused his attention on his hand, forcing his aching body to use the muscles. He reached up and wrapped his fingers around her wrist.

The sweet feel of her made him want to draw her closer. To curl her close to him. To feel her warmth and softness beside him.

Her other hand covered his, and together, they wove their fingers in a clutch so strong, almost desperate.

His yearning eased, calming into a reassurance that soothed some of the pain pulsing through his body. Susanna was here. She was safe.

And one day, Lord willing, she would be his.

CHAPTER 28

*S*usanna stared up at the peaks around them as the icy wind whipped at her hair, pulling the strands free from the braid she'd just refastened. It seemed nothing could be restrained from the wild freedom of this mountain wind. Not even the weight of her grief.

Warm hands wrapped around her from behind. Strong hands, enfolding her in the safety of the arms she'd come to love so much.

She leaned back against Beaver Tail, sinking into his strength, relishing the love he so freely offered. They'd not spoken of feelings or weighty matters in the two days since the fire. His pain had been obvious, even though he rose within an hour of that first awakening. He'd seemed light-headed, but she hadn't protested his activity until she saw him weave when he walked.

Thankfully, he'd settled back down on his bed pallet and hadn't taken long to succumb to sleep. He'd alternated between sleep and waking ever since then, and she'd tried hard not to worry over the knot protruding under the thick layers of his now-sleek hair.

His memory and speech didn't seem to be affected. God be praised for His abundant mercies.

The warm press of Beaver's mouth rested on her head, and she let her eyes drift shut. Her heart had been through so much turmoil these last days, yet resting in this man's hold, she could feel God's peace settling over her.

She wasn't whole yet. Maybe she never would be, not until she saw Pa in heaven one day, but the weight of grief didn't crush her any longer.

After long moments standing with Beaver, absorbing his strength, Susanna turned in his arms to see his face. Standing sideways in his hold, she studied his strong jaw. She cradled that strength in her palm, let her finger rest on the curve beside his mouth.

His eyes pierced her with a gaze that took her breath away. Her stomach flipped as longing surged through her. Her body prepared for the kiss she'd been craving, although she hadn't realized it before now.

Then, the corners of his mouth curved up, and his dark eyes danced. His face slipped into a smile that made her heart nearly burst inside her chest. Heavens, she loved this man.

He kept one hand tight at her waist and brought his other up to cradle her jaw. "Susanna, I planned to wait until you were ready, to give you time to grieve. But these past days have reminded me we can't count on how much time we'll have." His gaze intensified. "I want to spend as many days as I'm given with you. The love I feel for you is more than I ever thought possible."

The flurry of emotion his words stirred fanned through her, making her eyes sting with more thoughts and feelings than she could name. Overwhelming happiness rose to the surface. But a sadness tinged the emotion, the reality she would have to face. She couldn't commit her life to a man who didn't share her faith. Her love for the Father.

A flash of uncertainty slipped through his eyes. "Your pa spoke much to me of God. He said I wouldn't be able to make you happy unless I knew your God and accepted his love. I have done that. Caleb is teaching me, but there is much more I want to learn."

A wash of joy swept through her, spreading a tingle all the way down her back. Beaver had committed his life to God? Wanted to learn more and to serve Him? *Thank You, Father.* How could all this be true? It seemed too much, too wonderful a gift, even from the God who loved her.

Yet, one concern niggled in her mind. If Beaver chose her faith merely to make her happy, his commitment may not be real. She couldn't risk entering a union that would unequally yoke them. She'd seen the misery of that situation too many times to risk living out that possibility herself.

But this man... She clutched at his tunic, letting her eyes roam every handsome feature of his face. She'd never seen so much uncertainty in his eyes. Never seen his expression so unguarded, so exposed as he waited for her answer.

Her heart yearned to say yes. To accept his words and glory in his love. To tell him how she'd been falling for him a little more every day, and now she couldn't imagine leaving his side.

She couldn't, though. Not until she knew for sure. If she did this right, held staunchly to the directions God had given, He would guide her to the best path. *Lord, let that include Beaver. Please, Father.* But even if it didn't, God would sustain her. He would be enough. She had to cling to that.

Summoning every bit of strength she could muster, she worked for the best way to ask the question that would determine the course of her life. "Beaver, I don't... You shouldn't..." She drew in a breath to settle the churning in her mind. To help her form a coherent sentence.

His hand slid from her jaw into her hair, tightening a little as his body tensed. His gaze didn't close off, but the unguardedness shifted to urgency. "Say it, Susanna. Speak of what worries you." Tension gripped his voice, and she could taste his fear, maybe even desperation.

Dear God, don't let me hurt him. Breaking her own heart was one thing. But she wouldn't be able to stand bringing pain to this man she loved so much.

With another breath for strength, she forced herself to speak. "I don't want you to accept my God to make me happy. I want Him to be real to you." She pressed a hand to his chest, where his heart resided, doing her best to ignore the powerful muscle under her palm. "God loves you even more than I do, and He wants desperately for you to know Him. To trust Him with your life. You can't do that if you turn to Him only because you think that's what I want." *But that is what I want.* She couldn't speak those last words.

Instead, she watched his face, studied for any sign of what he might be thinking. She didn't expect the sheen of moisture glimmering in his eyes.

His Adam's apple dipped as his throat worked. Under her hand, his chest rose as he drew in a large breath. "Your father spoke of God's love, but he was near the end of his strength, so I turned to Caleb with my questions. I think I had been searching before that, although I told myself I knew well that no greater being existed. Yet something inside me craved." He raised his gaze from her, looking out into the distance.

She didn't dare breathe, didn't dare hope as she waited for his next words.

"I knew He was real, this God your father told me of." He lowered his face back to her as a sad smile crinkled the corner of his eyes. "But I wasn't sure I wanted to commit to Him. Not until the fire came. As the heat from the flames pressed around me, I realized how foolish I'd been. A reckless youth with no real power of my own. I gave my life to the God Who held it anyway. If I was to die, I begged for mercy. If He gave me more time on this earth, I committed every day left to follow Him."

His hand in her hair gentled. "I have much to learn, but I'll spend the rest of my life seeking Him." And then his eyes grew earnest again. Yearning. "I want to do it with you. Please say yes."

Joy overflowed inside her, bursting through every part as a laugh tumbled out. She pressed herself into him, resting her head against his shoulder as the tumult of emotion stole the strength from her legs. She couldn't stop smiling, couldn't stop laughing. Couldn't stop the happy tears from rolling down her cheeks.

He held her tight. Cradled her, his head tucking into her hair. Oh, this man... She breathed in the essence of him. The fragrance of grace.

Even in the darkest of nights, God had blessed her more abundantly than she could have ever foreseen.

EPILOGUE

Susanna couldn't remember the last time she'd felt so happy. Or so short.

With Caleb's massive frame on her left, nearly blocking out the sun, and Joel and French standing on her right as witnesses, she was surrounded, encircled by friends who had become so dear.

But it was the gaze of the man before her that made her feel cherished. The love shimmering in his intense regard. He'd pulled his raven black hair back into a leather strip, outlining every handsome angle of his face. She let her gaze drink him in, and her heart strained with the fullness of joy inside her.

This seemed too wonderful, that God would have blessed her with this man. That He would have orchestrated so many events—from her father's desire to follow in the steps of Lewis and Clark—even that those explorers had undertaken their travels in the first place—to the events that sent Beaver on the journey with his friends to take that same path.

All had led them to this place. To this moment. To this joining of lives. She squeezed her eyes shut as grateful tears welled. The Lord had even blessed them with an ordained minister. Their Heavenly Father truly thought of everything.

"What God has joined together, let no man separate." Caleb raised his gaze from the Bible in his hands and sent Beaver Tail a grin. "You can kiss her now if you want."

Beaver glanced at his friend and the corners of his mouth tugged in a smile that made her heart sing. She could look at that smile for the rest of her life and never grow tired of it.

But then he turned his gaze back to her, and the intensity in his eyes started a tightness that pulled all the way through her. A tension that drew her with an invisible tug. She could feel his lips even before he lowered his mouth to hers. The sensation was like coming home. Like she'd finally found the place she belonged.

All too soon he pulled back. But he slipped his hand around her, tucking her into his side as he turned to Caleb. The man was speaking to them. Congratulating them. But her mind couldn't seem to pull itself from that kiss. From the tingling that had spread all through her. She'd never felt so full, almost giddy.

The men either didn't notice or were kind enough not to comment as they all made their way over to the celebratory meal she'd left simmering all morning. The others talked and jested. Maybe her happiness had spread through the air, but she couldn't seem to focus on their words as she scooped out servings of stew for each of them.

She could easily feel Beaver Tail's gaze on her, and she allowed herself a few stolen glances as she worked. If someone had asked her only a year ago what her wedding day would be like, she'd never ever have imagined this to be it.

In fact, she'd have said she didn't plan to marry. Not unless her situation became desperate enough to require it. Thank the Lord He hadn't given her an inkling of His plan back then. She might have run the opposite direction, just from fear of the unknown.

She could never have imagined how good this day would be. If only Pa had been here. Yet she'd felt him all day, his presence nearby. Maybe those who'd gone before really did look down from heaven and watch loved ones who still missed them. Perhaps that was only wishful thinking. But she knew in her heart Pa would be smiling if he knew of this next step in her life.

She still missed him with a craving she couldn't put into words, but he would want her to step into this happiness with Beaver. He would look at her with that sparkle of love in his eye and tell her how pleased he was. How he'd known their Father above had just the right man planned for her.

A hand wrapped around her waist, its warm strength soaking through her to soothe the sadness. It was still a wonder how Beaver knew exactly when she needed him. There in front of the stewpot, she lay her head on his shoulder—just for a moment. A thank you.

He pressed a kiss to her hair. "I'm ready to ride out whenever you are."

She glanced behind them at the three men still talking amongst themselves as they ate. Pretending they didn't see the two lovebirds, most likely.

Just then, French glanced sideways and met her eye. He winked.

Heat flared up her neck, and she turned back to scoop the last of her own serving of stew. Leaning closer to Beaver, she murmured only loud enough for him to hear. "I think we should stay and visit awhile." They had final details to work out, after all.

With her bowl in hand, she and Beaver turned back to join the others.

"You want us to meet you at the three forks of the Missouri in four days or five?" Joel leveled his gaze on Beaver Tail, then shifted his focus back and forth between the two of them. "I imagine you'll be wanting to head out for your wedding night soon."

Were they all determined to embarrass her? Susanna did her best not to show even a hint of mortification, but she had to look down at her stew to accomplish it. She spooned a bite as the men kept talking.

"Five days. If we're not there, wait for us."

She glanced sideways at her new husband and caught the twinkle in his eye as he met her look. She'd happily extend their wedding trip longer than five days if given the chance. Time alone with this man—tucked away in a quiet cave somewhere with a roaring fire—sounded just about perfect. But she didn't plan to share those thoughts with the others.

Fortunately, Caleb had mercy on her and glanced skyward. "You couldn't have picked a better day to ride. I think the weather's gonna stay warm a few days." He lowered his gaze and gave Joel one of his off-kilter grins. "Maybe we'll find Adam before we all meet up, then we can all spend the winter with whatever friends he's made."

"I hope he's made friends and not enemies." Joel muttered the words, but they were loud enough for all to hear.

Susanna studied him. Was he worried about more than he'd told her? She wouldn't expect him to bare his deepest fears after knowing her only a few short weeks. But if she let her mind run rampant imagining what trouble Adam might have met with, she'd become as tight a bundle of nerves as Joel was.

A warm hand settled at the small of her back, and she glanced over at her husband. His eyes asked a question, and her heart responded with a leap. Yes, she was ready. It was time they start out on their new life. Together.

He rose with a lithe grace and took her bowl, stacking it in his. She'd not eaten much of the small amount of stew she'd dished herself, but in truth, her middle was too tied in knots to eat.

Beaver Tail handed the bowls to French. "You'll wash them?"

The smaller man nodded with a grin. "After I eat what's left."

"We're off then." Beaver reached for the satchel she'd packed. Hopefully she'd remembered everything they'd need, as he'd not added much to the load. Maybe he didn't require as much to survive as she did.

Beaver turned to her with raised brows. She nodded that she was ready, then sent the others a smile. "Be safe in your travels. We'll pray you find Adam before we meet again." She pushed down the churning in her middle. Goodbyes were hard, even in the happiest of situations.

As she and Beaver made their way to the horses, his hand slipped around her back again. She would never tire of his touch, of the way he made her feel so protected. When they reached the horses, he tied the satchel behind his saddle while she mounted.

He led his horse over to her and rested a hand on her mount's shoulder as he looked up. "Mind if we ride double?" The grin twitching the corners of his mouth made his teasing impossible to miss, and inspired a bit of the same in her.

"If you think this boy can handle it." She ruffled her gelding's mane.

In an easy movement, Beaver Tail slid up behind her. She leaned back into his strength, a solid presence behind her. He wrapped an arm around her waist and pulled her in tighter as his breath brushed her ear. "Let's ride, wife. We have much good awaiting us."

As she nudged her mount forward, with Beaver's gelding trailing behind them, the truth of his words washed through her. There would be so much good ahead, no matter where the trail led them.

Did you enjoy Susanna and Beaver Tail's story? I hope so!
Would you take a quick minute to leave a review where you purchased the book?
It doesn't have to be long. Just a sentence or two telling what you liked about the story!

To receive a free book and get updates when new Misty M. Beller books release, go to https://mistymbeller.com/freebook

And here's a peek at the next book in the series (Joel's story!), Hope in the Mountain River:

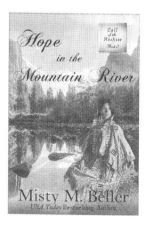

CHAPTER ONE

DECEMBER, 1830

BITTERROOT MOUNTAINS, FUTURE MONTANA TERRITORY

"Is he friend or enemy?" Elan's blood pounded through her veins as it did when the warriors from her tribe struck their targets with tomahawks—blow upon blow, louder and louder with each passing moment. She pulled her furs tighter around her shivering shoulders against the bitter wind whipping down the mountainside.

"I can't tell. They're..." Her faithful friend Meksem paused, then a tiny gasp slipped from her mouth in an icy cloud. "It's a *white* man." The shock in her voice thrust the words to a dangerously loud whisper.

"A French trapper?" Elan softened her own tone so she didn't alert the stranger of their presence. The trappers were the only *soyapo* who ever came to the Bitterroot Mountains. *White people*, they called themselves, from the northern country. She'd heard them speak of a place called Canada. Enough of these men had visited their camp that she'd become accustomed to their strange manners and learned some of their words.

"I don't know. There are two of them. No…" Another pause.

If only she had a clear view herself. Elan forced her legs to relax around her horse's sides. Everything in her wanted to ride the few steps forward beside her friend and peek through the trees to see the outsiders for herself.

But even that small movement could alert the strangers to their presence. Better to keep themselves hidden until they knew better what manner of persons they were up against.

With all her training among the braves, Meksem could likely protect the two of them from any harm these foreigners might plan. But sometimes stealth was a better feat than courage. Especially for two women alone in the mountains, facing white men who surely carried guns.

The emptiness in Elan's heart had stripped away any caution for herself, but for her friend, she had to be diligent. She couldn't lose Meksem—not to beast or man. Elan's eyes lifted to the angry gray sky. The coming weather couldn't be battled, though.

The clop of horses' hooves thumped loudly in the icy air as the strangers drew closer. There must be more than two traveling, as much noise as their animals created.

Finally, Meksem drew back from her perch among the cluster of trees and turned to face Elan. Instead of speaking aloud, she used the language of signs to share what she'd seen. *Four men and a woman.*

A woman? Elan's breath caught in her chest. These people must be friendly then. Unless the woman was a captive. She made the motions to ask, *All of them are white?*

Meksem shook her head, and her hands flew as she

answered. *All but one man. He is not of The People. Not Shoshone either.*

Elan's heart stilled as fear clutched her throat.

Blackfoot?

Even as she signed the question, her mind revolted against the answer. The Blackfoot were one of her people's most dangerous enemies. The stories of how they'd taken women and children captive and the awful way they'd treated them as slaves had been shared as warning in every lodge.

I don't know. Meksem's answer only stilled a small bit of the churning in Elan's middle. Maybe the man was Salish or from one of the other friendly tribes. After all, why would a Blackfoot brave be traveling so far south in the winter moons, especially traveling with a band of white people?

Her friend turned back to watch the strangers, and Elan braced herself for her first glimpse as the nose of a horse appeared between the trees. The moment Meksem had first caught the sound of riders approaching, Elan had spotted this perfect place to watch the strangers while keeping the two of them and their horses hidden.

The first sight she caught was of a horse with a long winter coat that had once been black, but long days in the sun had bleached the ends lighter brown. Its rider came into view, and something in Elan's middle tightened. He wore a fur coat and hat, much like the French trappers did, and she couldn't see much of his face except a glimpse of paler skin—the color of a white man's.

Yet something in his manner—maybe in his bearing, the way he sat atop his horse—struck a yearning inside her. He rode like a horseman, one capable of communing with his mount and moving as one. She'd seen this among some of the braves in their camp. After all, her people were known for their skill with horses and the unique spotted animals they raised. But she'd never seen a man who gripped her attention at first glance like this one.

When he'd nearly ridden past, she caught sight of the man riding behind him. This one truly did look like a Frenchman. Much like the trapper, Lebeau, who'd spent a winter in the lodge beside her own a few years back.

After the second man, a female passed by—a white squaw with light brown hair dressed in a beautiful set of buckskins and covered in a cape of fine wolf fur. She sat regally in the saddle—no mere serving girl, this one. Nor a captive.

Another horse climbed the trail close behind her, and the sight of raven hair poking out from under his fur cap made her chest tighten again. She couldn't see much of the man's face, only enough to agree that he was from one of the tribes. But which one?

The risk of showing themselves to find out wasn't worth any gain that might come from a meeting. Meksem knew the trail the two of them were following, as she'd passed through here several times on hunting trips, and they'd packed enough food to reach the great river. The only reason to reveal themselves would be curiosity to see what these people were about. Definitely not worth the risk.

After all, hadn't Elan chosen to take this journey to escape from people? Time alone was what she'd craved. Time to heal, if that were possible. Meksem knew how to keep silent and was an able guide and friend, so accepting her insistence on coming along hadn't been too hard.

Yet the long days of quiet hadn't eased the rending of Elan's body and heart yet. Nothing ever could. Not when her daughter's life had been crushed, ripped into bloody shreds by a single horrific act.

Chuslum had tried to save her. He'd done everything he could to rescue their only child. But his efforts hadn't been enough. No man could best a grizzly with only his hands, not even a brave as skilled as her husband had been.

Now, Elan was alone.

In one awful day, she'd been stripped of the two people who'd mattered most to her. How could she possibly go on? What was there without her child to give her life meaning?

Another man rode into view, bringing her focus back to the present. This stranger sat taller than the others, almost bear-like wrapped in his furs. At least they'd all dressed suitably for travel through the deadly winter in these mountains. The snow only came above the horses' knees for now, but the low thick clouds meant more would be falling soon. This group must not have seen the cave they had to have passed early in the day, or they would have taken shelter. She and Meksem were riding hard to reach that cave before the worst of the snow came in a fury.

When the last pack horse marched past their hiding place, Elan forced her mind to focus on sounds around them. The horses' hooves crunching snow, the squeaking of saddles. One of the men murmured, but the group had moved far enough away that she couldn't make out the words. Not even what language it might be.

At last, silence descended over the land, settling on them like a heavy shroud. Pressing so hard she had to work to draw breath. Why did this quiet she'd craved now feel like the press of death?

Meksem turned, and her perceptive gaze roamed over Elan's face.

Elan turned away from her friend toward the eastern path they'd been riding. "Ready?"

Her friend nudged her mount forward. "If we ride hard, we'll reach the cave before the snow comes. This will be a deep one."

Meksem was right, no doubt. Yet the fury of the oncoming blizzard was nothing compared to the desolation left by the storm raging inside her.

～

Joel Vargas eyed the darkening sky overhead, then signaled for a halt as he reined his gelding in.

"That storm will strike any minute, no?" From behind him, French peered up at the low clouds pressing down on them.

Joel scanned the rest of the group—Susanna, Beaver Tail, then Caleb in the rear. All these people he'd dragged into these treacherous Bitterroot Mountains. He'd expected the terrain to be rough—the cliffs steep and the footing dangerous. But he'd not expected the cold to be so fierce a man could freeze to death in an hour unless he bundled tight in furs.

And the snow already stood as high as the horses' knees. Now, they were about to get more? He'd never imagined such a place existed when he left Andalusia. The mountains in his Spanish homeland—at least where he and his brother had grown up—rose in majestic grandeur as these did, but the climate was so much more agreeable.

None of this frostbite and limbs so cold a man didn't dare make water until he first built a warming campfire.

"We passed a cave a few hours back. That would be a good place to wait out the storm." Beaver Tail spoke in his usual reserved manner.

Joel jerked his gaze to the man. "Why didn't you say something when you saw it?" And why hadn't Joel seen it himself? How did Beaver always manage to be one step ahead, even when Joel did his best to keep every one of his senses alert?

Beaver sent a glance around them, ever watchful. "I didn't think you'd want to wait half a day just to keep from riding in snowflakes."

The pressure in his chest pinched harder. Did his friends think him such a dictator he would risk their lives just to make a half-day's progress in their trek?

Yes, this journey was important. Every half day could mean

life or death for his brother—the brother he hadn't seen in over a year now. He didn't actually *know* if Adam was in danger. He only suspected so because Adam's note had said he'd find Joel in the summer. About five months ago.

While Joel had no certain knowledge of Adam's peril, he *did* know this snowstorm could be the death of them all if they didn't find proper shelter and a dry place for a fire.

Reining his horse around, he nodded toward Caleb. "Let's retrace our steps. We won't find Adam if we all turn to icicles."

The next hours dragged on as the temperature dropped. Not even the majestic views surrounding them—peaks rising up like cathedrals into the clouds—could overcome the miserable cold.

"Behind those two boulders just ahead of you." Beaver Tail's voice broke the interminable silence.

Joel craned his neck to see the cave his friend had spotted. He rode in the back of the line now, so he didn't get a glimpse of the opening until the others had reined their horses in a semi-circle around the spot.

Two stones stood as tall as men, palace guards in front of the cave's entrance, permitting access only through the narrow space between them. He could see why most people wouldn't notice the dark hole hiding behind the rocks.

But *he* should have seen it. He'd spent his life watching for danger, trying to spot potential hazards and possible protection. How had he missed this?

Beaver Tail had already dropped to the ground and padded forward to slip between the stone barriers. Ever the scout and protector.

Joel gripped his rifle as he slid from his own mount and stepped forward to follow his friend. Surely Beaver knew the chance that a bear or other animal had taken refuge inside, but just in case, Joel asked the question. "Think anything is in there?"

Beaver didn't even slow, just tipped his chin to throw his voice back to Joel. "Mayhap."

He was prepared then.

With the gun in Joel's left hand, he gripped the hilt of his knife with his right and followed his half-Blackfoot friend through the boulders. Joel could shoot a gun with decent aim, but he'd spent so many long hours on the ship from Andalusia perfecting his skills with a blade, he'd be quicker with that weapon in an attack.

Beaver Tail slipped into the darkness of the cave without a pause, even though the interior yawned black. Joel pulled out his knife, but kept the blade pointed downward as he used the fist of that hand to feel the air in front of him. Better not to run into anything.

Every one of his senses strained to hear a sound or catch a whiff of odor, something other than the dank scent of damp stone and decaying leaves. Even a shifting of shadows.

The low growl of Beaver Tail's voice was his first alert. "Show yourself."

Joel's chest tightened as he strained to hear or see the threat Beaver had sensed. He could make out Beaver's form now that his eyes were adjusting to the dim interior. But only darkness lay beyond.

Beaver's voice hadn't echoed through the space, so this cave must not be large. Joel stretched his right hand—the one gripping the knife—sideways as far as he could reach to see if his knuckles brushed the rock wall.

His hand touched fur, and he nearly jumped even as he jerked his hand back.

At the same moment, a tiny squeal—a gasp, really—filled the air.

A shuffle sounded in front, just as a hard body slammed into him.

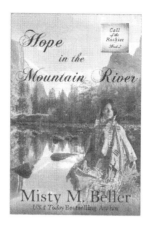

Get HOPE IN THE MOUNTAIN RIVER at your Favorite Retailer!

ABOUT THE AUTHOR

Misty M. Beller is a *USA Today* bestselling author of romantic mountain stories, set on the 1800s frontier and woven with the truth of God's love.

She was raised on a farm in South Carolina, so her Southern roots run deep. Growing up, her family was close, and they continue to keep that priority today. Her husband and children now add another dimension to her life, keeping her both grounded and crazy.

God has placed a desire in Misty's heart to combine her love for Christian fiction and the simpler ranch life, writing historical novels that display God's abundant love through the twists and turns in the lives of her characters.

Connect with Misty at www.MistyMBeller.com

ALSO BY MISTY M. BELLER

The Mountain Series

The Lady and the Mountain Man

The Lady and the Mountain Doctor

The Lady and the Mountain Fire

The Lady and the Mountain Promise

The Lady and the Mountain Call

This Treacherous Journey

This Wilderness Journey

This Freedom Journey (novella)

This Courageous Journey

This Homeward Journey

This Daring Journey

This Healing Journey

Call of the Rockies

Freedom in the Mountain Wind

Hope in the Mountain River

Light in the Mountain Sky

Courage in the Mountain Wilderness

Faith in the Mountain Valley

Hearts of Montana

Hope's Highest Mountain

Love's Mountain Quest

Faith's Mountain Home

Texas Rancher Trilogy

The Rancher Takes a Cook

The Ranger Takes a Bride

The Rancher Takes a Cowgirl

Wyoming Mountain Tales

A Pony Express Romance

A Rocky Mountain Romance

A Sweetwater River Romance

A Mountain Christmas Romance